MARABOU STORK
NIGHTMARES

Irvine Welsh is the author of seven works of fiction, most
recently *Porno*.

Irvine Welsh

MARABOU STORK NIGHTMARES

VINTAGE BOOKS
London

Published by Vintage 2004

21

Copyright © Irvine Welsh 1995

Irvine Welsh has asserted his right under the Copyright,
Designs and Patents Act, 1988 to be identified as the author
of this work

First published in Great Britain in 1995 by
Jonathan Cape

First published by Vintage in 1996

Vintage
Random House, 20 Vauxhall Bridge Road,
London SW1V 2SA

www.vintage-books.co.uk

Addresses for companies within The Random House Group
Limited can be found at: www.randomhouse.co.uk/offices.htm

The Random House Group Limited Reg. No. 954009

A CIP catalogue record for this book
is available from the British Library

ISBN 9780099435112

The Random House Group Limited makes every effort to ensure
that the papers used in its books are made from trees that have
been legally sourced from well-managed and credibly certified
forests. Our paper procurement policy can be found at:
www.rbooks.co.uk/environment

Mixed Sources
Product group from well-managed
forests and other controlled sources
www.fsc.org Cert no. TT-COC-2139
© 1996 Forest Stewardship Council
FSC

Printed in the UK by CPI Bookmarque, Croydon, CR0 4TD

for Trish, Davie, Laura & Sean

Zero Tolerance

The material used in this book is taken from the Zero Tolerance campaign which originated in Edinburgh. Zero Tolerance is the first campaign to use the mass media to challenge male violence against women and children. The campaign believes that there is no acceptable level of violence against women and children.

Foreword

Thanks time again. Always first and foremost to Anne, for reasons which you could write all the books in the world about and still not do it the slightest bit of justice.

Then to Kenny McMillan and Paul Reekie for providing me not just with stacks of ideas for this book, but also much of the information I needed to complete it, as well as numerous other East Terracing (now sadly, the East Stand) boys for their specialist info. To Kevin Williamson, Barry Graham and Sandy McNair for casting their beady eyes over the manuscript and providing useful feedback. It goes without saying that the above can't be held responsible for the many defects, only that such crap bits would have been more numerous without their intervention.

To the City of Munich local authority, without whose generous hospitality this book would not have been so quickly completed.

To all at the publishers, especially Robin Robertson and Nicky Eaton, and Lesley Bryce, the best editor in Western Europe. To Jeff Barratt at Heavenly.

To various pals in Edinburgh, Glasgow, London, Manchester, Amsterdam and other places whom I can always rely upon to drag me into clubs or pubs or onto the terraces for mischief whenever an outbreak of sanity threatens. You know who you are; nice one to each and every one of you.

Nods, winks, hugs and best wishes to all the punters and posses I've met up with over the last year at Pure, Yip Yap, Slam, Sativa, Back to Basics, The Ministry, Sabresonic, Desert Storm, The Mazzo, The Roxy, Sunday Social and Rez. Well done to all the DJs for keeping it going.

A very big thanks to my family for not being the one in this book.

Massive respect to all.

Irvine Welsh,
Amsterdam, October 1994

Scepticism was formed in Edinburgh two hundred years ago by David Hume and Adam Smith. They said: 'Let's take religion to the black man, but we won't really believe it.' It's the cutting edge of trade.

—P.R.

We should condemn more and understand less.

—Major.

Contents

part one

Lost
Empires

1 Another Lost Empire

It. was. me. and. Jamieson.

Just us.

On this journey, this crazy high–speed journey through this strange land in this strange vehicle.

Just me and Sandy Jamieson.

But they were trying to disturb me, trying to wake me; the way they always did. They willnae let this sleeping dog lie. They always interfere. When the cunts start this shite it makes things get aw distorted and I have to try to go deeper.

DEEPER. Things get dis

up – – – – – We're just
coming going to take
start your temperature,
I Roy. Have you got the
bedpan, Nurse Norton?
I lose control when they interfere – – – and Number Twos now Roy,
time for Number Twos.
 – Yes, he's looking brighter this morning, isn't he, Nurse Devine? You're brighter this morning,
Roy lovey.

Aye right ye are, take your fuckin hand oot ma fuckin erse.

DEEPER

DEEPER –
– – – – – – – – Sandy Jamieson is my best friend down here. A

former professional sportsman and an experienced hunter of man-eating beasts, I enlisted Jamieson's aid in a quest I have been engaged in for as long as I can remember. However, as my memory is practically non-existent, this could have been a few days ago or since the beginning of time itself. For some reason, I am driven to eradicate the scavenger-predator bird known as the Marabou Stork. I wish to drive this evil and ugly creature from the African continent. In particular, I have this persistent vision of one large blighter, a hideous and revolting specimen, which I know somehow must perish by my own hand.

As with all other events, I have great difficulty in recalling how Sandy Jamieson and I became friends. I do know that he was of great help to me when I first came here, and that is enough. I do not wish to remember where I was before. I am averse to my past; it is an unsavoury blur which I have no wish to attempt to pull into focus. Here and now, Africa and Sandy, they are my present and my future.

I feel a cool breeze in my face and turn to face my companion. He's in good spirits behind the wheel of our jeep.

— You've been at the wheel far too long, Sandy. I'll take over! I volunteered.

— Wizard! Sandy replied, pulling over by the side of the dusty track.

A large insect settled on my chest. I swatted the blighter. — Yuk! Those insects, Sandy! How positively yucky!

— Absolutely, he laughed, clambering over into the back of the vehicle. — It'll be great to stretch these damn pins! He smiled, extending his long, tanned muscular legs across the back seat.

I slid into the driver's seat and started up the jeep.

All Sandy and myself had in the world were this rotten old jeep, some limited supplies and very little money. The majority of our possessions had recently been expropriated by a cunning but somewhat morally deficient native fellow, whom we'd rather foolishly hired as a guide.

For a while we had planned to engage the services of some young native boys, but the undernourished specimens we had encountered had proved to be unappetising prospects . . . that is, manifestly unfit for the physical demands adventures with Sandy and I would inevitably place upon them. Eventually we secured the services of one shifty urchin who went by the name of Moses. We took this to be a sign of good luck. It proved anything but.

Moses hailed from one of the shanty towns that lined the banks of Lake Torto. While I have to admit that we were not in the position to be able to pay our manservants generously, our behaviour towards Moses scarcely merited the response of this roguish boy: the blighter did a runner with the bulk of our money and supplies.

I find this attitude of 'something for nothing' sadly prevalent amongst the non-white races, but I put the blame fairly and squarely on the shoulders of the white colonialists, who by assuming responsibility for GOD THAT
BLINDING BLOODY   up — — —   — Roy, I'm shining this torch
FUCKING   coming   into your eyes. Pupil dilation
                                                seems more evident. Good. Good.
SUN — — — — — — I'm

FUCK OFF

— Definitely more of a response that time, Roy. It's probably just a reflex, though. I'll try it again . . . no . . . nothing this time around.

Naw, cause I'm too quick for youse, you'll never find ays in here.

DEEPER
            DEEPER
                        DEEPER — — — — — — — Sandy is
masturbating in the back of the jeep and she is just laughing . . . eh
. . . what the fuck's gaun oan here . . . what's *she* dacin here . . . it's
just supposed tae be Sandy n me . . . I'm losing control and all I can
hear is her laughter and I see her face in the mirror; her face warped
and cartoonish as his semen shoots onto her blouse. Her face is like
. . . is like I want to . . . I'm feeling jealous. Jealous of Jamieson.
What I want is for her not to just sit there laughing, not to sit and
encourage him; I want to scream, don't encourage him you fucking
slut, but I have to concentrate on the road because I've never driven
before . . .

I can't keep my eyes off Sandy Jamieson. There is a sick tribe of demons lurking behind his generous if gormless facade. I am moved to shout, — You're a metaphor, Jamieson. You don't exist outside of me. I can't be angry with nothing, you're just a manifestation of my guilt. You're a projection.

This is ridiculous. Sandy's my friend. My guide. The best friend I've ever had but

But Jamieson now has his penis in her mouth. Its head bubbles her cheek outwards from the inside. It looks horrible, that swelling, that distortion of her face. Sandy's face, though, is even worse; it reddens and inflates, providing a contrast to his dark, shaven head and the whites around his dark green eyes. — I'm real enough, he gasps, — this rod is in your girlfriend's head.

In my mirror, while at the same time trying to keep my eyes on the dusty, winding track that they ridiculously refer to as a road, I see a blade come tearing out of her face. Panic sets in as I realise that the vehicle I'm travelling in is a structure now indivisible from my own body and we're dipping and flipping over, rising upwards in a shuddering rush into a buzzing wall of light. I'm gulping frenziedly at air which is so thick and heavy it feels like water in my lungs. I hear the shrieks of a large, predatory bird soaring past me; so close to my head I can smell the diseased remnants of carrion from it. I regain some sense of control over the vehicle only to find that she's gone and Jamieson is sitting in the front passenger seat with me.

— It was getting a tad crowded back there, he smiles, gesturing behind us to a trio of Japanese men in business suits who are occupying the back seat. They are excitedly snapping with cameras and speaking in a language which I can't make out but which doesn't seem to be Japanese.

This is totally fucked.

Is Sandy the best guide in all of this?

DEEPER
               DEEPER
                              DEEPER

Yes.

I'm starting to feel happier. The deeper I get, the further away from *them* I get, the happier I feel. Sandy Jamieson's expression has changed. He is reassuming the persona of a loyal friend and guide rather than that of a sneering adversary. This means I'm back to where they can't get to me: deep in the realms of my own consciousness.

But they keep trying; even from in here I can feel them. Trying to stick another tube up my arse or something similar, something which constitutes a breach of my personal no no can't have this . . . change the subject, keep control.

Control.

Sandy

DEEPER
              DEEPER
                        DEEPER ————————— Holy
Cow! Sandy exclaimed as an unwanted Marabou Stork flew past the passenger window. I knew that it was our bird, but pursuit was difficult, as I had little control over this vehicle. The bird was impossible to follow in flight, but later on we would endeavour to locate its nest on the ground and destroy the beast. As things stood, however, we were coming down slowly, with a strange hydraulic hiss, towards the surface of this tropical, forested terrain.

— I've absolutely no control here, Sandy, I defeatedly observed, pulling at levers and pushing at buttons, but to little avail. I threw my hands up in exasperation. I wanted to stay up here. It seemed important not to land.

— Any biscuits left, Roy? Sandy asked eagerly.

I looked at the packet on the dashboard. There were only three left which meant that the greedy blighter had scoffed most of them!

— Gosh Sandy, you're a Hungry Horace today, I remarked.

Sandy gave out a high, clear laugh. — Nerves, I suppose. I don't particularly want to land, but at least this place might have some proper tuck.

— I hope so! I said.

The craft descended implacably, coming down over what at first seemed to be a small settlement, but which appeared to be expanding continually beyond our line of vision until we saw it as a giant metropolis. We were hovering down into this old stone colonial building which had no roof; only the jagged remnants of glass around the periphery showing where one had been.

I thought that our craft would never squeeze through the gap and braced myself for collision. However, its dimensions seemed to alter to fit the shape it had to go through, and we touched down in a rather splendid hall with some interesting gothic stonework. This was obviously some sort of public building, its grandeur hinting at more affluent times and its poor state of maintenance indicative of a more sordid and less civic present.

— Do you think we're allowed here, Sandy asked shakily.

— I don't see why not. We're explorers, aren't we, I told him.

As we got out of our car (for this was what the vehicle now seemed to be, a simple family saloon car) we noted the presence of many people, wandering around aimlessly, and taking little notice of us. Some broken glass crunched under my feet. I started to feel more than a wee bitty paranoid, thinking that the natives would perhaps blame us for breaking the roof. While we were innocent, circumstantial evidence could certainly be weighted against us by an unscrupulous and malevolent set of officials in a corrupt regime, which to a greater or lesser extent meant any regime. I had absolutely no intention of getting back into that vehicle, nor, evidently, had Sandy; engaged as he was in the removal of his backpack which contained half our supplies. I followed his lead and swung my own pack over my shoulders.

— Strange little performance this, I noted, turning to Jamieson, who was surveying the scene with increasing distaste. Two white men walked straight past us, completely ignoring us. I was just starting to entertain the possibility that we were invisible when Sandy roared, — This is preposterous! I am a seasoned explorer and a professional footballer! I demand to be treated in a sporting manner!

— It's okay, Sandy, I smiled, placing a comforting hand on my friend's shoulder.

This outburst was certainly effective in registering our presence, but only at the expense of generating hostility from some of the citizens present. In particular, one band of youthful roughs were sizing us up.

Gosh and golly.

Damn and fucking blast.

— Sandy's the *enfant terrible* of British soccer, I limply endeavoured to explain.   up — — — Okay Roy?

Then I felt something — — — — — — — — — — — — coming

AH FEEL SOMETHING AH FEEL IT BUT YOUSE CUNTS CAN FUCK OFF AND DIE CAUSE YOUSE'LL NO GIT AYS IN HERE YA CUNTS

DEEPER
          DEEPER
                    DEEPER — — — — — Let's scarper
Sandy, I nodded, noting that the mood of the mob had turned sour and — — — coming up — — — oh fuck I've lost control again THESE CUNTS' FAULT, LEAVE AYS ALANE and now I feel the stabbing beak in my arm, it can only be the Marabou Stork but it's my injection, it's the chemicals, not ones that dull and chill my brain, not ones that make me forget because with these ones I remember.

Oh my God, what dae ah fuckin well remember . . .

Lexo said that it was important that we didnae lose our bottle. Nae cunt was tae shite oot; eftir aw, the fuckin hoor asked fir it. She'd've goat it fae some cunts anyway the wey she fuckin well carried oan and the fuckin fuss she made. Aye, she goat slapped aroond a bit, but we wir fuckin vindicated, British justice n that. She wis jist in the wrong place at the wrong time n anyway, it wis aw Lexo's fault . . .

. . . change the subject . . . I don't want this. I want to keep hunting the Stork. The Stork's the personification of all this badness. If I kill the Stork I'll kill the badness in me. Then I'll be ready to come

out of here, to wake up, to take my place in society and all that shite.
Ha. They'll get a fuckin shock, when they see this near-corpse, this
package of wasting flesh and bone just rise and say: — Awright
chavvy! How's tricks?

— Awright son!

AW FUCK! *THIR* HERE. ALWAYS FUCKIN HERE.
ALWAYS ASSUMING I WANT THEIR FUCKIN PRE-
SENCE. DAE THEY NO HAVE FUCKING VISITING
HOURS HERE?

My father. Nice to see you, Dad. Please, continue, while I doze.

— How ye daein? Eh? Well, that's us in another final. Disnae seem two whole years since the, eh
accident, but enough ay that. Another final! One-nil. Darren Jackson. Ah didnae go masel mind.
Tony wis thair. Ah wis gaunny go, bit ah nivir goat a ticket. Saw it oan the telly. Like ah sais, one-nil.
Darren Jackson, barry goal n aw. Tony made up a tape ay the commentary, like ah sais, a tape eh
made up. Eh Vet?

— Aye.

— Ye goat the tape then?

— What?

— The tape, Vet. Ah'm askin ye, ye goat the tape?

— Tape . . .

— Whit's wrong, Vet?

— Thir's a Jap ower thair, John.

— It's jist a nurse, Vet, jist a nurse. Probably no even a Jap. Probably a Chinky or somethin. Eh
son? Jist a nurse ah'm sayin, son. Eh Roy? Eh that's right son?

FUCK OFF AND DIE YOU DAFT AULD CUNT

— A nurse . . .

— Aye, the wee Chinky nurse. Nice lassie. Eh son? Lookin better the day though, son. Mair
colour. Like ah sais, eh Vet, like ah sais, Roy's goat mair colour aboot um.

— They nivir git it. Every other perr bugger gits it, bit they nivir git it.

— Eh?

— AIDS. Ye nivir see Japs wi AIDS. Here wuv goat it. In America thuv goat it. In India thuv goat
it. In Africa thuv goat it. Oor Bernard might huv it. No thaim, though. They nivir git it.

— What the fuck ye oan aboot? Chinky nurse . . . nice wee lassie . . .

— Ken how? Ken how they nivir git it?

— Vet, this husnae goat nowt tae dae wi . . .

— Cause they inventit it! They inventit the disease! So as they could take over the world!

— You fuckin stupit or somethin?! Talkin like that in front ay Roy! Ye dinnae ken what the laddie kin hear, how it effects um! Like ah sais, ye fuckin stupit? Ah'm askin ye! Ye fuckin stupit?

MUMMY DADDY, NICE TO SEE YOU IS IT FUCK DON'T WANT TO SURFACE DON'T WANT TO GET CLOSER TO YOUR UGLY WORLD GOT TO GO DEEPER, DEEPER DOWN, GOT TO HUNT THE STORK, TO GET CONTROL

DEEPER
        DEEPER
                DEEPER---------------
-------------------------------Jamieson.

We've somehow given the baying mob the slip and find ourselves on the edge of a run-down shantytown. A huge, festering garbage dump lies alongside a now poisonous lake. Malnourished children play in its squalor. Some of them come over to Sandy and myself, begging without really expecting any results. One little boy, a wild-looking creature with a face as brown as dark chocolate, stares intently at us, never averting his gaze. He is wearing nothing but old, dirty blue shorts and a pair of worn shoes without any socks.

— I say, Roy, what an extraordinary looking creature, Sandy smiled.

— Yes, a funny little thing, I said.

The little boy gave a loud, long laugh and suddenly poured out quite an extended speech. I couldn't understand a bloody word of it.

— Bantu, I suppose, Sandy said sadly. — Sounds all very splendid and lovely, but I can't make head nor tail of it!

We gave them some coins and Sandy produced a small bag of sweets. — If we only had a ball, I could do a bit of coaching, get a scratch game up, he said wistfully.

I looked up at the blinding sun. It had been relentless all day, but soon it would retreat behind the green hills which rose up over the Emerald Forest. This was a beautiful spot. This was . . . my thoughts were distracted by some shouts and the sound of the rattling of tin against the compressed clay track. Jamieson was

expertly shielding a Coca-Cola can from the rangy limbs of a group
of the local Bantu children. — There you go, you little blighters . . .
it's all about possession, he told them.

He was forever the sport.

While Sandy's interest in sports coaching and the development of
youth was touching, we had more pressing matters to consider. Our
vehicle had been left behind in the civic hall, neither of us caring to
travel in anything *quite* so unreliable. — We need transport, Sandy, I
told him, — our Stork must be nesting around here somewhere.

Sandy signalled for the kids to disperse. One tyke, our funny little
creature, glared at me in a sulky way. I hated to be the spoilsport, but
there was business to take care of.

Sandy crisply and clinically volleyed the can into the rubbish-
infested lake, then looked at me and shook his head sadly. — This is
not going to be quite as straightforward as you think, Roy. The
Storks are dangerous and formidable opponents. We're alone and
isolated in hostile terrain, without any supplies or equipment, he
explained. Then he looked at me with a penetrating stare, — Why is
slaying that large Marabou so important to you?

Damn and fucking blast.

This made me stop to consider my motives. Oh yes, I could have
gone on about the spirit of the hunt. I could have produced a welter
of damning evidence of the carnage that these despicable beasts can
perpetrate on other wildlife and game; on how they can upset the
entire ecology of a region, how they can spread pestilence and
disease through the local villages. Certainly, such reasoning would
have struck a chord with both Sandy's sense of adventure and his
humanitarian principles.

The problem is it wouldn't have been true. Moreover, Sandy
would have known that I was lying.

I cleared my throat, and turned away from the blinding sun.
Feeling a shortness of breath, I felt the words about to evaporate in
my throat as I prepared to speak them. I always seem to feel
something sticking in my throat. I cough, miraculously finding
strength, and carry on. — I can't really explain, Sandy; not to my
own satisfaction, so certainly not to anyone else's. I just know that

I've met that Stork before, in a previous life perhaps, and I know that it's evil. I know that it's important for me to destroy it.

Sandy stood looking at me for a few seconds, his countenance paralysed with doubt and fear.

— Trust me on this one, mate? I said softly.

His face ignited in a beautiful, expansive smile, and he gave me a powerful hug which I reciprocated. We broke off and gave each other the high-five. — Let's do the blighter! Sandy smiled, a steely glint of determination entering his eye.

Another two small black children from the football game approached us. Their clothes were in tatters. — Homosexual? One young boy asked. — I suck you off for rand.

Sandy looked down at the crusty lipped urchin. — Things may be bad little one, but selling your body to the white man is not the answer. He ruffled the child's hair and the boy departed, skipping across the path back down towards the settlement.

We moved on by foot, carrying our backpacks and heading out of the village towards the other side of the lake. The wind had changed direction and the smell from the rubbish was overpowering in the hazy heat. Ugly bugs of varied sizes swarmed around us, forcing us to beat a hasty retreat along the path. We ran until we couldn't go any further, although I must confess that was the royal 'we', for Sandy, as a professional sportsman, had quite an edge on me in fitness and stamina, and could probably have stuck it out a bit longer.

We set up camp with our provisions, enjoying a feast in a shady glade by the more picturesque side of the lake. We opened our packs to examine their contents.

— Mmmm! Pork pie; homemade of course, said Sandy.

— And what's this . . . golly, it's a cheese! How enormous. Smell it, Sandy, it's enough to make you want to start eating straight away!

— Gosh, I can't wait to get my mouth around that, Sandy smiled, — And that homemade bread! Can't we start?

— No, there are new-laid boiled eggs to begin with, I laughed.

— Gosh, all we're missing is some homemade apple pie and ice-cream, Sandy smiled, as we tucked in to our feast. Then, suddenly inspired, he turned to me and said, — I've got it, Roy!

What we need is sponsorship! Somebody to fund this Stork hunt. I
know a chap who'll sort us out with provisions. He runs the Jambola
Safari Park, access to which is a few miles' trek on the west side of the
lake.

I knew instantly whom Sandy was talking about. — Dawson. Mr
Lochart Dawson.

— You know him?

I shrugged non-committally. — I know *of* him. Then again, most
people know of Lochart Dawson. He sees to that.

— Yes, he has a flair for self-publicity, does our Lochart, Sandy
said, his tone implying an affectionate familiarity. I then recalled that
Sandy mentioned that he'd previously been in the employ of
Dawson.

Sandy was correct about the self-publicity; you just couldn't keep
Dawson out of the news. He was currently planning on expanding
his park by taking over an adjacent leisure reserve. Whether in the
long term Dawson actually envisaged any animals in what he
described as the 'superpark' was more open to conjecture. He had
made his money in the development of property, and there were
more profitable uses for land in this region than a Safari Park.
Nonetheless, Dawson could be useful.

— We'd have a smashing time at old Dawson's, I said eagerly.

— I'll bet he's got enough food to feed an army! Sandy agreed.

Suddenly we were interrupted by a chorus of frenetic squawking.
We looked back, and I saw them. Although one or two social
groupings could be evidenced, they were largely standing in
isolation from each other, in the rubbish by the lakeside. Some
squatted on their breasts, others paced slowly at a short distance.
One large devil; it must have had a wing span of around eighty and
weighed about nine kilos, turned its back to the sun and spread its
wings, exposing those spare filamentous black feathers.

The beast's throat patch was reddish; it had scabs of warty dried
blood on the base of its large, conical bill; its legs were stained
white with dried excrement. It was the large, bulky scavenger-
predator known as the Marabou Stork. More importantly, it was
our one.

— Look Sandy, once again I felt my words dry in my throat, as I pointed across the lake to the mountain of rubbish and the large bird.

The sheer evil power of the creature emanating from its deathly eyes shook us to the marrow.

— Come ahead then, ya fuckin wide-os! It squawked.

I felt sick and faint.

Sandy looked pretty fazed.

— Look Roy, we need more hardware to take on that bastard. Its bill must be razor sharp, containing the venom and poison of rotting carcasses: one scratch could be fatal. Let's see Dawson. His resort was once plagued by these beasts, but he found a way to sort them out.

THESE BEASTS ARE KILLERS. THEY ARE INTERES-TED ONLY IN MAYHEM. THEY CARE NOTHING FOR THE GAME . . .

up – – –

back

Eh?   coming

Aw fuck – – – – I'm

— We're away now, son.
Yir Ma n me. Like ah sais,
that's us away now.
CHEERIO SON! CHEERIO ROY!
— Cheerio Roy! Cheerio darlin.

Like yir Ma sais, that's us sayin cheerio. See ye the morn though son. Ah'll be in in the morn. CHEERIO ROY!

Aye, aye, aye. He's always so fuckin loud. Ah'm no fuckin deef, ya cunt! Sometimes ah just feel it would be so much fuckin easier tae just open my eyes and scream: FUCK OFF!

— The min-it choo walked in the joint dih-dih, I could see you were a man of dis-tinc-tyin, a real big spender . . .

What the fuck is this? Ma. She's finally fuckin blown it.

— . . . good loo-kin, so ree-fined . . .

— What ur ye daein Vet? Whit the fuck ye playin at?

— Bit mind they sais John, mind they sais that ah could sing tae um. The doaktirs said. Ken, wi the music hittin a different part ay the brain. That's how wi bring in the tapes, John. Ah jist thoat this wid mean mair tae the laddie, likesay a live performance. Mind eh eywis liked ays singing Big Spender whin eh wis a bairn?

— Aye, well music n singin, that's different like. Different sort ay things. That's jist singing you're daein. Ye couldnae really call it music, Vet. Like ah sais, ye couldnae really call it music.

— Bit ah could git Tony tae play the guitar. Make up a tape ay me singin Big Spender, fir the laddie's cassette player, John. Ah could dae that, John.

OH FUCKIN HELL, GOD PRESERVE US . . .

I could tell that my Ma was upset, and they had another blazing argument. I was relieved when they departed. So fuckin relieved. Even now they embarrass me. Even in here. I've nothing to say to them; I don't think anything of them. I never really had, besides I was anxious to get back to Sandy and our pursuit of the Stork. I hear a different voice now though, a sort of fluffy feminine voice, the voice of Nurse Patricia Devine. —That's the visitors away now, Roy.

Her voice is soft, mildly arousing. Maybe I'll get a bit of love interest into my little fantasy, a bit a shagging into things no no no there will be no shagging because that's what caused aw this fuckin soapy bubble in the first place and I'm being turned over in my decaying organic vehicle, and I can feel the touch of Patricia Devine.

Can I feel her touch, or do I just think I can? Did I really hear my parents or was it all my imagination? I know not and care less. All I have is the data I get. I don't care whether it's produced by my senses or my memory or my imagination. Where it comes from is less important than the fact that it *is*. The only reality is the images and texts.

— There's nothing of you, she says to me cheerfully. I can feel the frost in the air. The staff nurse has given Patricia Devine a dirty look for making a negative comment in front of the veg. Me who used to weigh thirteen and a half stone, too. At one time I was heading for Fat Hell, (Fathell, Midlothian, population 8,619) with a fat wife, fat kids and a fat dog. A place where the only thing thin is the paycheque.

Now I can hear that 'Staff' has departed leaving me with the simply Devine Patricia. Patricia is possibly an old hound, but I like to think of her as young and lovely. The concept adds quality to my life. Not a lot of things do at the moment. Only I add the quality. As much or as little as I want. If only they'd just fuckin leave ays tae get on with it. I don't need their quality, their world, that fucked-up place which made me the fucked-up mess I was. Down here in the comforts of my vegetative state, inside my secret world I can fuck who I want, kill who I please, no no no nane ay that no no no I can do the things I wanted to do, the things I tried to do, up there in the real world. No comeback. Anyway, *this* world's real enough to me and I'll stay down here out of the way, where they can't get to me, at least until I work it all out.

It hasn't been so easy recently. Characters and events have been intruding into my mind, psychic gatecrashers breaking in on my private party. Imposing themselves. Like Jamieson, and now this Lochart Dawson. Somehow, though, this has given me a sense of purpose. I know why I'm in here. I'm here to slay the Stork. Why I have to do this I do not know. I know that I need help, however, and I know that Jamieson and Dawson are my only potential allies in this quest.

This is what I have instead of a life.

2 The Scheme

I grew up in what was not so much a family as a genetic disaster. While people always seem under the impression that their household is normal, I, from an early age, almost as soon as I was aware, was embarrassed and ashamed of my family.

I suppose this awareness came from being huddled so close to other households in the ugly rabbit hutch we lived in. It was a systems built, 1960s maisonette block of flats, five storeys high, with long landings which were jokingly referred to as 'streets in the sky' but which had no shops or pubs or churches or post offices on them, nothing in fact, except more rabbit hutches. Being so close to those other families, it became impossible for people, as much as they tried, to keep their lives from each other. In stairs, on balconies, in communal drying areas, through dimpled-glass and wire doors, I sensed that there was a general, shared quality kicking around which we seemed to lack. I suppose it was what people would call normality.

All those dull broadsheet newspaper articles on the scheme where we lived tended to focus on how deprived it was. Maybe it was, but I'd always defined the place as less characterised by poverty than by boredom, although the relationship between the two is pretty evident. For me, though, the sterile boredom outside my house was preferable to the chaos inside it.

My old man was a total basket case; completely away with it. The old girl, if anything, was worse. They'd been engaged for yonks but before they were due to get married, she had a sort of mental breakdown, or rather, had her first mental breakdown. She would have these breakdowns intermittently until it got to the stage it's at now, where it's hard to tell when she's *not* having one. Anyway, while she was in the mental hospital she met an Italian male nurse with whom she ran away to Italy. A few years later she returned with two small children, my half-brothers Tony and Bernard.

The old boy, John, had got himself engaged to another woman. This proved that there were at least two crazy females in Granton in the early sixties. They were due to be married when my Ma, Vet (short for Verity), reappeared in the lounge bar of The Anchor public house. As Dad was to remark often: Ah jist looked acroass n met yir Ma's eyes n the auld magic wis still thair.

That was that. Vet told John she'd got the travelling out of her system, that he was the only man she'd ever loved and could they please get married.

John said aye, or words to that effect, and they tied the knot, him taking on the two Italian bambinos whom Vet later confessed were from different guys. I was born about a year after the wedding, followed about a year later by my sister Kim, and my brother Elgin, who arrived a year later again. Elgin got his name from the Highland town where John reckoned he was conceived.

Yes, we were a far from handsome family. I suppose I got off relatively lightly, though I stress relatively. While my own face and body merely suggested what people in the scheme would, whispering, refer to as 'the Strang look', Kim and Elgin completely screamed it. 'The Strang look' was essentially a concave face starting at a prominent, pointed forehead, swinging in at a sharp angle towards large, dulled eyes and a small, squashed nose, down into thin, twisted lips and springing outwards to the tip of a large, jutting chin. A sort of retarded man-in-the-moon face. My additional crosses to bear: two large protruding ears which came from my otherwise normal-looking mother, invisible under her long, black hair.

My older half-brothers were more fortunate. They took after my mother, and, presumably their Italian fathers. Tony looked a little like a darker, swarthier version of the footballer Graeme Souness, though not so ugly; despite being prone to putting on weight. Bernard was fair, slim and gazelle-like, outrageously camp from an early age.

The rest of us took 'the Strang look' from the old man, who, as I've said, was an A1 basket case. John Strang's large, striking face was dominated by thickly framed glasses with bottom-of-Coke-bottle lenses. These magnified his intense, blazing eyes further. They had the effect of making him look as if he was coming from very far away then suddenly appearing right in your face. It was scary and disconcerting. If you were in possession of a Harrier Jump-jet, you could have chosen either his chin or forehead as a landing pad. He generally wore a large brown fur coat, under which he carried his shotgun when he patrolled the scheme late at night with Winston, his loyal Alsatian. Winston was a horrible dog and I was glad when he died. He was instantly replaced by an even more vicious beast of the same breed, who also rejoiced in the name Winston.

I later had cause to be less than pleased at the first Winston's demise; the second one savaged me badly. I was about eight, and watching a Superboy cartoon on the television. I decided that Winston Two was Krypto the Superdog and I tied a towel to his collar to simulate Krypto's cape. The dog freaked out and turned on me, savaging my leg so badly that I needed skin grafts and walk with a slight limp to this day . . . only now I don't walk at all.

I feel a spasm of hurt at that realisation. Remembering hurts.

— Dinnae tell nae cunt it wis Winston, Dad threatened and pleaded. He was terrified in case they took the dog away. I said it was an unprovoked attack by some of the strays which congregated on the wasteland adjacent to our block. It made the local paper and the Tory council, who hated spending the snobby ratepayers' money on anything to do with our scheme, grudgingly sent an environmental health van over to round up the savage pack-beasts for extermination. I spent four months off the school, which was the best part of it.

As a kid I did the normal things kids in the scheme did: played fitba and Japs and commandos, mucked about on bikes, caught bees, hung around stairs bored, battered smaller/weaker kids, got battered by bigger/stronger kids. At nine years old I was charged by the polis for playing football in the street. We were kicking a ball around in a patch of grass outside the block of flats we lived in. There were no

NO BALL GAMES signs up, but we should have known, even at that age, that as the scheme was a concentration camp for the poor; this like everything else, was prohibited. We were taken up to court where my mate Brian's dad made a brilliant speech and embarrassed the judge into admonishing us. You could see the polis looking like tits.

— A fuckin common criminal at the age ay nine, my Ma used tae moan. — Common criminal.

It's only in retrospect I realise that she was fucked up because the auld man was away at the time. She used to say that he was working, but Tony told us that he was in the jail. Tony was awright. He battered me a few times, but he also battered anybody who messed with me, unless they were his mates. Bernard I hated; he just stayed in the hoose and played with my wee sister Kim aw the time. Bernard was like Kim; Bernard was a girl.

I loved catching bees in the summer. We'd fill auld Squeezy detergent bottles with water and skoosh the bee as it sucked at the nectar on the flower. The trick was to train a couple of jets on the bee at the same time and blast it to fuck, the water weighing down its wings. We'd then scoop the drenched bees into a jar and then dig little prison cells for them in the softer material between the sections of brick at the ramp at the bottom of our block of flats. We used ice-lolly sticks as the doors. We had a concentration camp, a tiny Scottish housing scheme, for bees.

One of my pals, Pete, had a magnifying glass. It was great getting a shot of it. I used to like to burn the bees' wings, making them easier prisoners. Sometimes I burned their faces. The smell was horrible, the smell of burning bee. I wanted the glass. I swapped Pete an Action Man that had no arms for his magnifying glass. I had earlier swapped the Action Man fae Brian for a truck.

I was embarrassed when any of the other kids came roond to the hoose. Most of them seemed to have better hooses than us, it was like we were scruffs. That's how I knew the old man was in the jail, there was only my Ma's wages for doing the school dinners and the cleaning. Thank fuck my Ma did the dinners at a different school than the one I went to.

Then my Dad came back. He got work in security and started daein the hoose up. We got a new fireplace with plastic coals and twirly things inside a plastic funnel which made it look like heat rising. It was really just an electric bar fire but. My Dad was awright at first; I remember he took me to Easter Road for the fitba. He left me and Tony and Bernard and my cousin Alan in my Uncle Jackie's car ootside a pub. They bought us coke and crisps. When they came out they were pished from drinking beer and they got us pies and Bovril and mair crisps at the fitba. I was bored with the fitba, but I liked getting the pies and crisps. The backs of my legs got sair, like when my Ma took us tae Leith Walk tae the shops.

Then I got a bad battering fae my Dad and had to go to the hospital for stitches. He hit the side of my head and I fell over and split it on the edge of the kitchen table. Six stitches above the eye. It was barry having stitches. The auld man didn't understand that it was only clipshers I put in Kim's hair. — It wis jist clipshers, Dad, I pleaded. — Clipshers dinnae sting.

Kim just gret and gret like fuck. She wouldnae stop. It was only clipshers as well. Just clipshers. It's no as if it was bees. They have these pincers at the back, but they dinnae sting. I think Devil's Coach-Horses or Earwigs were their real names.

— Look at hur! Look what yuv fuckin well done tae yir sister ya silly wee cunt! He gestured tae Kim, whose already distorted face twisted further in contrived terror. The auld man thumped me then.

I had to tell everyone at the casualty that I was mucking aboot wi Tony and I fell. I had headaches for a long time eftir that.

I remember once watching my Ma, Vet, scrubbing the tartan nameplate on the door of our maisonette flat. Somebody had added an 'E' to our name. Dad and my Uncle Jackie went around the stair cross-examining terrified neighbours. Dad was always threatening to shoot anybody who complained about us. Other parents therefore always told their kids not to play with us, and all but the craziest ones complied.

If the neighbours were terrified of my Dad and Uncle Jackie, who was really just Dad's mate but we called him 'Uncle', they were also pretty wary of my Ma. Her father or grandfather, I could never

remember which one, had been a prisoner-of-war in a Japanese camp
and he had gone slightly loopy; a direct result, Vet claimed, of his
cruel incarceration. She grew up indoctrinated with tales of Jap
atrocities and had once read this book which contended that the
orientals would take over the world by the turn of the century. She
would scrutinise the eyes of my few friends, proclaiming them
unsuitable if they had what she considered to be 'Jap blood'.

I think I was about nine or ten when I first heard the auld man
mention South Africa. It seemed that no sooner than he mentioned
it, we were there.

— See us, Vet? Meant fir better things. Me wi aw they security
joabs. Nae prospects. Like ah sais, meant fir better things. This
country's gaun tae the dogs. Aw they strikes; cannae even git yir
fuckin bucket emptied. They trade union cunts: hudin the country
tae ransom. Sooth Efrikay, that's the place. Like ah sais, Sooth
Efrikay. Ah ken thuv goat problems in Sooth Efrikay n aw, but at
least thuv no goat this fuckin Labour Governmint. Ah'm gaunny see
aboot gittin us ower thair. Oor Gordon wid pit us up, nae danger.
Ah'll take us oot thair, Vet. Fuckin well sure'n ah will. Think ah'll
no? Ah'm askin ye! Think ah'll no?

— Nae Japs . . .

— Aye, bit git this though, Vet. Thir's nae Japs in Sooth Efrikay.
Nane. That's cause it's a white man's country, like ah sais, a white
man's country. White is right oot thair, ah kid ye not. Like ah sais:
Sooth Efrikay, white is right, Dad sang, all high and animated. His
large flat tongue licked at a stamp which he stuck on a letter. It was
probably a letter of complaint to somebody. He always wrote letters
of complaint.

— Jist as long is thir's nae Japs . . .

— Naw bit this is Sooth Efrikay. Sooth Fuckin Efrikay Vet, if yi'll
pardon ma ps n qs.

— Somewhair ah kin git tae dry clathes . . . they Pearsons . . .
eywis in the dryin green . . .

— Eh! Ah fuckin telt that cow! Ah fuckin telt hur! Ah sais tae hur,
nixt time ah fuckin see your washin in that fuckin dryin green whin
ma wife's tryin tae wash, the whole fuckin loat's gaun doon the

fuckin shute intae the rubbish! Fuckin ignorant, some people, like ah sais, fuckin ignorant. Bit see in Sooth Efrikay Vet, we'd huv a big hoose like Gordon's. Dry oor clathes in the sun, in a real fuckin gairdin, no in some concrete boax wi holes in it.

Gordon was John's brother who had left to go to South Africa years ago. Possibly John's closeness to 'Uncle' Jackie was due to him seeing Jackie as a brother substitute. Certainly at the drunken parties he frequently hosted, when squads of guys and couples would pack into our egg-box after closing time, he seemed at his happiest telling old stories of himself, Gordon and the Jubilee Gang, as he and his hippy-beating Teddy Boy mates used to call themselves.

— It wid be nice tae huv a real back gairdin . . . I remember Ma saying that. I remember that clearly.

It was decided. Dad's word generally went in our family. We were making plans to go off to South Africa.

I didnae really ken whether or no I wanted to go. It was just eftir that that I lit my first really big fire. I'd always liked fires. Boney nights were the best nights of the year in the scheme, Guy Fawkes because you got fireworks, but Victoria Day n aw. We'd go doon the beach tae get wood or find other boneys in the scheme and raid them. Sometimes, though, we got raided ourselves. You would get cudgels and stanes and try to defend your bonfire against raiders. There was always fights with stanes in the scheme. The first thing I learned tae dae was tae fling a stane. That was what you did as a kid in Muirhoose, you flung stanes; flung them at radges, at windaes, at buses.

It was something to do.

The fire, though, that was something else. It was eftir the boney. I had a lighted torch and I put it doon the rubbish chute. It ignited the rubbish in the big bucket in the budget room at the bottom of the building. Two fire engines came. Ma mate Brian made ays shite masel.

— Ooohhh! You'll get taken away, Roy, he telt me with wide-eyed glee at my fear.

Ah wis shitin it, nearly fuckin greetin n aw that. Brian kept taking the pish, but I'll gie him his due, he never telt nae cunt. The polis came roond every door and asked aw these questions. My Dad said nothing. — Never tell these cunts anything, he used to drum into us. It was the one bit of sense I ever remember him talking. He was really chuffed about the fire as well, because Mrs Pearson from up the stairs had her washing ruined by the smoke. It rose from the budget room to the drying greens above it.

— Serves the cow fuckin well right, like ah sais, the fuckin ignorant boot. Shouldnae be monopolisin the fuckin drying greens whin thir's people wantin tae hing oot a washin! That's what she fuckin well gets!

It dawned on me that the auld man was probably prime suspect in the lighting of the fire. He was chuffed to have a cast-iron alibi; he was playing in his dominoes league match up at the Doocot when it started. He was so chuffed that I wanted to tell him it was me, but I resisted the temptation. The cunt could change moods quickly.

Sometimes me and my pals used to go out of the scheme, but it was usually just doon the beach. Me, Pete, Brian, Deek (Bri's brother) and Dennis, we would think aboot running away and going camping, like in the Enid Blyton books. We usually just got as far as the fuckin beach, before getting fed up and going hame. Occasionally we'd walk to snobby bits like Barnton, Cramond or Blackhall. The polis would always come around and make us go hame, though. People in the big hooses, hooses that were the same size as our block, which sixty families lived in; they would just go away and phone the polis. They must have thought we were gaunny chorie aypils or something. Aw I wanted tae dae was tae watch birds. I got an interest in birds, used to get loads ay books on them fae the library. I got this from my auld man, I suppose. He was really interested in birds as well.

I mind ay askin ma Dad if we would live in a big hoose like the ones in Barnton when we went tae South Africa.

— Bigger than thaim though son, much bigger. Like ah sais, much bigger, he telt ays.

The funny thing is that it was in the period when we were preparing to go to South Africa that I have some of the most vivid memories of John, my Dad. As I've indicated, he was a little bit crazy and we were all frightened of him. He was far too intense about things, and got himself worked up over nothing. I worried about the shotgun he kept under the bed.

Our main point of contact was through television. John would take the TV pages from the *Daily Record* and circle the programmes to watch that evening. He was a keen nature freak, and as I mentioned, particularly interested in ornithology. We both loved the David Attenborough style nature documentaries. He was never so happy as when programmes on exotic birds came on the box and he was very knowledgeable on the subject. John Strang was a man who knew the difference between a Cinnamon Bracken Warbler and, say, the Brown Woodland variety.

— See that! Bullshit! A Luhder's Bush Shrike, the boy sais! That's a Doherty's Bush Shrike! Like ah sais, a Doherty's Bush Shrike! Jist as well ah'm tapin this oan the video!

We were the first family in the district to have all the key consumer goods as they came onto the market: colour television, video recorder and eventually satellite dish. Dad thought that they made us different from the rest of the families in the scheme, a cut above the others. Middle-class, he often said.

All they did was define us as prototype schemies.

I remember the note he sent to the BBC, smug in his knowledge that for all the research capabilities he imagined them having at their disposal, their presenter had got his facts wrong. The reply was initially a great source of pride to him:

Dear Mr Strange,

Thank you for your letter in which you point out the factual error in our programme WINGS OVER THE BUSH which was transmitted last Thursday.

While this particular nature documentary was not made by the BBC, as commissioners of the group of independent film-makers who produced the programme, we accept liability for such inaccuracy in our broadcasts.

While we at the BBC strive for accuracy in every area of our broadcasting activities, errors will inevitably occur from time to time and keen members of the viewing public with specialist knowledge like yourself provide an invaluable service in bringing such inaccuracies to our attention.

The vigilant and informed viewer has a key role to play in ensuring that we at the BBC maintain our high standards of broadcast excellence and adequately fulfill the responsibilities of our charter, namely: to educate, inform and entertain.

Once again, thank you for your correspondence.

Yours sincerely,

Roger Snape
Programme Controller, Nature Documentaries.

The old man showed every fucker that letter. He showed them in the pub, and at his work with Group Six Securities. He freaked out when my Uncle Jackie pointed out to him that they had misspelled his name. He wrote a letter to Roger Snape saying that if he was ever in London, he would kick fuck out of him.

Dear Mr Snap,

Thank you for your letter in which you show yourself to be an ignorant person not spelling my name right. I just want you to know that I do not like people not spelling my name right. It is S-T-R-A-N-G. If I am ever in London I will snap you . . . into small pieces.

Yours faithfully,

John STRANG.

The only things which seemed to give Dad enjoyment were drinking alcohol and listening to records of Winston Churchill's wartime speeches. Pools of tears would well up behind his thick lenses as he was moved by his idol's stirring rhetoric.

But these were the best times. The worst were the boxing lessons he gave us. He had a thing about me being too uncoordinated, especially with my limp, and considered Bernard too effeminate. He bought us cheap, plastic boxing gloves and set up a ring in the living-room, with four confiscated traffic cones defining its perimeters.

Bernard was even less interested in the boxing than I was, but Dad would force us to fight until one or both of us broke down in tears of misery and frustration. The gloves caused a great deal of scratching, scarring and tearing, and it looked as if we'd been slashing rather than punching each other. Bernard was older, bigger, and heavier-handed, but I was more vicious and had quickly sussed out that you could do greater damage with slashing swipes than punches.

— C'moan Roy, Dad would shout. – Punch um, punch um, son . . . Keep that jab gaun Bernard . . . dinnae fuckin slap um like a pansy . . . His coaching advice was always a bit one-sided. Before the fights he used to whisper to me: — You're a Strang son, mind that. He's no. Mind that. Right? Mind, yir fightin fir the Strang name. He might git called a Strang, but eh's no. Eh's a fuckin crappin eyetie bastard son.

On one occasion when I had marked Bernard's eye and swollen his lip, John could scarcely contain himself: — Keep that fuckin jab in ehs eye, Roy! Poke ehs fuckin eye right oot!

I kept jabbing away at that reddening queer face, my body tight with concentration as Bernard's eyes filled with petulant unease.

BANG

      QUEER-FACED CUNT

BANG

      TAKE THAT YA FUCKIN SAPPY BIG
      POOF

BANG

I opened up his eye above the brow with a tearing twist of the glove. I felt a jolt of fear in my chest and I wanted to stop; it was the blood, splashing out onto his face. I was about to drop my hands but when I looked at Dad he snarled at me to fight on: — GO FIR THE KILL, NAE FUCKIN PRISONERS!

I battered into the fearful face of my broken-spirited pansy half-brother. His gloves fell by his sides as I kept swinging wildly, urged on by John's frenzied cries. Bernard turned his back on me and left the room sobbing, running up the stairs and locking himself in the toilet.

— Bernard! Ye'll huv tae learn tae stick up fir yirsel! John smirked, a little worried as Ma would not be pleased when she came back from the shops in Leith and inspected the damage. On that particular occasion, I came off the best, but it wasn't always like that. Sometimes it was me who beat a humiliating retreat, overwhelmed by pain and frustration.

At such times I envied my younger brother Elgin, silently rocking or gently humming, trapped in a world of his own, exempt from this torture. Perhaps Elgin had the right idea; perhaps it was all just psychic defence. At times I envied Elgin's autism. Now I have what he has, his peace and detachment from it all.

As for me and Bernard, those fights made us fear Dad and hate each other.

Bernard was

Ber no I've no time for this.

Now the nurses are back. They're doing something to me.

THIS IS ALWAYS UNPLEASANT

Turn the cabbage, prevent him rotting away . . .

I have to go deeper.

Deeper.

DEEPER

DEEPER

Away from them.

Better.

Now it's time to go
                    to
                           the
                                hunt — — — — — — — —

There is one lush green national park which is unique. Nowhere else in the world does such a park exist in a major city. Only a few miles separate the centre of the city from this park where game animals and the large carnivores which prey on them exist in the splendour of half a century ago

— — — Easter Road Nairobi got to stop this shite deeper deeper — — — —

The area of the park, around fifty square miles, is small in comparison to other faunal reserves in this part of the   **again** —   - just bad news,
world, but the park nevertheless   **up**   I really made a fool
possesses a diversity of   of myself. Once he
                               coming   got what he wanted
environments   **I'm**   he was off, off like a shot
The entrance . . . — — — — — — **aw fuck**   into the night, back to his life
                                  and there I was, left alone, again.
                    Left with nothing. I should have known. I should have known.

    I'm not deep enough. I can hear her. Nurse Patricia Devine. She's confessing to me, her vegetable priest, he who cannot affirm or condemn. I've found my perfect role.

    — You always think that the next one will be different and I suppose I let my emotions get the better of me, got all carried away and read what I wanted to read between the lines. He was so charming, so wonderful, so understanding but, yes, that was before he got me into bed . . .

    Sobbing sounds.

    — . . . Why am I telling you this . . . why not . . . it's not as if you can hear me, it's not as if you'll ever wake up . . . oh God, I'm so sorry I said that . . . I'm just upset, I didn't mean that, I mean some people do wake up . . . they do get better . . . I'm just not myself just now Roy, you see, I let this one get right into my head as well as into my pants. Letting them into your pants is bad enough, but when they get into your head . . . it's like . . .

No

Don't want this

DEEPER

          DEEPER

                    DEEPER --- Mwaaa! A loud, nasal sound. The sound of an adult Stork threatening a human intruder. I look around and Sandy Jamieson is boldly starting the ugly bird down.

— Net the bastard, Roy! Net the cunt! he shouts.

My psychic quality control is bloody bloody bloody damn well fucked and everything has changed and suddenly I'm standing with a ball at my feet on a football pitch. I slam it into an empty net. A couple of players in the same jerseys grab me in celebration; one of them seems to be Lexo, oh fuck naw, no Lexo, and I try to get free but he willnae let ays go and over the shoulder of his crushing bear hug I see Jamieson looking deflated, his hands resting wearily oan his hips.

3 The Pursuit Of Truth

The old man had always been a nutter, but it seemed to me that he started to lose it really badly when we were preparing to move to South Africa. He probably knew he was a fuckin loser and this was his last throw of the dice to make something of his life. His nervousness was apparent, he was smoking more than ever. He would sit up most of the night, either with my Uncle Jackie or even sometimes with Tony, who was only fourteen but was very mature in certain ways for his age. Anytime we were out and he saw a young lassie, Tony would mutter, — Ah'd shag the fuckin erse oafay that . . .

From an early age Tony hung around with girls fae the scheme. He was always driven by hormones and completely oblivious to any other forces like logic or conscience which might serve as a counterbalance. It was inevitable that he would get some dopey cow up the stick, which he did. Her father came round to the house looking for justice. John instantly freaked out, threatening to blow him away with his shotgun. I remember this incident as I was trying to watch Superboy on the telly. The introduction was in full swing and Superboy and his loyal friend Krypto were flying through the air, dedicated to what the commentator described as 'the pursuit of truth'. I remember looking down at Winston Two, who sat curled up in front of the electric fire. I stared at the soft-breathing beast and thought of how his rib cage could be so easily shattered by simply jumping on it with a pair of heavy boots. I had a pair of heavy boots. It was something to think about. The scar tissue on the wounds Winston Two had given me tingled.

Elgin was sitting on the settee, his expression vacant, lost in a world of his own.

My concentration, divided between fantasising the slaughter of my canine assailant and watching Superboy, was shattered by my father's voice coming from the front door and ricocheting around the concrete blocks of the scheme.

— YOU KEEP YIR FUCKIN HOOR AY A DAUGHTER AWAY FI MA FUCKIN LADDIES OR AH'LL GIT MA FUCKIN SHOTGUN N FUCKIN WELL BLAW YIS AW AWAY!! RIGHT!!

I stealthily sneaked outside to see the guy timidly capitulate, leaving his daughter to face the alternatives of abortion or single parenthood. His conversation with the old man probably convinced him that these were sounder options than marrying into my family.

I crept back into the living-room, leaving my father bellowing at the retreating man, as every net curtain in our block and the one opposite twitched. John Strang was at it again. A bit later he came in, shaking, and Tony followed him sheepishly, tears in his eyes. My Dad looked down at me. I kept my attention on the set but he snapped, — Roy! Doon tae the shoaps fir ays. Forty fuckin Regal!

— How's it ey me that hus tae go? How no Elgin? It was a stupid thing to say. It just came out in my anger at being disturbed from my telly programme.

My Dad shook with rage. He gestured over to my brother who was now rocking on the couch. On sensing that he was being referred to, Elgin let out a steady mmmmmmmm.

— He cannae go! HE CANNAE FUCKIN WELL GO!! Ye fuckin well ken that, ya stupit wee . . . use the brains God gied ye, Roy. Like ah sais, the fuckin brains God gied um, he turned to Vet.

— It's no as if he's a stupid laddie . . . my Ma said to him.

— A dreamer, that's whit the school sais! Like ah sais, a dreamer. Heid stuffed too fill ay they fuckin comics!

I felt a horrendous tremor rumble through me as Dad's eyes burned with inspiration. — Ah'll fling aw they daft comics oot! How wid ye like that! Eh? Ah'm asking ye! How wid ye like that!

— Ah'll go . . . ah'll go . . . I helplessly whined.

— Think ah'll no? Eh? Think ah'll no? Ah'm asking ye! Think ah'll no?

— No ehs comics fir fuck sakes, John, Ma pleaded. — No the laddie's collection ay Marvel comics.

There was self-interest underpinning her concern as my Ma was a big fan of the *Silver Surfer*.

— Well then, git! Dad snorted. — N dinnae think thit yi'll no huv tae improve yir schoolwork, son!

I was putting my coat on in the lobby when Dad came out. — Ah   jist gaun . . . I said, terrified of those intense, blazing eyes.

He put his hands on my shoulders. My head was bowed. — Look at ays, he said. I looked up, but I couldn't stop my eyes from watering. — Whit's wrong? Look son, ah ken thit ah'm harder oan you thin the rest. It's cause you're the one wi the brains, son. Ah ken that. It's jist thit ye dinnae use these brains. Like ah sais, brains, he tapped his large forehead. — Ah hud brains n ah didnae use thum. Ye dinnae want tae end up like me, he said, looking genuinely tormented with remorse. — Sooth Efrikay, it'll aw be different thair though, eh?

— Aye. N wi'll be able tae go tae a Safari Park, Dad? I asked.

— Ah've telt ye! Ah'm gaunny git a joab as a Park Ranger. Wi'll be practically livin in a Safari Park.

— Barry, I said with genuine enthusiasm. I was still at the age where, despite being embarrassed at their weirdness, I essentially believed in the omnipotence of my parents. I skipped along to the shops.

The old man was right though. I was a dreamer, stuck in my own world for much of the time. I'd have my head buried in the adventures of the *Silver Surver* and the *Fantastic Four* and the likes. This was because I never really fitted in anywhere. I was quiet at school, but had got intae trouble for stabbing a laddie with a compass. They were laughing at me. They called me Dumbo Strang or the Scottish Cup because of my ears. On top of all my other Strang defects, I had to be cursed with those protruding lugs. I was, though, working out a simple formula: if you hurt them, they don't laugh, and I can't stand anybody laughing at me. I had learned that I could take pain. Physical pain I could take. If you can stand pain you're going to give any cunt problems. If you can stand pain and you arenae feart and you're angry. Pain I could stand. Them laughing at me; I couldnae take that.

The teacher and the headmaster expected me to feel guilty for what I had done. They expected me to fear them. I didn't fear them. I lived in a houseful of sociopaths so the disapproving threats of middle-class teachers calling me a warped, evil and nasty little creature didn't bother me, they just lowered my self-esteem further, became a set of terms of reference for me to embrace.

But it wasn't as if I was disruptive at school; I was nothing. I withdrew as much into anonymity as I could. I wanted to be invisible. I wanted nobody to see the misshapen, twisted Dumbo Strang. I just sat at the back of the class and daydreamed.

At home in my bedroom, I rubbed my cock to illustrations of Sue Storm, The Invisible Girl, in my *Fantastic Four* comics. The drawings of Sue being kidnapped and restrained were the biggest turn-ons. Sometimes you got well-defined tits, arse and lips in the drawings.

I wonder now if the pursuit of the Marabou is about anything as fundamental as the pursuit of truth. I'll have to go deeper to find out.

DEEPER
            DEEPER
                        DEEPER————————Now I'm back in the hunt, heading deeper, because I feel the heat and see the light. On my face, in my eyes. I feel the warm, dusty sweet air in my lungs and cough and wonder if it registers in my slumbering near-corpse up in the other world.

We had got back into town and Sandy, forever the sport, had traded our photography equipment for an old jeep. — All this has to do is to get us out to Dawson's. He'll see us alright, Sandy smiled.

— But your equipment, Sandy . . . I felt awful, knowing how keen Sandy was on photography. He always said ruefully: the camera never lies.

— Photos won't be much good against the Stork. We need

hardware, and Dawson's the chap to get it for us. The time for photographs is later on!

— I can't wait, I said excitedly. — I can think of lots of things I want to photograph!

We found cheap lodgings in a poor area of the town and spent the evening drinking bottled beer in a spartan hut of a bar.

— Do you have any food? Sandy asked the bartender.

— We have the best homemade steak pie and mashed potatoes in Africa, said the barman, — followed by the most scrumptious apple crumble absolutely drenched in whipped cream!

— Gosh, that's just what we could do with after all that travelling, Sandy said eagerly, and we sat down to a feast.

Despite the bartender's enthusiasm, the food simply wasn't up to scratch. That night I experienced a fevered, alcoholic sleep. The Storks were pursuing me in my dreams. Then it was the group of youths from the large, municipal building. I woke up more than a few times covered in sweat. On one occasion I came to absolutely terrified, after having been followed by something which did not reveal itself, but which I could sense lurking in the shadows. This thing suggested such horror and evil that I dared not trust myself to the mercies of sleep. I left Jamieson slumbering heartily and sat up at an old, marked wooden table, writing up my notebook.

The next morning we set off. The burning, sweltering sun had turned the dark continent into a vast furnace. I was weary and out of sorts. Nothing felt right. My bare legs in my khaki shorts stung with pain every time they came into involuntary contact with the hot body of our jeep. Avoiding such unwanted bonding was impossible when we were shaking in gravelly ascent towards the Alpine Moorlands, our four-wheel-drive vehicle still struggling to negotiate the rough surface and steep inclines.

My discomfort lifted as almost imperceptibly we found ourselves travelling through an environment I can only describe as paradise. My awareness of it started as we passed through a magnificent belt of juniper and podocarpus, and I began rushing on the magical fragrances that filled the air, before we reached the high altitude bamboo forest with its mighty gorges, sylvan glades and fast trout streams.

— Isn't this heavenly! I exclaimed to Sandy.

— I'll say, Roy, Sandy agreed, tearing open a packet of chocolate biscuits. – Munchie wunchies, he smiled.

We drove past a couple of elephant and buffalo herds grazing in a grassland clearing and Sandy even claimed to have spotted a rare black rhino. Ahead was our destination, one of Dawson's lodges, No. 1690, which lay approximately 7,000 feet above sea level in the heart of the forest.

On our way up a particularly challenging incline, Sandy passed over the large joint he had been smoking. After a couple of enthusiastic tokes I was feeling somewhat out of sorts. Generally, when I take drugs of this type I can reserve a small central part of my brain for sobriety. This becomes a lens, through which I can, with concentration, view the world with a certain

clarity – – – but it – – – was all fuckin

falling apart eftir jist one fuckin toke . . .   – Time

this shouldnae be happening   up   for your

– – – shouldnae be – – – – – – – – – – – coming   injection, Roy

Simply Devine, Patricia.

Sidney Devine.

I'll be back, Sandy.

— Your girlfriend looked nice. I hadn't seen her before. Still, I suppose I'm quite new on this ward.

What girlfriend? Surely that fat hoor wisnae back. Some mistake surely. She'll be gettin fucked by somebody else long ago and good riddance. And I gave that fuckin boot a ring. Fuckin joke. Git back tae Fathell, Dorie my love.

No don't talk about her that way don't talk like that about Dorie who isnae real nowt's fuckin real

Stay cool

— I think she's a bit shy. Very pretty though. You're a bit of a dark horse, aren't you Roy?

I've not got much to say for myself, Patricia. Plenty to think about though.

— You know Roy, I heard all about you. It came as a shock to me.

— Right Nurse Devine, let's get him changed.

— Oh, Staff, Right.

Caught again Patricia, caught blethering to the veg.
Fuck getting changed.
Fuck getting shaken aboot like a pea in a whistle . . . this whistle

the whistle

This requires DEPTH.

D

     E

          P

             T

                 H-------------------

After circling around on a path on the periphery
of the forest for a while, we eventually pulled
into a yard. The lodge was a strange building,   k   – Still quite
constructed on stilts. The smell of diesel from   c   heavy aren't
our vehicle was overpowering. It smelt like   u   you, Roy?
hospit not hospitals ------------   f   Isn't he, Tricia?
                                         – Yes, he certainly

is . . . I feel really bad about us moving him into the corridor like this, Bev.

    — I know Tricia, but it's only going to be for a couple of nights, then he'll have his room back.
Won't you, Roy?

Ah dinnae gie a fuck where ye pit ays. Stick ays oot wi the rubbish
fir aw ah care, ya cunts.

    — I think it's terrible though. Some rich private patient needs the room, so a long-term, coma
victim is dumped in the corridor until the wealthy case is ready to go . . .

    — The hospital needs the funds these people bring in though, Tricia.

    — Well, I'm just glad I'm not on duty when we have to explain to the family what he's doing in
the corridor.

Deeper.

Can't I get some shagging interest in this? Conjure up a fleshy hologram of Nurse Patricia Devine and fuck her no no no

Dawson

Dawson, who looks like a criminal seal, eyes alert and open in all that blubber . . .

What does Patricia Devine look like

HAIR

EYES

TEETH

COMPLEXION

TITS

ARSE

MINGE

LEGS

It needs a woman in this not as a real person just for the shag interest just for

DEEPER
  DEEPER
    DEEPER
      DEEPER
        DEEPER
          DEEPER
            DEEPER
              DEEPER
                DEEPER – – – – – Dawson . . . on our arrival at the lodge he had stolen over to me, completely ignoring Sandy, and shaken my hand with a theatrical warmth. He let his eyes hold mine for a few seconds of contrived intimacy and boomed in a deep,

affectedly sincere voice, — Roy Strang. I've read so much about you in the papers. A pleasure to meet you.

— You're no slouch in the publicity stakes yourself, Mr Dawson, I commented.

— Lochart, please; call me Lochart, he implored. He grinned idiotically for a few more rather excruciating moments then once again looked penetratingly at me. There was a snidey, manipulative aspect to his eyes which was totally incongruent with the open, garrulous set of his mouth. He reminded me of nothing more than a desperate old queen attempting to score in a singles bar, apparently casual but ever conscious of the remorseless clock. He looked mildly uneasy for a brief second or two, as if he was reading my thoughts, and then cackled, – We'll, I hope that my publicity is a little more, eh, salubrious, than yours. But they say that there's no such thing as bad publicity. That is an adage that I have at least some sympathy with.

This conversation was becoming rather upsetting. — I don't believe that to be the case. Few people would welcome what I've gone through . . .

— All this self-pity, Roy! Very disappointing, he boomed, slapping my back, his hand making a sound like a wet fish hitting a slab. Then he ushered me through to a library, leading to a conservatory at the back of the Lodge. As we moved towards the French windows, he plucked a book from the shelf and handed it to me. — For you, he smiled. I looked at the title:

YOUTH IN ASIA

I stuck it in a plastic bag I had been carrying.

— I see you have the toolkit handy, he smirked. Damn and fucking blast, I felt a little uneasy at this statement. I started to remember something, no, not remember a thought, but an experience, I started to *feel* something unpleasant and was happy when Sandy came through and interrupted this sensation before it could flower into recall.

Sandy had said something about a jeep. Our rusty ancient blighter had buggered up badly on reaching the lodge. As Sandy had

suspected, Dawson was pleased to sell us an old one from Jambola
Park, at about three times the normal price. — This one, he smiled,
and looked at Sandy in a way which caused him to visibly twitch, —
is surplus to requirements.

As well as being ripped off with the jeep, we were forced to
accompany Dawson on a visit to his favourite spot in the hills, a place
he visits regularly for its natural beauty. We had to walk about two
and a half miles from Lodge 1690 and it was now overpoweringly,
miserably hot; a smudge of sweat on the back of Jamieson's shirt had
become a large heart. I made reference to this and Dawson smiled
approvingly, lavishly, from his one-man buggy. Sweat trickled
down my legs. Sandy looked quite fresh but Dawson, despite the
motor cart, was saturated and breathing in a laboured, heavy
manner. One of the wheels of his vehicle crushed a snake, mashing
the animal into the path. His head poked out the side of the cart and
grinned hideously back at us.

— Unfortunately, only one available, he'd smiled widely as he'd
twisted his girth into the motorised cart. Starting it up, he had, with
snapping jocularity, bade Sandy Jamieson and I to follow him on
foot. Dawson's skin was the colour of barbecued tandoori chicken;
clashing vividly with a Brylcreemed shock of brown, thinning hair,
white and blue eyes, and pearly teeth which seemed permanently
hanging out to dry. He also appeared to be covered in a strange,
translucent oil.

Dawson stopped the buggy, climbed out and swept a doughy
paw around his terrain. Our track wound around the precipice of a
spectacular gorge, which swung down towards a fast-flowing river.
— Not bad for a lad who left home with the less than princely sum of
ten pounds sterling in his pocket, he smugly observed.

I saw a dead rodent by the side of the path. I picked it up by the
tail. It had a fat slimy leech attached to it. I dropped it and looked at
Sandy. — I came to Africa to study parasites, I told him, glancing
back at Dawson. Sandy appeared a little bit uneasy, and gestured at
me to keep my voice down.

I remembered Sandy saying that he once worked for Dawson.
Gosh and golly.

Our destination was a building which on the outside looked rundown and ramshackle, but internally was very stark, modern and functional, its harshness only dissipated by a number of large, exotic plants in pots. We were greeted by a stout, middle-aged African woman, who made a particular fuss of Lochart Dawson.

— This is great pleshah, Missuh Dossan, she smiled.

— On the contrary, Sadie, the pleasure is always mine in visiting your fine establishment.

His smile made me feel as if I'd eaten or drank something decidedly unpleasant.

— For my guests, he smiled, turning to Sandy and myself. — You see, I own this place, and I use it as a sort of unofficial hospitality suite for potentially special customers. Special being defined as those who can advance the interests of Jambola Park PLC. This facility was specifically constructed on the impetus of the board of Jambola Park PLC, of which I am a member.

Dawson owned seventy-eight per cent of the Jambola Park PLC shares.

At that point Sandy went to light a cigarette but stopped after noting the look of disapproval on Dawson's face. He extended his palms and looked at me in appeal. I shrugged briefly.

I felt the hand of the African woman called Sadie rest on my shoulder. — You are veh tense, she said. — Would you like me find girl massage you neck? Perhaps bit more than you neck?

— Eh . . . if I could just have a glass of water, please.

Dawson curled his lips downwards in disapproval. — Yes, Sadie, the water. For myself and Mr Jamieson as well. I should imagine you two are rather thirsty camels after your exploits.

— I'll say! I nodded appreciatively.

Sadie departed but returned quickly with a tray on which sat three glasses and a pitcher of iced water. Also now in attendance were three young white girls. They looked skinny, malnourished and dirty and their eyes were thickly clouded over.

I sipped at the water which was so cold that it made my teeth hurt.

— So you are, like Mr Jamieson, a hunter?

— Yes, though perhaps not as successful as Sandy . . . I started.

Dawson interrupted me with a nasty smirk. — I would hardly say that Mr Jamieson has been particularly successful on the trophy hunting front. I must say, though, that I've found it persistently difficult to find hunters who look like bagging trophies. What is your specialisation, Roy?

— Sharks mainly, but also scavengers.

Dawson raised an eyebrow and gave a knowing nod. — And you, Mr Jamieson, still hunting the maneaters?

— Eh, yes, said Sandy nervously, — I mean, with only spears to rely on in defence, African villagers are effectively helpless in the face of lion attacks on their settlements . . .

— Yes, smiled Dawson, — in nearly all cases the maneater is an animal well past his prime. He has lost all his youthful agility and is simply not up to the capture of wild game for food.

— Man, though, is easy to procure, Sandy said, the unease of realisation coming into his voice.

— Oh yes, agreed Dawson with a slow, sly nod, — oh yes. Then he looked intently at Sandy and, with his face strangely blank and dead, said in a teasing tone out of synch with his expression: — I'd like to ask you, Mr Jamieson, have you an awareness of the role of ritual?

Sandy, obviously fazed, looked across at me, then back at Lochart Dawson. — As a sportsman, he began, but Dawson raised a Pillsbury Dough-boy hand to silence him.

— A sportsman. How . . . anachronistic. I should not have addressed such a statement to a sportsman. His voice went low and mocking at the term 'sportsman'. — The role of ritual is to make things safe for those who have most to lose by things not being safe. Wouldn't you agree, Roy?

— It's not a concept I've thought about exploring deeply Lochart, though I have to confess it does have a certain prima facie appeal.

Dawson seemed irritated that I was not getting into things with him. — And my proposal that the sportsman is an anachronism? Is that a concept you've had time to explore? His pitch is now challenging.

— I'd probably need to have the proposition defined in a little more detail before I would presume to comment.

— Very well, Dawson smiled, tucking his shirt into his trousers and belching, — I contend that sport, like everything else, has been replaced by business.

Dashed if I didn't find myself arguing in spite of what I'd intended. — Up to a point. Sport though, when it has a cultural locus, becomes a source of identity to people. Lose such sources of identity, and you have an atomised, disjointed society. Sport can move some people in a way that the profit motive can never. Our values have become obscured and warped to the extent that the means for self-actualisation, i.e. money, has become an end in itself. One of the ends is the appreciation of sport. Another might be art. Another might be the precipitation of chaos.

Dawson chuckled pneumatic-drill style, his flesh wobbling steadily as he laughed. — Yes Roy, sport does move the masses, but they only gain any relevance insofar as they are involved in the economic process, insofar as they become consumers. Sport has to be packaged to the masses, leisure has to be sold to them in a way they understand. Yes, in the past people had families, communities. There was a sense of living together. Through this they developed a shared understanding of the world, developed different cultures. Now not all of these cultures are in empathy with the profit system, and therefore they have to be replaced by another, stronger, richer culture, or at least assimilated into it. Families and communities have to be broken up further, have to be taken to where the work is, have to be denied at all costs meaningful interaction with each other. They have to live in, as our American friends call them, subdivisions. They have to be economically and physically subdivided . . .

I smiled and cut in, — And the old culture replaced by advertisers and marketeers telling people what to enjoy. Easy when they have no other ponts of reference, e.g. other people in the same economic and social circumstances. So through the media you have people in different economic and social circumstances telling them what to consume. The key is the increasing of choice through the process of subdivision you alluded to. The increasing experiencing of leisure and sport indirectly, has encouraged a decrease in real participation, which is direct communion. Therefore you have the replacement of one or two really decent experiences with loads and loads of crap things.

— Yes. But what you're doing is merely illustrating my point.

— Or you mine. Perhaps sport has colonised capitalism rather than the other way around. The rampant self-promotion of businessmen in the eighties is an example. They refer to themselves as main players and their vocabulary is a sporting one; whole new ball games, level playing fields, moving goalposts, and all that.

Dawson looked a bit shirty. — Yes Roy, but we have colonised sport and plundered its language . . .

— But perhaps the superiority of that terminology illustrates that sport and the sporting instinct are sovereign and that capitalism is just a branch of sport, a warped, inferior branch of sport, sport with money . . .

— In which case, then, it disproves your contention that the pursuit of profit, the only truth, cannot be self-actualising, if the accumulation of that wealth has sporting elements.

— No, it proves it. Capitalism has had to graft on sporting culture, the culture of games, in order to make the pursuit of money seem a worthwhile endeavour in itself.

— Look, Dawson began, exasperated, — you obviously don't understand the process of debate. Anyway, it's time to water the plants.

He snapped his fingers and began rubbing at his groin through his flannel trousers. The three girls took up position in front of him, squatting over some of the plant pots.

Unzipping his flies and removing a stumpy, semi-erect penis from his trousers and pants, Dawson masturbated himself hard as the girls discharged hot, steamy urine into the soil of the robust plants. He came powerfully, looking like a man going into cardiac seizure, gasping like

like

like somebody else. Just somebody else.

I REMEMBER   up the road tae the Ferry Boat.
                        up   A guy had a fit
I REMEMBER   up   a fit at this party
                   up   eftir my Uncle Jackie glassed him
Coming back up .   the boy was nearly fucked for good

I REMEMBER the party we had in the lounge bar of the Ferry Boat
public house, a couple of days before we set off for London on our
way to Johannesburg. They booked the top bar. Everyone was
there. We were allowed in; me, Kim, and Gerald with our lemonade,
Tony was allowed beer. It was brilliant.
    Mum serenaded John with 'Big Spender'.

    The minute you walked in the joint,
    I could tell ye were a man of distinction,
    A real big spender.
    Good lookin, so refined,
    Suppose you'd like to know what's goin on in ma mind.

    So let me get right to the point do-do,
    I don't pop my cork for every man I see.
    Hey big spender,
    Hey big spender,
    Spend a li-ril time with me.
                    do-do-do-do-do

  — Still got the voice, Vet, Uncle Jackie said.

    So would ye like tae have fun, fun, fun,
    How's about a few laughs, laughs, laughs,
    Let me show you a good time,
    I could show you a good time . . .

    I sat in the corner with Bernard and Kim, munching on our Coke
and crisps. I was enjoying myself. My Ma was a good singer,
especially with the band backing her, and I was drinking in the

applause she was getting. I felt like royalty. The only ghost at the feast was Elgin. It had been decided that he wasn't coming to South Africa with us.

He had got a place at the GORGIE VENTURE HOSTEL FOR EXCEPTIONAL YOUNG MEN. There, it was explained, he'd be properly looked after by specialist staff. My Gran would visit, so would my Uncle and Auntie Jackie. (They were called John and Jacqueline respectively, but when they got together, neither had wanted to surrender their accustomed name of Jackie, so they were both known by that title.) One day, Dad had told us, we would send for Elgin. Kim was heartbroken, but I was relieved. To me it was one less embarrassment to have to worry about and I still had plenty.

I remember that night. It was good until Ma spoiled it by getting pished and acting like a slut. Dad punched this guy who'd been chatting her up. Uncle Jackie then glassed the guy's pal, and the polis came and broke up the party. Dad was done for causing a breach of the peace, which resulted in a minor fine for him, while Uncle Jackie got six months for malicious wounding. The guy went into shock following the attack and his heart stopped. He had to be revived by the ambulance crew. They were quite near at hand, coming from the Western General. Now they've shut down the accident and emergency there, so he probably would have died if it had happened today.

— Ah nivir fuckin well touched um! Jackie roared unconvincingly as blood spilled from the man's twitching body and he and Dad were huckled into the station which was right next door to the pub.

I remember walking home with Tony, Bernard, Kim and Ma down Pennywell Road. The night had ended in disaster, our last proper night in Scotland, and it was all Ma's fault. I hate to see women who should have dignity acting like sluts. I hate because it

No way.

Deeper

```
                          deeper. In fact I'm further up
              get         because I can hear Patricia
              can't       Devine telling me that
This is disturbing because I        I have a visitor. I'm so
                                    conscious, I'm almost
                                    awake. I fear waking up.
```
I fear it more than ever.

Patricia Devine's voice; cloying, but yet with a harshness to it. When we're alone together she tells me all about her life. I want to gather her up and protect her and love her because of all the hurt and disappointment she's suffered. I want to do this to make up for my . . . there's nothing to make up for. It was all Lexo's fault.

I've revised my image of what Patricia looks like. I see her now as slightly older than I first imagined, formerly very attractive but now a little gone to seed. Perhaps a bit over made-up and carrying a couple of extra pounds. She never married that surgeon. She seems a bit like the air hostess I saw on that plane to Johannesburg, the first time I'd flown. Bitter, having failed to marry the pilot. Travelling from one ugly airport building to another, from one systems built airport hotel to another. The glamour of flight my arse. What was she? The airways bike. Even at ten years old, I knew what she was like.

Patricia is similar. After the doctors, it's the male nurses, then perhaps the technicians. She'll be on the porters soon. Downwardly mobile sexually. You're simply Devine though, Patricia. If only I could brush your tears away. No. I know you too well now. I'd just be another source of hurt and betrayal to you. You scream desperation. It's going to take an exceptional piece of luck to arrest your decline, to break this sad cycle.

Why is it that I can only see people in the negative, only recognise them through their pain and their thwarted ambitions?

Because I'm a

— Yes Roy, it's your visitor friend from yesterday. She's back, Patricia says. Yes, we have company. I can tell by Patricia's tone. She has her in-company voice on; sugary, pretend intimate but in reality anything but.

The visitor does not respond. It is a she though. I can smell traces of her perfume. I think I can smell it. Maybe I'm just imagining I can smell it. Whatever, it's oddly familiar. Maybe I fucked her once.

I went through a phase when I fucked loads of women. This was after I discovered that all you had to do was be what they wanted for about twenty minutes. I suppose we're talking about a certain type of woman here. Each time you went through that bullshit act to get closer to them, you got further away from what you wanted to be. At the time it made me feel good about myself because I was younger. This shagging period represented a change in what I was doing before, which was not getting a ride and this was not a good place to be, for all sorts of reasons. Now it seems a very good place to be, but that was then. I doubt if a shag would make me feel good about myself now. I doubt if I'll ever fuck again. It wasnae about sex anyway, no at that time, what it was about was . . . oh fuck all this shite. Stick to the Stork; maybe if I could kill the Stork.

No.

I'll never fuck again.

I hear the nurses leave, their sensible shoes clicking on the floor. I'm alone with my lady friend. I wonder who she is?

— It's funny seeing you here, Roy. It's been a long time.

Who the fuck are you?

— I'm sorry to be the bearer of bad news. It's your old pal Dempsey. Alan Dempsey. He's no longer with us, Roy. I thought you'd like to know that.

WHO ARE YOU?

It's no good. I hear her steps start up and fade. She's leaving.

Dempsey. Ali Dempsey. Demps. Total Niddroid. One of the top boys. One top boy deid, another a cabbage. The Cabbage and Ribs.

The bearer of bad news departs but the sound of her leaving becomes the sound of someone else appearing.

— Yir gaun back tae yir right fuckin room, son. Ah goat they cunts telt. Ah sais, youse cunts git ma fuckin laddie back in that room or ah'll git ma fuckin shotgun right now n yis'll be needin mair fuckin beds thin ivir by the time ah've fuckin finished!

— The laddie disnae need tae hear that, John. It's aw sorted now, son. We goat them aw sorted oot.

— Too fuckin right we did. Eh hen? Telt these cunts the score.

— Yes, well you'll have to leave now, Mr and Mrs Strang. I need to get Roy prepared.

— Aye, wir gaun . . . bit naebody better try n move him ootay this room again . . . right! Cause like ah sais, ah'll be right doon here!

— Nobody's moving Roy, Mr Strang. Now let's just keep our voice down shall we, it might upset him.

Aye, right.

— Aye, well, so long as youse mind what ma man sais!

— Yes Mrs Strang.

— Tro Roy!

— Cheerio son. Mind son, we'll no lit thaim dae nowt tae ye. Like ah sais . . . cheerio Roy!

CHEERIO YA FUCKIN RADGE.

Nurse Beverley Norton is getting me sorted. Patricia must have finished her shift. Talk to me in your soft Coronation Street accent, Nurse Norton. Just like Dorie's . . . naw, no Dorothy's.

— We've got a visit from Dr Park this afternoon, haven't we, Roy loovey? Got to get you all nice and spruced up for Dr Park.

Fire ahead Nurse Norton. Never mind auld Strangy here. Roy Strang. Strangy fi Muirhoose. A vegetable now likes, but still a sound cunt. Still a top boy. Now Dempsey's wormfood though. The rest? Who the fuck kens. Two years ah've been here. Thir probably in Saughton, or worse, in some tenement or Gumley's, Wimpey, or Barratt box with a bird and brat checkin oot B&Q's wares. Sittin in front of the telly. Are they cabbages too? C'mon you cabbage. Not as much as me: a biodegradable piece of useless shit incapable of fulfilling its intended purpose in this life, just as incapable of passing on to the next one.

Thank fuck for a childhood in a large Scottish housing scheme; a wonderful apprenticeship for the boredom that this kind of semi-life entails. Pull the fuckin plug.

Wonder how Demps kicked it?

Thank fuck for Sandy Jamieson. Time

to

go

back

down

under

Bruce————

——————— It's all about good service, old Dawson explains
to us, wiping large remnants of a substantial starter from his face.

Sandy and I eagerly set to work on our hors-d'œuvre although we
both found that we were rather full after them.

— We haven't been *quite* so hungry today, Sandy said.

— I blame this confounded heat, I nodded, — but I could make a
meal of this homemade bread and butter alone!

Our food is served by a strange creature, the likes of which I had
never seen before. It was stunted and furtive, and although its
short-arsedness seemed to suggest a range of possibilities, it was too
dour looking to be a leprechaun, too ugly to be a pixie and too
clumsy to be an elf. Its malevolence seemed far in excess of what one
might expect from any self-respecting imp. Dawson informs us that
it is his faithful manservant, Diddy. Sandy tries to avoid making eye
contact with the dwarf valet as he ladles copious amounts of
vegetables onto Dawson's plate, a contrast, it has to be said, to the far
less liberal helpings he furnishes us with.

— Take Diddy here. He used to run this reserve. Now all he does
is skivvy. I had to dismiss him from a position of executive
authority. He was yesterday's man, incapable of taking us onto the
next phase. Is that not so, Diddy?

Dawson slowly enunciates the phrase *incapable of taking us onto the
next phase*.

— Yes, Mr Dawson, Diddy solemnly replies.

— And how do you feel to be serving my food now, Diddy?

— It's an honour and a privilege to serve Jambola Park PLC in any
way I can, Mr Dawson.

— Thank you, Diddy. Now please leave us. We have matters to
discuss: executive matters.

Diddy scuttled out the door.

Dawson reclined in his chair and let out a loud, appreciative belch.
— You see Roy, Diddy may have no class, but he possesses an
important quality. Not really important any more in top execs, they
can always be rewarded, but crucial in footsoldiers. I'm talking, of
course, of loyalty. Good old Diddy; aye ready to serve the empire.
Men like him have been rewarded by men like me ever since the
British set foot in this godforsaken continent.

— The hun never sets, I smiled, and Dawson raised a lascivious
eyebrow in fruity acknowledgement.

— And if I may say so, Diddy has been rewarded handsomely,
Sandy ventured.

It was a remark which Dawson largely close to ignore. I kept
forgetting that Sandy was once in the employ of 'Fatty' Dawson.

— Wonderful food, Lochart, I smiled.

— Yes, said Sandy, — especially after that simply *horrid* stuff we
had in town.

— That *was* beastly, I agreed, — the chap in the bar made so much
fuss about it as well. It's so difficult to get good service nowadays.
You're lucky to have Diddy.

Dawson rubbed his swollen hands together and let his face take on
a serious bearing. — You see Roy, humans have a wretched
tendency to pledge devotion to insitutions rather than individuals.
This can be problematic for people like myself who require loyalty in
service. What happens, of course, is that one simply buys the
institution. Of course one is changing this institution at the same
time to suit one's business plans and, yes, many people do notice
this. Fortunately, tribal loyalties are pretty well-honed and the fools
can't help but to subscribe.

— Goodwill is one of the greatest assets an organisation can have,
Sandy remarked.

— Tremendously difficult to quantify on the balance sheet
though, Dawson smiled, directing his remark at me rather than
Sandy. Sandy began rocking in his chair and letting out a low sound.
— Mmmmm.

— So what does this mean, Lochart? What sort of a role do you

perceive for Sandy and myself? I asked, impatient to discover where
Dawson's game was leading us.

As you may know, he smirked, — I'm planning to take over a
debt-ridden park which lies adjacent to us. I've made a reasonable
offer, but I've been subjected to the predictable, tiresome cries of
asset-stripping and child-molesting and so on and so forth. Kicking
Lochart Dawson around is something of a thriving industry in these
parts. Well, I've news for the loudmouths, I've never run away from
anything.

— So where do our interests converge?

— I want the land they have. It's over two hundred square miles.
With my smaller park joined to these resources, we could be in
business. Big business. I'm offering opportunity, Roy. I'm offering
vision. However, there will always be malcontents who choose to
resist progress. The neighbouring park, Emerald Forest, is infested
by the most vicious and unscrupulous predators/scavengers on this
continent. I'm referring, of course, to your old friends . . .

— The Marabou Storks.

— I hear that there is one you're interested in? The leader?

— You hear correctly.

— I want to help you take him out. I'll put all my resources at your
disposal.

— Well, we need a couple of pump-action shotguns, some maps
. . . explosives . . .

— Anything! Dawson bounded across and shook my hand. —
Well, as they say, let's kick ass, or rather, you chaps kick ass. I'm
going to disappear for a while. It's, eh, the family; slightly jittery
about all this. We also have a hostile media to contend with.

Dawson barked instructions to Diddy to kit us out, and we were
off.

4 Leptoptilos Crumeniferus

The Marabou Stork is a predator. The Marabou Stork is also a scavenger. These qualities make it detested and despised by human beings. Humans are into animals whose qualities they covet, and hate ones whose characteristics they vainly like to feel are not at all 'human'. The world we live in is not run by cuddly, strong bears, graceful, sleek cats or loyal, friendly dogs. Marabou Storks run this place, and they are known to be nasty bastards. Yes, even the vulture does not get such a bad local press.

Fatty Dawson was sold on the concept of taking out the leader, creating a vacuum, and watching the birds turn on each other and tear each other apart in disarray. I knew that this would not happen. I knew that these birds were far more sophisticated and organised than Dawson gave them credit for. Dawson was from the west; he didn't understand these creatures. Another leader would swiftly emerge. You couldn't eradicate the Marabous, they were purely a product of their environment, and this scabrous environment totally supported them. The best you could hope for was to perhaps force them into a temporary migration. Nonetheless, I was happy to let both Dawson, and my guide Sandy, believe that the eradication of the leader was an appropriate strategy for ridding the Emerald Forest of the Marabou Stork.

For me it was personal. There was only one Stork I wanted, one of those beasts which had to die. I sipped some cool water from my canteen. My lips had dried in the heat. I removed a tube of Vaseline from my coat pocket to apply to them, just as Sandy emerged naked from the river, where he had been taking a dip to gain respite from the omnipresent heat.

He looked at me tensely, then glanced around at the deserted

wilderness. There was nothing and nobody about for miles. He
rolled his eyes   naw   he

– One could think of other uses for that, Roy, he smirked –––––––
–––– naw   didnae roll
                               his eyes
                                          Sandy and I
                                                    urnae like that it wis
jist mates muckin aboot –––– DEEPER
                                   DEEPER
                                              DEEPER ––– he quickly got
into his clothes.

Sandy and I were well-kitted out for the task at hand. Tooled up
with rifles, shotguns, explosives and carrying absolute *stacks* of
provisions: jam, English Breakfast Tea, tins of beans, soup,
desserts, all that sort of stuff. Stuff that doesn't go off in this confounded heat.

    I did, however, notice some reticence on Sandy's part concerning
what on the surface seemed to be a fairly straightforward task.

    — What's your opinion of Johnny Stork, Sandy old man? I asked
him.

    — They are evil incarnate, Roy. They have to be stamped out for
the good of the game, Sandy replied, ashen-faced.

    — You don't have any concerns about us not being up to the task
do you, Sandy? I enquired.

                                         up –––– time will tell.
    — Time will tell, he said   up
grimly, time will tell. –––––– up

What the fuck is this?
       — But I think he's going to come out of it. There's definitely increased signs of brain activity.
I wouldn't be surprised if he could hear us. Take a look at this, Dr Goss . . .
    FUCK OFF!
The cunt wrenches open my eyelids and shines a torch into them.

Its beam shoots right down into my darkened lair and I skip into the shadows to avoid its light. Too quick for these cunts.

— Yes, we're definitely getting some sort of reaction. A very positive sign, says one of the doctors, I forget their names, they all sound the same to me.

— I don't think you're doing enough to help us, Roy. I don't think you're doing enough to get well, says the other. I'll call him Middle-class English Cunt One and the other Middle-class English Cunt Two in order to differentiate them.

— I think we have to increase the stimulus and the number of tests, says Middle-class English Cunt Two.

— Yes Dr Park, says Nurse Beverly Norton.

— Those tapes his family brought in. Keep them going, suggests Middle-class English Cunt One.

So I'm to be subjected to increased harassment, and my energies, which should be concentrated on getting me deeper, deeper into my world, my story, my hunt, now have to be diverted into keeping these fuck-wits out.

— Listen Roy. We're doing our best for you. You have to want to get better, says Middle-class English Cunt One, bending over me. I feel his rancid breath in my nostrils. Oh yes, just you keep that up ya cunt, because if I do come out the first thing ah'm gaunny fuckin well dae is tae rip yir fuckin queer English face apart wi ma chib . . . but fuck, naw man, naw . . . ah'm gettin too fuckin close tae the surface, cause ah feel masel at the top ay the ladders which run up the side ay the deep deep well, half-way down being my lair, further down still the beautiful blue skies of Africa, the world ah just drop into but now I'm right at the fuckin top, right at the top, pushing at the trapdoor and some shards of light are coming through . . .

I *feel* his rancid breath

DOWN

DEEPER

DEEPER ------

—Funny, I thought that there was something there for a bit . . . must just be my imagination. Anyway, let's move on. Thank you, Nurse.

Exit the bools-in-the-mooth cunts.

—Did you hear that, Roy! Two doctors today! Dr Park *and* Dr Goss. And they're pleased with you. You have to work a little bit harder though, lovey. I'm going to put on the nice tape that your mum and your brother made for you. That brother of yours, Tony, is it? He's a saucy one and no mistake. I think he's interested in some of our younger nurses. Anyway, here you are:

> The minute you walked in the joint,
> I could see ye were a man of distinction,
> A real big spender . . .

Thank you but no fuckin thank you Bev-ih-leey, chuck. Bring back Patricia Devine. Come back Patsy, Patsy De Cline, all is forgiven . . .

Suppose you'd like to know what's goin on in ma mind.

DEEPER
            DEEPER
                        DEEPER — — — — — — — — — — — — — —
— — — — — — — — — — — Peace.

part two

The City
Of Gold

5 Into The City Of Gold

Our first home in South Africa was a few rooms in Uncle Gordon's large house in the north-eastern suburbs of Johannesburg. Uncle Gordon was fond of saying that we were as 'far away from Kaffirtown (Soweto) as it was possible to get and still be in Jo'burg'.

Though I was just a kid, my impression of the city was of a drab, bleak modern place. It looked spectacular from the sky as we circled over it on our way to landing at Jan Smuts International Airport, named, John proudly told me, after a South African military man who was a big pal of Winston Churchill's. It was only when we saw it from the ground that I realised it was just another city and that they all looked better from the sky. Close up, downtown Johannesburg just looked like a large Muirhouse-in-the-sun to me. The old mine dumps provided a diminishing backdrop to the ugly skyscrapers, highways and bridges which had long replaced the shanty homes of the first gold pioneers who made the city. I was so disappointed as Ma had told me on the plane that it was called the City of Gold, and I had expected the streets to be literally paved with the stuff and the buildings composed of it.

Gordon's place in Kempton Park was certainly salubrious enough, but all there seemed to be at the end of his driveway was a tree-lined road leading to more houses and grounds. No kids played on the deserted streets, the place was dead. I just stayed in most of the time, or played in the garden, hanging around with Kim. It was okay, though: there were plenty of things to see around the house.

Gordon lived on his own with his black housekeeper, and it seemed bizarre that he should keep on a house of that size. It was probably just to show the world how much of a success he was, financially at any rate. Emotionally, life in the Republic had not been

so rewarding for him. There had been a wife, but she had departed
long ago, all traces of her obliterated. Nobody talked about her, the
subject was taboo. I'd put the shits up Kim by telling her that
Gordon had murdered her and buried her body in the grounds. This
was plausible, given the way Gordon appeared. Straight away I
clocked him as a true Strang: weird as fuck.

On one occasion I took my tormenting of Kim too far, and she
freaked really badly, spilling the beans, resulting in me getting a
good slapping from my Ma. As she belted me, I remembered Vet
saying: — I'm only daein this cause if yir faither finds oot n he does it,
ye'll ken aw aboot it. That was true as Kim was my Dad's favourite
and teasing her always carried the extreme risk of incurring his
wrath. While it was quite a healthy slapping, I took it with a sense of
relief, recognising the truth in her words. She was actually doing me
a favour and I sensed her heart wasn't in it; but unfortunately she was
instinctively quite good at violence. She stopped when my nose
started to bleed heavily. Though my ears rang for a few days I didn't
even sulk or feel bad about her or Kim after. Everyone seemed
lighter, happier. It was a good time.

I knew fuck all about politics at the time, but even I soon sussed
that Uncle Gordon was what I suppose I'd now call an unrecon-
structed pro-apartheid white supremacist. He had come to South
Africa about fifteen years previously. His story, which he was fond
of telling anyone who'd listen (I heard it literally dozens of times that
year) was that he and two of his pals were sitting in the Jubilee Cafe in
Granton, thinking about what to do to with their lives. They
thought of emigration to Canada, Australia or South Africa. They
decided to take one each and Gordon arbitrarily picked SA. They
were supposed to report back to the Jubilee in ten years' time, but
they never showed up. The cafe had shut down anyway. — We were
silly laddies, Gordon remarked, — but it was the best break I ever
had.

Even at the time, as an eleven-year-old, I thought that his story
was romanticised bullshit.

There was no doubt that Gordon had done well, at least
materially, from the system. After taking a few menial but

well-paid-compared-to-the-blacks-doing-the-same-thing sort of jobs, he set up a property management agency in Johannesburg. It took off, and he diversified into property development. By the time we arrived, Gordon had this large suburban home, a mansion, really, and a fair-sized timber farm out in the veld of the Eastern Transvaal, on the road to the Kruger National Park. He also had offices in Durban and Cape Town as well as property interests in Sun City.

I think the old man thought that he was just going to walk into a top job in Gordon's business. I can recall Gordon saying to him over breakfast, — Look John, I'll get you fixed up here. Don't worry about that. But I won't have you working with me. I'm a great believer in keeping business and family apart.

I remember this fairly vividly, because it resulted in an argument, and the recurrence of the tense atmosphere I was used to feeling at home and had naively thought that we had left behind in Scotland.

Kim started· crying, and I recall putting my arm around her, displaying a tenderness I didn't really feel in order to try and shame my parents into stopping shouting. It proved completely ineffective. I sat with a sad, baleful expression watching the tears roll down my sister's large face. Vet's pus was pinched with tension and John and Gordon both shook visibly. This was the beginning of the end of my father's South African dream.

·Dad eventually landed a job as a security guard in a supermarket at a shopping mall in a white working-class district a few miles away. Gordon assured him that it would just be a temporary measure; a first step on the ladder, as he put it. He got Ma a job, typing and filing at a city-centre office in a business run by a friend of his.

I was due to start at the Paul Kruger Memorial School with Kim in a couple of weeks' time. Bernard had enrolled at the Wilheim Kotze High, while Tony had found, again thanks to Gordon, a traineeship as a chef at a hotel in the city.

Before we started school, however, Kim and I were left at Gordon's with Valerie, the large African woman who was his housekeeper. She was very cheerful, always singing us Bantu songs. She had left her family to come and work here, sending the money back out to the place she came from. We quickly built up a relationship with her, as she was warm and friendly and made a fuss of us. This ended abruptly one day; Valerie suddenly acted cold, off-hand and distant, telling us to get out from under her feet. Kim was puzzled and saddened at this change, but I knew that Gordon had spoken to her.

Later on, my uncle, who had taken a particular interest in me, came home and took me aside, ushering me into the large garage which adjoined his house. — I don't want you getting friendly with Valerie. She's a servant. Always remember that; a servant and a Kaffir. She'll never be anything other than that. They seem friendly, they all do, that's the way with them. But never forget, as a race, they are murderers and thieves. It's in their blood.

He showed me a scrapbook he kept of cuttings from newspapers which highlighted what he referred to as 'terrorist atrocities'. I recollect being frightened and fascinated at the same time. I wanted to sit and read the scrapbook from cover to cover but Gordon snapped it shut and looked me in the eye. He placed a hand on my shoulder. His breath smelt sweet and rancid. — You see, Roy. I'm not saying Valerie's like that, she's a good person in many ways. But she needs to be kept in her place. Don't let all that cheerfulness fool you. She's got a chip on her shoulder. They all do. These people are different to you and I, Roy. They are one stage up from the baboons you'll see out in the veld. We had to take this land and show them how to develop it. We made this beautiful country, now they say they want it back. His eyes grew large, — Do you understand me?

— Aye, I nodded doubtfully. I was staring at the black hairs which grew out of his nostrils and wondering when we would get to see the baboons out in the veld.

— Think of it this way, Gordon continued, smugly inspired, — if a nasty, stupid, lazy, bad-smelling person had an old garden shed that was falling to pieces and wasn't being used, then you come along and say, I can make something of this shed. So you take on the responsibility of making the garden shed into something better. You put your heart and your soul into rebuilding it, and over the years, through your sweat and toil, it becomes a grand, beautiful palace.

Then the lazy, stupid person with the dirty-coloured skin which gives off a bad smell comes along and says: — That's my shed! I want it back! What do you say?

— Get lost! I said, eager to impress.

Gordon, a thin, spindly man, with tired, watery eyes, which could suddenly glow with violence, beamed and said: — That's right! You're a true Scotsman, Roy! A real Afrikaaner! He smiled at me. Gordon always seemed to hold you in his gaze a second or two more than felt comfortable. I didn't know what an Afrikaaner was, but it sounded alright; like a true Scotsman.

I started to look at Valerie in a different light. She had had babies in the bush, knowing that she couldn't feed them, because as Gordon had explained, blacks couldn't organise themselves, couldn't do anything right. Even the good ones needed white people to look after them, to provide them with jobs and homes. It was important not to get too friendly with them though, he told me, because they got excited and reverted back to a primitive state. — You remember your dog, Winston, wasn't it?

— Yes, I said. Winston Two was in kennels somewhere. He had to spend six months in quarantine before he could join us. I was not looking forward to his reappearance.

— Remember you got him all excited?

— Yes.

— What happened?

— He bit me.

Of course, Winston did more than just bite me, he practically took my leg off. Even now, three years later, after skin grafts and intensive physio, my limp was still apparent.

Gordon looked at me intensely, – Kaffirs are like that. Get them excited, they're liable to turn around and   up   – You're very bite you! He snapped jokingly, tickling me with   up   bony, Roy, what his long fingers – – – – – – coming   up   are you? I'll bet up – – – – – – – – – – – – – up up up   you've always been nice and slim though.

You could do with some meat on these bones, Roy Strang. We're going to have to make sure you eat. That's what we're going to have to do. Yes we are.

Leave ays alane ya fuckin daft cow

DEEPER
         DEEPER
                   DEEPER ----- We're driving
back out through the shantytown and heading towards Lake Torto
in an attempt to pick up the trail of the Stork.

Sandy was recounting a tale from his lion-hunting days: — I recall
one little girl running through the village crying: 'Simba mamma
wae!', which means, roughly: 'A lion has one's mother', and sure
enough, this beast had seized the child's mother by the thigh and
bitten the poor woman through the neck. On hearing our cries, it
had dropped its kill and made off into the long grass. I headed after it,
making speedy progress through the foliage in time to see the brute
entering a thicket on the other side of an open range. Taking a steady
aim, I fired, the bullet striking the beast and rolling him over. The
blighter rose instantly, however, and unfortunately my shot with
the second barrel wasn't so keen; I completely missed him. Crossing
the clearing, I heard a growling challenge. Imagining that the brute
was severely wounded and would before long succumb to the effect
of the bullet I'd dispatched into him, I considered that discretion was
the better part of valour and thought it prudent to retrace my steps
for about thirty-five yards and simply await developments.

— Crikey, I said, enjoying the scent of eucalyptus in my nostrils, —
What happened?

— Well, after a lapse of about an hour I became a tad restless and
decided the time was ripe to explore the bush. Of course, I fully
expected to find the blighter dead. All was silent, so I cautiously
entered the dense undergrowth and began to follow his trail. He had
clearly lost a considerable amount of blood and appeared to be
limping badly. After a few yards of progress I could discern the
tawny form of the lion, crouching completely motionless, head
between paws, eyes glinting in the shade and staring steadily at me;
but the thing was, the bugger was only about ten blasted yards
away!

— Gosh . . .

— Well, I raised the bloody rifle pretty damn sharply, but without
giving me time to aim and fire the bloody brute somewhat

unsportingly charged at me, roaring savagely. I promptly let him have it, the bullet striking the left side of his head and smashing his shoulder. My third shot knocked him down and I thought; that should be *quantum sufficit*, but I'll be blowed if the bugger wasn't straight up again and coming on as strongly as ever!

— Bloody hell, Sandy, what did you do?

— It wasn't what *I* did, old man. I was rather fortunate that Tanu, a stout-hearted native from the village, had followed me, and the brave chap raised his spear and drove it with all his might into the brute's shoulder. The lion seized my courageous ally, though this gave me time to reload and I took up position and furnished the brute with the contents of my second barrel. Another shot finished him. God, I remember the celebrations in the village. They were overjoyed at the news of the killer lion's demise. They fashioned garments from its hide and amulets from its bones and we indulged in some pretty damn prodigious beer-drinking that evening!

— How was the native chap?

— Tanu . . . dear Tanu . . . unfortunately the poor blighter didn't survive the mauling, Sandy said, tears welling up in his eyes.

I let my hand fall onto his knee and gave it a squeeze.

— A fucking brave chap, Sandy sniffed.

We drove down the dusty road in silence for a while. Then, as we cruised along the track that straddled the west side of Lake Torto, I spotted someone. — Look Sandy! It's that young lad, from the football game.

— Yes, a funny little creature! Sandy smiled.

We stopped the jeep alongside him.

— Lift? I asked. — Ride? You like ride?

He looked suspiciously at us.

— What's Bantu for 'ride', Sandy? I turned to my companion. Sandy seemed different. This heat, it was making me hallucinate . . . his face looked a scaly reptilian green.

— I've dem well forgotten all the bloody fucking shitey cunt radge Bantu I ever cunting well learned! Sandy groaned, punching the jeep's body in exasperation.

I'm losing it. Concentrate.

— Never mind, Sandy, I said, turning back to our ragged young friend. — Ride? Brm! Brm! It's alright! We won't hurt you! Get into the jeep!

For some reason Sandy was rummaging through the medical supplies. A forked tongue darted out his head as he lisped in a strange voice: — Come and share some lemonade with us, young fellow. You must be *absolutely* parched!

The little urchin's face lit up in a delightful smile as he eyed the bottle of lemonade, and I thought that he was going to climb into the jeep.

— C'moan little fellow, we'll have some fun! Sandy said. Then he went, — Ye want a fuckin ride ya wee cunt, ah'll gie ye a fuckin ride awright . . .

No no . . . it wisnae like that, Sandy n me urnae like that . . .

The native boy turned on his heels and ran away. Sandy looked distraught.

— Never mind, Sandy, I smiled, — It's just the way they're brought up.

— Yes Roy, he beamed largely, — and anyway, it's just simply heavenly being on our own.

— Tell me another one of your lion adventures, I requested.

Sandy thought about this for a while, then said, — Oh, no Mr Strang. Methinks it's time for one of your shark hunting tales.

— Hmmm, I considered, — did I ever tell you about the spot of bother I got into with Johnny Shark down in Natal province?

— I don't believe you did.

— Well, I was down in Natal investigating attacks on local divers. Some suspected that one of our old friends the Great White, or at least a Tiger shark, was responsible. For some reason, I had my doubts; the bite marks on the survivors' legs seemed inconsistent. Those doubts were confirmed with a vengeance when I was diving alone near the scene of these attacks. I found myself confronted by *Carcharhinus longimanus*.

— The Oceanic White-tip shark, Sandy gasped.

— You know your sharks, Sandy. Anyway, this brute was circling around me. It must have been in excess of three metres long.

The Oceanic White-tip is very aggressive. This was the shark responsible for the slaughter of survivors of the *Nova Scotia*, when that ship sank off the Natal coast. In a similar scenario to your little encounter with the lion, this bugger came twisting towards me, just as I was about to let fly with the explosive harpoon.

— Oh my God, Sandy said, his eyes widening.

— Before I could react, the beast had fastened onto my leg. I felt no pain, however, and I took my knife and thrust it into the creature's snout. This caused the beast to loosen its grip. I quickly jammed my harpoon gun into his jaws to prevent them from closing again on my leg, then I prised my wounded limb off the monster's bed of teeth. The creature began thrashing around, trying to get the explosive gun from its mouth but, fortunately for me, only managed to detonate the device, blowing its own face to pieces. I still have a little memento from that brute . . . I showed Sandy the scars on my leg.

— Gosh, he said.

We drove on, swapping tales, until night settled around the lake. We could hear the trumpeting noises the flamingos made as we drove along the track, our headlights cutting through the darkness. We were growing very tired. Somewhat fortuitously at that point, our maps indicated that there was a hut nearby and we managed to locate it fairly easily.

With our spirits lifted, we found that we were not too weary to conduct a thorough examination of our new abode. The building was constructed on high stilts and it looked out from deep in the forest down a slope over the still lake. I gleefully anticipated the morning appearance of the rising sun which would shine straight into our hut from above the lavish green hills.

Sandy exclaimed in unbounded delight as he opened cupboard after cupboard. — Towels! Cutlery and crockery! Bedding! And look, in the refrigerator: bottles of pop!

— We could light the stove to heat the room up, I suggested, pointing to the old stove in the middle of the room. It seemed as if the hut, which was really more like a small lodge, hadn't been occupied in ages.

– No, we don't need to, Sandy said, – not the way we're facing. That sun will be simply pouring in before too long! If it gets cold we could always wrap ourselves up in one sleeping up bag. It was a practice I indulged in with up the native boys, in order to up preserve heat – – – – – – – – coming up

– right up the fuckin erse man. Dirty fuckin cow that she wis, Roy, tellin ye. Thing is, ah'm no even that bothered if Hannah finds oot.

Ah mean, she kens ah've been playin away fi home, but wi her sister . . . well, ah suppose that's different right enough. It's just that she'd try n stoap ays fi seein the bairns Roy, you dinnae ken how spiteful that cunt is . . . ah fuckin gied her it tight the other day thair, telt a few home truths . . . here, ah bet if ye did wake up you'd have some stories to tell though Roy, eh? Mind you, might no be that bad. Gittin a bed bath fi the nurses everday. Ah'd be up fir that. Thir's a couple in here ah'd fuckin ride in a minute man, ah'm tellin ye . . .

Tony. You're visiting me. Fuck. This is a rare treat

— The thing is, her sister, she's gantin oan it . . .

The Big Ride

Shut up

— . . . bangs like a fuckin shitehoose door in a gale, ah'm tellin ye . . .

SHUT UP

— . . . thir aw the same, though, these daft cunts . . . fill their heids fill ay shite n they cannae wait tae whip thir fuckin keks oaf . . .

SHUT THE FUCK UP YA SICK MISOGYNISTIC WOP CUNT IT'S AFRICA AH WANT TAE THINK ABOOT

DEEPER

DEEPER – – – – – – I'm out of range of that crazy spic clown's rantings, but I can't get deep enough to hunt the Stork. I'm deep enough to remember, though.

I remember.

After Uncle Gordon's lecture, I avoided Valerie. I now looked upon her with a mixture of fear and contempt. I quickly put Kim in the picture about her and we kept out of her way, occasionally playing some mean tricks on her to ingratiate ourselves with Gordon; hiding stuff in different cupboards and that sort of thing, which caused her a great deal of distress. We made up nasty songs with words like 'coon' and 'Kaffir' and 'nigger' in them and sang them lustily around the house. Dad and Gordon would laugh approvingly at us.

I ingratiated myself with Gordon successfully; I ingratiated myself too much. Since coming to South Africa, all I had wanted was to get to see some of the wildlife I had read about in my books. One day Gordon came home and took me out with him for a drive into the bush to show me some animals. I was excited, as we had two sets of binoculars and had packed a large picnic. It was hot and I drank a lot of Coca-Cola. Due to this, and my excitement, I got sore guts and had bad trapped wind. I was rubbing my stomach, it was agony. Gordon pulled over by the side of the road and told me to lie down flat on the back seat. He started rubbing my stomach, feeling me, then working his hand slowly inside my shorts and down over my genitals. I just gave a nervous giggle. Part of me didn't really believe that this was happening. Then I felt a diseased spasm wrench through me and I began to tense up under his touch.

— It's alright, it's all connected up, he smiled, — the stomach, the bladder . . . I know what's wrong here.

Then he opened my trousers and told me that I was a good boy while he started stroking my cock, masturbating himself with his other hand.

His face reddened and his eyes glowed strangely, yet appeared unfocused as he seemed to struggle for breath. Then his body jerked before relaxing and a sharpened concern came into his eyes. He spent a few minutes massaging my stomach again, until I farted and burped a couple of times.

This incident stayed in my mind, but the funny thing was that we had a great day out after that. I filled six pages of my notebook with what we'd seen: a Black and white colobus, a Side-striped jackal, a Clawless otter (in a stream by the forest) a Black-tipped mongoose, a porcupine and an African hare on the mammals front, while in terms of birds it was really fuckin ace: European grey wagtail, African marsh owl, Golden-rumped tinkerbird, Olive thrush, doves of the Pink-breasted and Red-eyed variety, African snipe (which might have been a Jack snipe, I couldn't be one hundred per cent sure) and a Steppe buzzard.

I couldn't wait for my next trip, though this anticipation was tainted with a sense of unease and reservation as Gordon's abuse of me continued. It sometimes took place on drives, but often in the garage when he would come home from work during the day on some flimsy pretext. The funny thing was that it didn't really feel like abuse at the time, it felt mildly funny and amusing watching Gordon making a drooling tit of himself over me. I felt a sense of power, a sense of attractiveness, and a sense of affirmation that I hadn't previously experienced, during those sessions in the garage.

I used that power by extorting gifts from Gordon, my most lavish being an expensive telescope. In order to appear even-handed and avoid drawing suspicion, he had to sort out Tony, Bernard and Kim with costly gifts as well. John and Vet, feeling inadequate and jealous, with their meagre salaries, said that he was spoiling us and that caused a bit more aggro.

I loved South Africa. Even when we moved into our own place, a few miles away from Gordon's in a poorer area, we still had a big house with a back and front garden, and I had my own room. Through blackmail I had built up a huge library of nature books, mainly relating to African wildlife. John and I became big pals at this time. Our mutual interest in the natural world and animals flowered into an obsession. All our free time was spent in natural history museums, the zoo or local game reserves; or, chauffeured by Gordon, just driving out of the suburbs into the veld, trying to see some of the animals we'd identified from the books. The zoo was disappointing; the animals looked plastic and drugged. There was something sad and broken about them. I had to pretend to be enthusiastic as the zoo trips meant a lot to the old man; because the zoo was served by public transport, it was the only place he could take me on his own. He was planning to take driving lessons. Although sightings in the parks and bush were more irregular, they were more exciting.

Often Gordon engineered trips so
that Dad was working and we   fingah . . . the man
could be alone together.   Gold   with the midas touch,
This was my life in the City – – – of   A spider's touch.

SWITCH THAT SHITE OAF

                                      Such a cold finger,
                                      Beckons you . . . to enter his web of sin,
                                      But don't go in . . .

The Garage.

— Time for a bedbath, Roy.

DEEPER

          DEEPER – – – – – – Bernard and Kim showed little
interest in wildlife. When Gordon asked Tony if he'd like to come
along, Tony told him, — The birds I'm into are of the two-legged
rather than the winged variety. He was still shagging everything in
sight; usually the women who worked or resided in his hotel.

Gordon took us on the Blue Train to Bloemfontein down in the
Orange Free State. We were going to the zoo there to see the famous
Liger, the beast that was a cross between an African lion and a
Bengali tigress. I felt disappointed, then sad, when I saw this creature
in its enclosure. To me it seemed a misfit, a freak, something that
should never have been, would never have been but for human
intervention. I felt sorry for it. The most enjoyable part of that day
had been the journey. I had the best ice-cream I've ever eaten on the
train down, which was a really luxurious vehicle: ten times better
than any crap British shite. To me, everything in South Africa was
ten times, naw, one hundred times better than anything in fuckin
Scotland.

The most memorable trip, though, was a family outing organised
by Gordon to the Kruger National Park in Eastern Transvaal.
We drove out to Gordon's timber farm, stayed at his lodge for

a few days, then journeyed out towards the park, approaching it from the more rugged north-eastern end, which backed onto the Mozambique border.

At the time the security forces were advising people travelling in the area to take care. We were continually being stopped by uniformed police. Gordon explained that it was all due to terrorist activity. He used the term 'terrorist' freely. The terrorists seemed to get around, on the telly, in Gordon's scrapbooks, in the conversations he had with his friends at the *braais*. When I asked what a terrorist was, his face took on a sharp, intense bearing and he said: — A terrorist is a nasty piece of scum; a jealous, warped, evil, murdering immoral shitbag!

I was still no wiser as to what a terrorist actually was.

The Kruger was brilliant. I saw some lions stalking wildebeest and zebra, but did not see any make a kill. Some cheetahs had got hold of a baby wildebeest but got little from it before two lions chased them away. Kim gret at the baby wildebeest getting wasted, and Vet agreed that it was a shame.

— Si law ay the wild bit, Kim, Dad explained, putting his arm around her, — like ah sais, the law ay the wild.

Gordon gave me a matey wink and raised his eyebrows as if to say that lassies were daft, no like us guys.

It was a great time, really exciting, and the lodge we stayed in was luxurious.

The only thing which disturbed me was seeing a group of ugly birds waddling into a flamingo colony and scattering the beautiful pink creatures across the waters of a small lake. They just fled in sheer panic. I had never seen anything as horrible looking as those predators. They were like bent-over beggar-demons, their large beaks gave them a laughing look totally at odds with their dead eyes. I saw one of them trying to swallow a flamingo's head. It was a sick sight. The severed head of one large bird in the jaws of another.

— That's the Marabou Stork, my Dad sang triumphantly, drinking in the carnage through his binoculars, — like ah sais, the Marabou Stork. Bad bastards thaim, eh, but it's nature like.

That night I had my first Marabou Stork nightmare.

6 Huckled In
The City
Of Gold

South Africa was a sort of paradise to me. Funnily enough, I felt at home there; it was as if it was the place I was really meant to be, rather than shitey Scotland. When I thought back to Edinburgh I recollected it as a dirty, cold, wet, run-down slum; a city of dull, black tenements and crass, concrete housing schemes which were populated by scruffs, but the town still somehow being run by snobs for snobs.

I was glad when we moved away from Gordon's to our own place, but I missed what I had grown to think of as my refuge. Part of Gordon's house was built on top of an old well, and in the basement of the garage there was access to the well, via a trapdoor. The well had a set of metal rungs going down into it, and although I was told to keep away, I used to climb down there and just hang from the rungs, suspended in semi-darkness. I'd hear Gordon sneaking around above, looking for me to touch me up. The things he wanted to do were getting heavier and I was getting more scared. Gordon said if I told anyone I would get the blame; John, my Dad, would believe him and not me. I instinctively knew that this was true. So whenever I went into the garage I'd hide in the well.

The well wasn't very deep, perhaps about twenty foot at the most. Gordon claimed that it was not a well, but was part of an old access point to mineworkings where the prospectors who built the city dug for their gold. At the time, I took this with a pinch of salt, but given Johannesburg's history, it was possible. The bottom of the well seemed solid and blocked with rubble, though I could never bring myself to go right to the foot of it and stand free of the rungs. I would just sit in my semi–darkened lair, enjoy the peace and fantasise. I was sorry when I had to leave the well, as glad as I was to be getting away from Uncle Gordon.

As I said, I loved South Africa. For Dad, though, the honeymoon never lasted. He was fucked off with his security job. It wasn't quite what he had envisaged. Moreover, the social life was getting to him. He was fed up with the characterless suburban roadhouses or the *braais* in gardens, parks and campsites where South Africans did their serious drinking. He was craving the traditional social vice of the lowland Scot; a good, old-fashioned pub crawl in an urban city-centre environment. Gordon had tried to get him into South African culture. My uncle had become a rugby enthusiast and he took us along to a few games at Ellis Park to try to get us interested. — Poofs game, John would snort, — but ah suppose it's something tae dae. He would leave us and spend most of his time at the stadium bars. I hated rugby even more than football. So did John and nothing less than a good piss-up would suit him.

It was a drinking session in downtown Johannesburg that led to us leaving South Africa and returning to Scotland.

At the time I had just settled into the Paul Kruger Memorial. The kids were pretty thick, seeming to me to be even farther behind than at my old school, which was according to all reports, one of the crappest in Scotland, which also meant Europe. The only drag was having to wear a school uniform. I suppose I didn't mind too much, as I could wear long flannels rather than shorts. I was self-conscious of the scars on my legs.

On my first day at the school I was introduced as a 'new boy from Scotland' and shown the map of South Africa. My first piece of homework was to memorise the provinces and their capitals:

CAPE OF GOOD HOPE   CAPE TOWN
NATAL   PIETERMARITZBURG
ORANGE FREE STATE   BLOEMFONTEIN
TRANSVAAL   PRETORIA

One major difference was that the kids here, though easily as thick, were much more docile and well-behaved. Actually doing schoolwork was acceptable. The teachers were okay; my interest in nature and wildlife was positively encouraged. They were nice to me, my accent mattered less to the teachers in South Africa than it had done to those in my native city. Once I got over this culture shock, I found myself relishing the acquisition of knowledge. Schoolwork became interesting and I lost my urge to escape into the Silver Surfer and my other comic-book fantasies. I couldn't learn enough about things. I had, for the first time, ambition of a sort. Before, when people had asked me what I wanted to be, I would have just shrugged; I might have said a soldier, just because it seemed good fun shooting at people, like just a daft kid's thing. Now I was into being a zoologist. On my eleventh birthday I could see possibilities: good grades here, followed by the same at high school, a university place at Witwatesrand or Pretoria or Rand Afrikaans studying zoology or biology, then some field work, post-grad stuff, and there I'd be. I saw a career path.

The old man's piss-up blew that away. It showed me that I'd been a daft cunt to ever have had those dreams.

I recall the day it started. It was a clear Thursday afternoon and looking north-west you could see the Magaliesberg mountain range which towered over the city. I was out in the garden kicking a ball about with my mate Curtis. I was getting hot but I hadn't changed out of my school uniform. I went to do that, then I was going to Curtis's house for tea. He often came to ours, but I was less embarrassed by Mum and Dad now. They seemed happier and lighter out here, and strangely, their eccentricities were more tolerated as there was quite a mix of different white kids in our neighbourhood, likesay Greek and that, and some whose parents spoke no English. Anyway, I nipped in to get changed and I overheard my Ma and Dad talking.

The old man's restlessness was apparent. He would still circle the television pages for our viewing, only now they were the listings of the *Johannesburg Star.* — Fuckin thirty-six rand a year fir this shite, he moaned bitterly that early evening. The television licence fee had gone up. — It's no that, Vet, he implored my Ma, who had said nothing, — it's no thit ah grudge it. It's jist thit wi dinnae want tae become slaves tae the telly aw the time.

— Switch it oaf well, my Ma said.

— Naw . . . naw . . . that's no the point ah'm tryin tae make, Vet. Yir misunderstandin the point ah'm trying tae make. Like ah sais, it's no the telly thit's wrong; it's jist thit thir's nowt else. Like, ah mean tae say Vet, they fuckin braais, or whatever the fuck thir called, thir awright bit thir no ma cup ay tea, ken? Whit ah'm tryin tae say Vet, is thit ye cannae even git oot fir a fuckin pint, ken whit ah mean? Thir's no like a local; nae fuckin pub fir miles, jist that fuckin daft wee place roond at the Mall. Even Muirhoose hud a fuckin pub! Likesay in the toon though but Vet, thir's tons ay pubs doon in the city. Ah wis thinkin thit ah might just go doon thair the morn eftir work; git a couple ay pints wi Gordon, doon in the city likes. Like ah sais, a couple ay pints.

— Well, go oot fir a pint then, Vet snapped, angry at being distracted from her magazine.

— Mibbee ah'll just dae that well, mibbee jist dae that the morn. Fae work like, ken?

I saw a contented smile point his face as he sat behind the *Star*.

So the next day Dad finished his shift, and instead of coming home, went downtown to meet Gordon in his office, after a visit to the boxing museum at Hanson and Kerk Street. After Gordon finished they went out drinking in bars around his office in the Main Street/Denvers Street area. Gordon had soon had enough, and took a taxi home, imploring John to do the same. By this time, though, the old man had a couple of guys from Liverpool in tow and was into a real night on the pish.

Johannesburg's city centre is a drab, functional business area; totally deserted after six o'clock in the evening. Gordon kept telling John that it wasn't safe to wander the streets after dark, presumably in case he ran into someone like himself. My Dad's brother always talked about how lawless the city centre was at night; he went on and on about the gangs of black workies from rival tribes who lived in the hostels and ran amok in the city centre after dark, mugging and beating up each other and anyone else who crossed their path. All this did was set the old man off in a belligerent, aggressive frame of mind. If any cunt wanted trouble, he'd be game. After Gordon told us that John had said to him: — Whin the Luftwaffe wir bombin London, the big brass telt Churchill tae stey safely indoors instead ay gaun fir a walk in the park. Churchill jist turns roond n goes: Aye, right. Whin ah wis a wee laddie the nurse couldnae stoap ehs fae walkin in the park. Now thit ah'm a growin man, that wee cunt sure as fuck isnae. Ah rest ma case, my father had said smugly.

Anyway, John and the scouse guys staggered up Delvers towards Joubert Park. They had a great night out and drunkenly swapped phone numbers, arranging to do it all over again. John lurched into a cab that was parked outside one of the big hotels.

What happened next was contentious. John's version of the story, which I'm inclined to believe, because for all his faults the old man wasn't a bullshitter, he didn't have the imagination for one thing, was that he fell asleep in a taxi. When he woke up, they were parked in a disused layby in Germiston, with the driver rifling through his pockets. Now Germiston is a busy railway junction district to the south-east of the city which is dominated by the largest gold refinery in the world. We lived on the road out to Kempton Park, which is north of the city centre.

John assaulted the taxi driver with such force and vigour that several of the man's teeth were produced, in a plastic bag, by the prosecution in the courtroom, as a theatrical piece of evidence. The taxi driver claimed that he was trying to get this obnoxious drunk who was giving him the run-around out of his car, when he was violently assaulted. John got sentenced to six months' imprisonment. It seems that he was made an example of by the authorities, anxious to clamp down on violence in downtown Johannesburg.

Vet was well fucked up. I remember her at that time; chain-smoking and drinking cups of tarry coffee with around eight sugars in it. We left our new home in northern Johannesburg and stayed briefly at Gordon's before making plans to return to Scotland. John would follow once he'd served out his sentence. Kim and I were devastated at the prospect of going back. We'd settled. I could see myself right back in the same life, the same school, the same scheme.

I was gloomy in my resignation, only a sick anxiety brought on by the dread of leaving occasionally alleviating my depression. Edinburgh to me represented serfdom. I realised that it was exactly the same situation as Johannesburg; the only difference was that the Kaffirs were white and called schemies or draftpaks. Back in Edinburgh, we would be Kaffirs; condemned to live out our lives in townships like Muirhouse or So-Wester-Hailes-To or Niddrie, self-contained camps with fuck all in them, miles fae the toon. Brought in tae dae the crap jobs that naé other cunt wanted tae dae, then hassled by the polis if we hung around at night in groups. Edinburgh had the same politics as Johannesburg: it had the same politics as any city. Only we were on the other side. I detested the thought of going back to all that shite.

Bernard had hated South Africa from the start and couldn't wait to get home. Tony was ambivalent. He'd been shagging a few birds, but wanted to see his old mates. Being older, though, he had a vibe, a vibe about all the political trouble which we never really knew much about.

Maybe in retrospect I could say that there was a strange mood amongst the whites my folks socialised with. It's just possible, though, that I'm inventing it with the benefit of hindsight. Did everybody really seem a wee bit edgy? Probably. The only real talk I remember was of what people (and I do remember there were some dodgy looking cunts Gordon hung around with) referred to as the selling out of Rhodesia, which was now called Zimbabwe-Rhodesia. That and the constant references to terrorists. Gordon spoke Afrikaans and preferred the Afrikaans papers like *Die Transvaler* and *Die Vaderland* to the *Rand Daily Mail* and the *Johannesburg Star*. He once took us to the Voortrekker Monument which dominates the southern approaches to Pretoria and rabbited on about the great trek. This seemed to affect him in the same way Churchill's wartime speeches did my Dad.

Once Gordon took us to the Museum of The Republick Van Suid-Afrika. It was an interesting place to visit. The information boards in the museum mirrored what I'd read in my school textbooks:

The white citizens of the Union are mostly descendants of early Dutch and British settlers, with smaller admixtures of French, German and other West-European peoples. The White man originally came to South Africa as a soldier, farmer, trader, missionary and general pioneer, and owing to his superior education and his long background of civilisation he was able to provide the necessary leadership, expertise, technical skill and finance among races who were for the most part little removed from barbarism.

South Africa is the only country in the world where a dominant community has followed a definite policy of maintaining the purity of its race in the midst of overwhelming numbers of non-European inhabitants — in most not still administered as colonies or protectorates either the non-whites have been exterminated or there has been some form of assimilation, resulting in a more or less coloured population. Indeed, far from the extermination of non-whites, the advent of the European in South Africa has meant that whole native communities have been saved from exterminating each other. It is not generally realised that scarcely a century ago Chaka, chief of the Zulus, destroyed 300 tribes and wiped out thousands upon thousands of his fellows.

Gradually, however, the remnants of the tribes which survived the internecine wars were able to settle down to a peaceful, rural way of life under the protection and with the assistance of the white man. In the traditional homelands, which cover an extent about as large as England and Wales together, nearly one-half of the Bantu live and lead a simple pastoral life as their ancestors did through the centuries before them — happy, picturesque people living the most carefree existence imaginable.

Thus we find that here on the southern tip of the African continent, amidst overwhelming numbers of non-European inhabitants, a small white population has made its home and is founding a new nation, with a way of life and an outlook of its own. It is due to the initiative of these people, to their knowledge and skill that South Africa has become the most advanced state on the African continent, and, as sure as night follows day, they

will evolve a form of co-existence which will allow every
race to live its full life and to contribute, in accordance
with its own abilities, to the welfare of the country.

After the museum we went back to Gordon's where he was having a
barbecue with some of his friends. There were always *braais* at
Gordon's. Some men were sitting in his lounge, watching the
television which showed riot police breaking up a black demonstra-
tion. They were cheering on the riot police. One tall, blonde woman
who looked like an actress came through and smiled at me. Then she
turned to a fat guy with a beard and said, — I see that the Kaffirs are
taking a dem good beating.

— They shid ten the ficking gihns en those apes, he snarled,
slugging from a bottle of beer and belching. There was such a stupid
malevolence on his face that I instinctively felt that, despite what the
school, the Government and my family were telling me, that
something wasn't quite right. I stopped to listen as the news bulletin
changed to the Rhodesian situation.

— Botha's fucking sold out our people in Rhodesia, Gordon
fumed.

— Yes, but it's tactical, Gordon, one man smiled, — it's buying us
favours in the world community. God knows, we may soon need it.

— You're talking like a flaming red, Johan, the fat guy with the
beard snapped, — we should be standing by our own. They let
twelve thousand ficking terrist skim walk into kemps with their
weapons for this bastard ceasefire. I say it's a gelden opportunity to
shoot the ficking lit of them. Just turn the ficking guns on those Zanu
so-called Patriotic Front red terrist animals and blow them to pieces
just like they do to decent bloody farmers.

Gordon sat with tears welling up in his eyes as he watched the
pictures of the Patriotic Front guerrillas march into the camps and
lay down their weapons, the condition for the ceasefire and the
commencement of the free elections. — I can't believe it. I can't
believe that they would do it. P. W. Botha. Maggie Thatcher.
Fucking whore! Fucking treacherous fucking stupid communist
fucking whore!

It was a good thing that John was in the nick at this point. I remember the last time Gordon had ranted about Thatcher's treachery, John had been standing leaning against the patio doors. He stiffened up and turned around. — Hi! C'moan Gordon, it's no Maggie Thatcher's fault. The best fuckin leader Britain's hud . . . the best peacetime leader. Like ah sais, the best. She pit the fuckin unions in thair place right enough. Jist gittin bad advice, fae they cunts in the civil service n that. That's whit it wid be! Dinnae fuckin slag off some cunt ye ken nowt aboot! Like ah sais, you dinnae ken whit she did fir Britain!

— I know she's sold Rhodesia down the fucking river, Gordon said weakly, obviously a little intimidated.

There was loads of political talk, but I suppose that apart from the odd vibe of discomfort, I thought it was just   up   – Just turning this up,
what boring auld cunts spraffed about.   up   Roy.
At that time ah didnae really unders – – – up

> So would ye like tae have fun, fun, fun,
> How's about a few laughs, laughs, laughs,
> I could show you a good time . . .

FUCK OFF AND TURN THAT SHITE OFF . . .

DEEPER
DEEPER
DEEPER – – – – – and although
the eggs were cooked to perfection and the toast was crisp and the coffee strong, rich and aromatic, there was something strangely amiss that morning we left the hut.

It was the silence. I couldn't hear the flamingos on the lake. I picked up the binos. Nothing.

— Where are they, Sandy?

— This is absolutely puzzling. I'd like to take a closer look.

— We drove down to the shore of the lake. There was immediate evidence of carnage. I saw pieces of dead birds. Then we heard a rustling and some squawking and noted some vultures still chewing

at a flamingo carcass. Sandy raised the rifle and fired a shot at them.
One toppled, and the others flapped their wings and waddled away.
They moved back quickly, the slain vulture joining the flamingo in
providing a feast for the other birds.

— Vultures are only cannabalistic under extreme conditions,
Sandy observed. — Those poor blighters must be starving.

At that point I saw a pink, swan-like head and neck which had
been severed from a body. — Our flamingo colony has been routed,
I declared.

— Yes . . . by the Marabou Stork, Sandy nodded sagely.

– Maybe we should take our clothes   nowt. What the fuck
off and go for a little dip, I suggested   suggest   wis ah oan
. . . naw naw that wisnae it − − −   fuckin   aboot?
− − − coming up − − − − − ah didnae

                                                                                    Politics.
That's what.

The politics of South Africa. Shite, that's what that was to me. It
caught up with us, though, caught up with us all in an even bigger
way about a fortnight before we were due to head back to Scotland. I
was out with Uncle Gordon at his timber farm in the Eastern
Transvaal. When we stopped the jeep, he looked around over that
sweeping arrangement of trees. I was a bit nervous. Because we were
going away, I worried that he'd want to do more than just touch me
and wank himself off. He'd kept this up over the year, although his
opportunities, with us in our own place and me at school, were few
and far between. This time he didn't even try to touch me. He just
ranted. He seemed seriously disturbed.

— This is mine. My farm. I'm a Jubilee boy Roy, a penniless
Scotsman from Granton. There I was nothing, another skinny teddy
boy. Here, I count. No fucking Kaffir is going to take this away
from me!

— They'll no take your place, Uncle Gordon, I said supportively,
all the time my mind playing with the delicious image of him lying in
the gutter in drapes outside the Jubilee Cafe, clutching a bottle of
cheap wine. We went back to his ranch house and had some drinks,

then went around to the woods so as I could look at some animals with my binoculars. We spotted a Moustached green tinkerbird and a Whalberg's eagle, both pretty rare in the Transvaal. Gordon's heart wasn't in it though and he soon returned to the ranch house. I was left alone to wander around the edge of the forested plantation and it was while I was stealthily trying to get closer to a shitting Bush duiker that I heard the explosion.

I almost shat myself, and I'm sure it helped the duiker's defecation too, the animal shooting off into the forest. I turned back and saw the blazing jeep. As I said, I knew nothing about politics. Despite frequent reports of guerrilla activity by a militant off-shoot of the ANC in Eastern Transvaal, Gordon refused to take heed. For some reason, he'd climbed into one of the four-wheel-drive Range Rovers outside the ranch, switched on the ignition and was blown into oblivion.

The funny thing was, I wasn't scared. I just thought that the terrorists have got Uncle Gordon. I had no real fear that they would do anything to me. I don't know why; I just didn't. I went back towards the house. The warm humid air was even heavier with the odour of gasoline and burning flesh: the smell of Gordon, barbe- cuing nicely in the blazing truck. I'd never smelt anything like it. While it's impossible for that much meat *not* to smell I had always imagined that humans would smell like bacon. When I was really wee my Uncle Jackie used to tell me that he ate cheeky wee laddies and that they tasted just like salty pork. I recall though that the smell of Gordon was so sweet I thought that if I hadn't known it was human flesh I would have wanted to taste it; would have enjoyed it. All I could see of Gordon was a charred thin, black arm and hand hanging out of the burning body of the vehicle. The smell changed briefly to that of one I could only describe as burning shite as my Uncle's guts popped and splattered as they incinerated in the flames. I went indoors and sat down and phoned my Ma back in Johannesburg.

— Roy, what is it! Ah'm up tae ma eyes in it! she moaned. Gordon had her preparing food for another *braai*.

— Ma, Uncle Gordon goat blown up. Eh's deid, n ah cannae git hame, like.

She gasped loudly and after a long silence said:— Don't move! Jist stey thair!

I sat and waited. I put on the telly and watched some cartoons. The polis came in a helicopter about twenty minutes later. It was fuckin barry being in the helicopter. They took me way up, and I saw, at close range, a magnificent Long-crested eagle, soaring over the thick forest. We landed with disappointing haste and transferred to a car, which drove me to the station where I was reunited with Vet, Kim, Tony and Bernard. Vet hugged me and Tony ruffled my hair. Kim kissed me, which embarrassed me in front of the polis. They had become good pals: the best cops I'd ever met. Bernard was as jealous as fuck of the attention I got: I felt like a hero.

Everyone said I was brave. It was a good time for me, a good farewell to a place I loved. Even Gordon's death, save the minor inconvenience of not being able to extort more presents, left me unmoved. As far as I was concerned Gordon was a sneaky, big-heided poofy auld cunt and it was good riddance. The only person really hurt was John, when we went to visit him in the prison, and his sadness seemed to be based on the loss of Gordon as he was fifteen years back, a 'skinny fucking teddy boy', rather than a crusty old Boer.

His death was actually of some practical benefit to my father. The authorities took a compassionate view of our circumstances and released him early from prison. He came back to Scotland about a month later than the rest of us. Winston Two, who had only been out of quarantine for a few months due to a blissful bureaucratic mix-up, was now banged up again, awaiting release to Scotland.

7 Escape From The City Of Gold

I remember the drabness of Heathrow, followed by the depressing connecting flight north of the border. We were all fucked anyway after the long journey from Johannesburg, but they had cancelled a couple of planes because of ice on the runway. London was freezing; Scotland would be even worse. It shows how dense and in a world of my own I had been eighteen months before, because I had been almost as excited that we were stopping off in London as I was that we were on our way to Johannesburg. I thought of London as somewhere just as distant and exotic; I had been surprised on the outward journey when we arrived there so quickly. Returning though, I saw London for what it was: the grizzled fag-end of the British Islands.

On our last day, I'd had to say goodbye to my friends at school and to my teachers. It was strange, but I seemed to be popular there; a big cheese, a top boy, numero uno. My best pals were called Pieter and Curtis. I was a bit of a bully to Curtis. Pieter was too. He was quite a wild cunt and was well pissed off that I was going back. It was good to have someone miss you. Most of the other kids were a bit slow and sappy. I would miss Pieter but, as this was the first time I'd discovered that I had a brain, the person I would miss most was Miss Carvello, one of my teachers. She was beautiful, with big, dark eyes. I used to wank about her, my first real wank, like, when you get spunk. She told Vet it was unfortunate that I was leaving South Africa as I had come on leaps and bounds at school and was 'university material'. This unfortunate phrase was to be thrown back at me in all my subsequent under-achievement.

I wanted to stay in South Africa. What I had gained there was a perverse sense of empowerment; an ego even. I knew I was fuckin special, whatever any of them tried to tell me. I knew I wasn't going to be like the rest of them; my old man, my old lady, Bernard, Tony, Kim, the other kids back in the scheme. They were rubbish. They were nothing. I was Roy Strang. Maybe I had to go back, but it was going to be different. I wasnae gaunny take any shite.

Back in Scotland, when John finally came home, we had a family meal to celebrate. Everyone was there, not quite everyone, Winston Two being back in quarantine, and Elgin still at THE GORGIE VENTURE FOR EXCEPTIONAL YOUNG MEN. It was considered too off-putting to have him home at the dinnertable, and I confess that I had been one of the principal advocates of keeping him away. Only Kim, Vet and Bernard argued for his presence, but John, as always, had the last word. — It widnae be fair tae the laddie, disorientate um, like ah sais, disorientate um.

The dinner was excellent. Ma made broth, then spaghetti carbonara with sprouts, broccoli and roast tatties heaped on top soas you could hardly see the pasta or the sauce, followed by sherry trifle. The bottles of Liebfraumilch were heartily drained. I'd never seen a table so loaded with food. We seldom ate around the table as a family, generally balancing plates on our laps as we jostled for position around the telly. This, we were told, was a special occasion.

There was, however, a tense atmosphere in the house at the meal; Tony's face was heavy with sweat as he ploughed into the food, while Kim pushed hers around. Bernard had had a violent argument with John earlier and instead of sitting down had sort of collapsed into the chair, ashen-faced and trembling. He was trying to cut a piece of roast tattie, his breath making high little sounds which could have come from the throat of a dog. Later on Kim was to tell me that Dad had heard from Mum about something Bernard had done with another laddie and had threatened to cut his cock off.

Mum and Dad had obviously argued about it and were both wound up so tightly as they sat at the table that the air around them seemed to gel. I ate nervously and quickly, anxious to excuse myself, feeling that one wrong word or dubious gesture might spark off a massacre.

— These tatties are hoat . . . Kim said inanely.

John glared venomously at her. — Well, thir nae fuckin good cauld! Yir Ma's gone tae a loat ay trouble tae make this meal, Kim! Show some appreciation! Like ah sais, some appreciation!

This was really worrying, as John seldom gave Kim a hard time; she was, after all, his favourite. Kim pouted and lowered her head. She looked as if she was contemplating doing what she often did to get attention and bursting into tears, but had decided against it and was struggling to consider what other action she could take.

Vet got in on the act. She turned to Tony and snapped: — Tony, take yir fuckin time. You n aw, Roy. That food isnae gaunny jump up n run away bichrist.

I had always though of my Ma as young and beautiful. Now she seemed to me to look like a twisted, haggard old witch, staring out at me from behind a smudged mask of eyeliner. I noted the strands of silver in her long black hair.

She and rest of them could fuck off. Ah wis going to be strong. Strong Strang. Ah wis gaunny make sure every cunt kent ma fuckin name.

Ah wis gaun . . .

DEEPER

DEEPER into the Marabou Stork nightmares.

8 Trouble
In The Hills

Old 'Fatty' Dawson looked absolutely beastly when we met up for a rendezvous and progress report at his secret guest lodge in the Jambola. His shifty, slimy eyes were blackened and his tanned flesh hung slack and wobbly on his jaw. He was not a happy man and it was more than obvious that we were the source of his disquiet.

Granted, we had failed to establish where our Stork was nesting. There were very few clues. In all frankness, Sandy and I had been rather treating it as a bit of a holiday and Dawson was not amused. There was no warmth in his greeting. He ushered us to sit down around a corner of his oak boardroom table. Then he left for a minute. Sandy turned to me and whispered: — Fatty Dawson's looking rather wild, he said, a little edge of panic creeping into his voice.

— Well, I'm blowed if I know what he's so steamed up about. It's not as if old Johnny Stork has . . .

At this point Dawson came back into the room and squeezed into a chair beside us. His doughy hands drummed the table, then he let out a sigh. — I'm surrounded by homoerotic prats who can't get it together to hunt those murderous beasts! he snapped contemptuously at us. Sandy looked vaguely guilty. This irritated me, as we had done nothing wrong. I was about to say something when Dawson turned his blotchy face away from us towards his valet, Diddy. — Either that or incompetent malcontents. The short-arsed man-servant mumbled something and shuffled out the room looking at his feet.

I considered that it might make for better sport to wind up Dawson rather than to oppose him outright. We still needed the fat oaf. There was little prospect of locating our Stork without his backing. — Take it easy, Lock, I smiled. — Unwind. Crack open a beer or two . . .

— How the hell can I be expected to relax when it's all caving in around me! he snapped. — This Emerald Forest park is rife with Marabous who only care for destruction, and here, in my own back yard, at the Jambola, the local natives are getting restless . . . SADIE! he screamed. – SADIE!

His black madame, the foreign lady, entered the room. — Yes Missah Dossan?

— What the fuck is happening, Sadie? *You* tell me . . . somebody tell me! It's Lochart Dawson this, Lochart Dawson that . . . oh yes, let's all put the boot into Lochart Dawson! Forget conveniently how Lochart Dawson saved this park from extinction!

Sadie shook her head sadly, — We all knows you our fren Missuh Dossan. We knows dat we don have nuthin till you comes heah an makes us all strong. All our people, dey respecks an loves you Missuh Dossan. Is only some of dem youth who is rebellious in de way dat young boys is. Dem boys will be punish badly for deh sins Missuh Dossan.

Dawson put both his hands behind his head and rubbed his neck. Then he gasped slowly. — I'm not a man who is intolerant by nature Sadie, but I am a great believer in examples being made and punishments fitting crimes and all that sort of stuff. Anything else sends signals to the bad eggs that they've won the battle. Well, my message to them is that they most decidedly have not. Those so-called rebels, when you round them up, see to it that I get to oversee their discipline personally. Baiting Lochart Dawson is becoming something of a thriving industry in these parts. Well, this is one enterprise I won't be encouraging thank you very much. You can tell them that Lochart Dawson has never run away from anything in his life and he doesn't intend to start now.

— Yessuh, Missuh Dossan.

— Of course, he bleated petulantly, — there may come a time when Lochart Dawson may just decide that it's all not worth the hassle and simply walk away. Then where would you all be, eh?

— Oh laud, Missuh Dossan, no go leave us, please no go leave us! You is speshul pehsun Missuh Dossan. We loves you veh much an we can no cope without you! Please no go!

Sadie was now at his knees, holding onto his legs. He ruffled her dark hair. — That's fine, Sadie. Thank you.

The woman rose and departed with tears filling her eyes. She deserved an Oscar.

— They seem to like you, said Jamieson, sycophantically stagey.

— Yes they do, Sandy. I can honestly say that, on the whole, I am a much admired and appreciated person. There are a minority, however, who seem to think that Lochart Dawson's a soft touch, a figure of fun. Well, when they are brought in as prisoners by my security forces, we'll see just how much a figure of fun I am after the questioning procedures.

I raise an eyebrow in Dawson's direction.

— It's a vice of mine, Roy, Dawson explained. — Questioning. I love to question. It's in my nature. I question everything. I question why so much is spent on state benefits to the unproductive while grants for business development for the go-ahead are so low. Indeed, I question why state benefits exist at all.

I smile at him. — Extremely visionary stuff, Lochart, not at all the type of questioning based on perpetuating the narrow economic interests of an already wealthy but spiritually impoverished elite at the expense of their more financially disadvantaged bretheren. Truly the type of questioning which will help enable mankind as a species to self-actualise and fulfil its cosmic destiny. There's a real sense of deep philosophy underpinning it all.

Dawson studied my expression to see if I was mocking him. It seemed as if he couldn't quite tell, but decided to give me the benefit of the doubt. — That's it, Roy! You're a true philosopher! He smiled, flashing pearly teeth and presenting expensive bridgework for my examination.

— You'll sort out those ungrateful malcontents, Lochart, I said encouragingly.

— They forget that they asked me to come here, Dawson said. —

The same as those people in the Emerald Forest. I did this for them.

— Oh, Emerald Forest invited this takeover bid, did they? I asked, intrigued.

— I can't say any more about it now, Roy. Unfortunately I've not got the same freedom as the hot-heads to go around making all sorts of accusations. Lochart Dawson doesn't have that luxury; I'm bound to be silent by the dictates of company law and my position as a board member of Jambola Park PLC. Now, onto other business. What progress on the Stork problem?

— We've not located the nest yet, as I indicated to you last night on the telephone. It's all not bleak though . . . Sandy, I turned to Jamieson who rose and went to his rucksack and, on producing a large map of the area, spread it over the table.

Putting on a pair of steel-framed spectacles, Sandy began, — This map indicates the principal flamingo colonies in the area, and the patterns of flamingo migration.

— So what? We're talking about Marabous here! Dawson boomed.

— Please let me finish, Sandy retorted with a touch of cocksure assertiveness which filled me with a quick flush of admiration. I watched Dawson grudgingly defer. Sandy continued, — The pattern is emerging of rapid movement of the flamingo colonies from the area around Lake Torto up towards the border.

— We can't afford to lose our flamingos . . . Dawson gasped.

— Yes. But there's more. The only thing that could cause mass desertion of flamingo colonies on that scale is the presence of large numbers of the scavenger-predator we know as the Marabou Stork.

— Yes . . . but . . .

— The Storks have routed every flamingo colony they've come across. The next undisturbed ones are up on the north-eastern banks of Lake Torto. That's where the Marabous are headed next.

Dawson raised an appreciative eyebrow.

— And so, I said with what I thought was a rather dramatic pause, — are we.

— There is, however, Sandy added, cashing in on his increased stock with Dawson, – one thing we – – – SUPPOSE YOU'D LIKE TO KNOW WHAT'S GOIN ON IN MA MIND

FUCK OFF!

— Just turning this up for you, Roy. The Doctor says as loud as we can have it.

Patricia's back.

— You certainly have some family, don't you Roy? Ha ha. I was propositioned last night by your brother. Tony.

Don't do it, Patricia.

— He's not my type, though. The married type, if you know what I mean. Good-looking, though. Can't really see much of a resemblance to you . . . oh God, I didn't mean it that way. Still, you seem to do alright. Your girlfriend was in. Doesn't say anything. Still, it must be upsetting for her to see you like this.

Who the fuck is that? Surely not Dorothy. Surely she's found another fat boyfriend, had her first fat kid even. Settled into a Wimpey or Barratt number in Fathell, Midlothian, or even Fathell, Fife. No. It would be Fathell, Manches . . .

NO. IT WASNAE DORIE.

Her that mentioned Dempsey. That's who it'll be. Her. Who the fuck is she?

— At least she stuck by you, Roy. She obviously doesn't believe that you're the bad one they're all making out. That's how I feel too. I can see the good in you, Roy. When I shine the torch into your eyes I know I can sometimes see something and I know it's good.

Aye, aye, Patricia. How the fuck would you ken?

I'm mad about the boy

MAD

DEEPLY MAD

DEEPER – – – – Aw aye, this yin. Ah mind ay ma Ma givin it laldy wi this yin. She sang it to me on my birthday. I was embarrassed, surprise, surprise. The daft party we had in my hoose. The funny thing was that when we came back tae Scotland the council housed us in the same maisonette block, on the fifth floor instead ay the fourth one. This was regarded as a come-down in status for my Ma. The poorest families tended to be at the top floor. The funny thing was, neighbours told us, they had only just re-let our old flat after it had been standing empty for the best part of our eighteen-month African safari.

Dexy and Willie, the two mates from school and scheme; I had just started the secondary; they were there. They were scruffy cunts glad to be let intae some cunt's hoose, even if it wis the Strangs. My mate Pete never came, he made some excuse. Brian was there, though. He'd just come back tae the scheme n aw; tae stey wi his auld man eftir being in Moredun wi his auntie. His Ma had left them and his auld boy had sort ay cracked up. They all looked nervous and furtive as Ma belted it out, half-pished . . .

> Even though there's something of the cad
> About the boy . . .

The new school.

Ma's intervention blew my cool, ruined my plan to be free from embarrassment, to take no shite from any cunt who would try to brand me a freak. By and large, though, things went well. I could, of course, have played up to being Tony Strang's brother, but that would also have identified me with Bernard, and that raging poof was two years above me at school. He was a constant source of shame, but was never tormented as he had no scruples about playing up to being Tony's wee brother. I hadn't wanted any of that shite though. I was into doing what people expected me to do least. At the school, as a Strang, they had expected me to be a basket case, so I was bright. Because I was bright, they expected me to go to university. The drab consensus that I was 'university material' had followed me all the way from Johannesburg. There was no way. No cunt told me what to do.

I arrived at the secondary school heavily suntanned from South

Africa; my ugliness now mildly exotic. There were loads of kids from the primary and from the scheme who remembered Dumbo Strang. In particular, there was a fat kid called Tam Mathews.

That poor cunt Mathews. All the time he was watching swotty Strang from the back of the class, he must have been totally unaware that I was psyching myself up for that moment. Mathews became my first victim. I was glad it was him; glad because he was big, tough, loud and stupid. This time it would be mair than just the spike on the compass.

He spat on the back of my neck as we were leaving the classroom. At school we used to kid on we were gobbing on the back of each other's heids, like blowing out compressed air. This cunt really did it but. I felt the thick spittle run under my collar, down the back of my neck.

I could see a flicker of disbelief, then hesitancy in his eyes as I squared up to him. He said something which brought a few laughs from the kids who had gathered round to witness Dumbo Strang's humiliation, but the laughter turned to gasps, to ooohhhss as I produced a small hunting knife from my pocket, one which I'd bought from Boston's of Leith Walk, and stabbed Mathews three delicious times; twice in the chest and once in the arm. I then went to the next period class.

The teachers and the police got involved, although Mathews, to be fair, didn't shop me, he just collapsed in the playground and was taken to the hospital.

I simply spoke nicely to them all. After all, I was now Roy Strang, a hard-working, intelligent pupil; university material. Thomas Mathews, the teachers fell over themselves to testify to anyone that would listen, was not a hard-working, intelligent pupil. He was a bully and a thug. Yes, the police knew the Mathews family. They also knew the Strangs, but I was far too convincing in my mummy's boy role for them to make that association. The consensus was that, obviously, the Mathews boy must have put the fear of god into poor Roy Strang for the boy to be so scared he had to carry a knife. Nobody remembered the compass back in primary. No charges were brought: Ma and Dad never even found out.

Life at school was easier after that, once that basic principle was established: you didnae fuck aroond wi Roy Strang.

Out of school, it wasn't so easy. I remember one Saturday night I was sitting in reading a new *Silver Surfer* I'd got from Bobbie's Bookshop. It was late and I cringed inside as I always did when I heard my auld man ask my auld girl: — Fancy some chips, Vet?

— Wouldnae mind . . . my auld girl said coyly and teasingly, as if he was talking about sex.

— Roy, git ays a fish supper n what is it you're wantin, Vet?

— Ah'll huv fish . . . naw, a white puddin supper . . . naw, a mince pie supper wi two pickled onions. Naw . . . make it haggis, a haggis supper. That's it definitely. A haggis supper. Naw, fish! Fish!

— Christsake . . . two fish suppers before yir Ma changes her mind!

— Aw Dad . . . I moaned. I hated going to the scheme chippy this late at night. The pub next door, The Gunner, would be emptying. It was okay when he was down there, he brought the chips hame. It was horrible for me though, so I hated the nights he stayed in. You were on a fuckin doing fae aw the aulder wide cunts and the junkies who'd try to rob you. Cause nae cunt fucked aboot wi him, the auld man never saw this.

I made my way out into the stair and headed down through the darkness of the shopping centre. I saw two boys coming towards me and tensed, but I relaxed as it was only my mates Pete Bowman and Brian Hanlon.

— Pete, Bri.

— Roy.

— Whair yis gaun?

— Hame.

— Whair yis been?

— Commie pool, then up at ma big brar's, Pete said.

— Chum ays doon tae the chippy well, I ventured.

Pete touched his eye and laughed, – Aye, that'll be fuckin right. N ye'd better watch, Roy. Hamilton n some ay the third-year cunts are hinging aboot doon thair.

— Ah'm no bothered, I smiled, shitein it.

— Ye gaun tae Easter Road oan Setirday? Brian asked.

There was no way ah wis gaun tae any fuckin fitba. — Aye, probably, I said.

— Come doon fir ays well, Brian said.

— Aye, right.

— Tro Roy.

— Tro Pete, tro Bri, I said as they departed.

I walked on into the darkness. A drunk shouted at me, but I ignored him and charged doon towards the chippy. The light coming from it was the only sign of life in the centre. As I was getting served, trying to act nonchalant as the raucous drunks and nutters from the pub joined the queue and shouted at each other, I noted with a sinking feeling that Hamilton and his entourage were standing outside the shop.

I waited and by the time I got my stuff, they were away. I breathed a sigh of relief and huddled the hot chips to my chest as I walked through the centre into the cold night. I was just starting to unwind when Hamilton came flying out of a stair door and stood in front of me. There were two other guys with him, and two lassies.
— Hi pal, gies a chip!

— Ah cannae, it's fir ma faither, I said.

Hamilton was sixteen. I was still not yet fourteen. This was a different league to Mathews. The other guys were even older. One guy with long, curly blond hair was about eighteen. — Leave um, Hammy, ehs jist a fuckin bairn . . . he said.

— Git um in the fuckin stair, Hamilton laughed.

His mate, another third-year cunt called Gilchrist was sniggering, — Ken whae this cunt is? Eh chibbed Davie Mathew's brar. Thinks eh's a fuckin wide-o.

They pushed me into the stair. I held onto the chips as tightly as I could. All I could think of was what my auld man would say if I let them get tae the chips.

Hamilton had masses of teeth. Protruding teeth. He reminded me of a piranha fish; so many teeth it can never close its mouth. He gleefully pulled a knife on me. — So ye cairry a blade, eh?

— Nup, I said.

— Heard ye hud yin it the school but, eh. Ye a wide-o, aye?

— Nup, I shrugged, still holding onto the chips.

Hamilton laughed and then did a strange bird-like dance in front of me strutting and twisting his head from side to side.

— Leave um, Hammy, ah'm no fuckin jokin, the older guy said laughing, and wrestling Hamilton playfully away from me. One of the lassies came over to me. She was at our school too. Me, Pete and Bri just called her The Big Ride. I'd wanked aboot her before: I'd wanked aboot her tons ay times if the truth be telt. I remember once we were watching a nature programme in Bri's hoose and there wis these two praying mantises and the lassie praying mantis was eating the laddie praying mantis's heid while they were shaggin. We used to joke that that was what shaggin The Big Ride would be like. Ah remember saying that ah'd never shag The Big Ride unless I could tie her doon first.

— Goat a girlfriend, son? she asked, chewing gum so slowly and deliberately that it made her lovely face seem long and horselike. While this made her look uglier, it strangely and paradoxically made her seem even more sexual.

In spite of my fear I felt a twinge in my groin. — Nup, I said.

— Ivir hud yir hole? Hamilton sneered. Gilchrist laughed.

I said nothing.

— Leave the perr wee cunt, the blond guy laughed. — C'moan, Hammy, lit um go.

Then I saw who the other lassie was, it was Caroline Carson from our year, her; a lassie that was in some of my classes. She was alright. Dead nice likes. I just wanted to die.

The blond guy must have caught my shock of recognition, because he put his arm around her, — This is ma wee girlfriend, eh hen? he said with teasing lecherousness.

She twisted away from him laughing, — Dinnae Doogie . . . She seemed a bit embarrassed that somebody had found her with these cunts. I took her for a nice lassie likes.

At that point Hamilton slapped me across the face. I stood staring at him, still holding the chips. — Gie's a fuckin chip! he snapped. I stood looking at his glaring, violent eyes, feeling the side of my face where his hand made contact throb in a strange harmony with my balls.

Then I saw something change in his eyes. It was a kind of startled, ugly impulse that we shared but which I couldn't define.

It was something we shared.

I kept staring at him. I wisnae scared any mair: no ay him. I was scared of my auld man, but no Hamilton. He knew it. All I felt was anger at him, and anger at masel fir being too weak tae oppose the cunt.

— Fuckin wide cunt! he roared, moving towards me with the blade. The blond guy held him and at the same time pushed me away, out the stairdoor, but they all came out after me.

I just held the chips. I knew at any time I could have stopped this nightmare by saying: Tony Strang's ma brar, but I didnae want tae. This was me. This was Roy Strang we were talking aboot.

Roy Strang.

I just held the chips.

— What team dae ye support? Hamilton asked casually, as if nowt hud happened between us, as he put the knife back in his pocket.

— Hibs, I said.

I wisnae really interested in fitba, but Dad and Tony were Hibs fans and so were most of my mates in the scheme, so it seemed a safe bet.

— Hebs! Hebs! he repeated, mimicking my unbroken voice.

He ripped the paper of my wrapper and dug out a few chips. I stood frozen. I tried to speak out but I couldn't say anything. — HMFC ya cunt! he snapped and, grabbing my hair, he hauled my head doon and booted me in the face. I felt my bottom lip rip on my bottom front teeth and the sour taste of my own blood fill my mouth.

I held the chips and lifted my head slowly, shaking with anger and frustration.

— Fuck off Hammy, ya Jambo cunt, the big, blond guy shouted and charged after Hamilton and they had a mock fight as I sneaked off, my lower lip tasting like a large piece of rubber in my mouth.

When I got home my Dad looked at me, then at the torn wrapper, which I had vainly tried to disguise. — They chips. Somebody wis tamperin wi they chips!

I told him that I'd got hungry on the way home and had eaten a few chips. He looked hard at me, — What happened tae yir mooth? My knees felt weak and I didn't have the strength to carry on the unconvincing lie. It would only wind him up further. I kept my eyes on the floor and told him the story. I looked up and caught Kim's wide eyes staring at me, punctuating my misery with the occasional: — Ooooohhhh. Bernard, naewhair tae be seen when they were looking for some cunt tae go for the chips, was fighting hard to stop his mouth twisting into a smile and losing. We were all waiting for my auld man to freak and smack me across the heid, but he just looked sadly at me.

— Ye'll huv tae learn tae fuckin well stick up fir yersel, Roy. Yir a Strang, or supposed tae be, he told me wearily, shaking his head in contempt.

I swore I'd get revenge on that cunt Hamilton, but I never did, the cunt goat sent tae the approved school at Polmont, then just vanished off the scene. Gilchrist, his sidekick, moved to another school in another part ay the toon. That cunt I did meet up wi again. Him and the slags.

That wis later but.

Things at the school were easier though. While the news went aroond that Hamilton had gubbed ays, as he was a third-year cunt and hard, that was no disgrace. Indeed, the fact that I hudnae really shat oot increased my stock. In school and roond the scheme it was basically just me, Dexy, Willie, Bri, Monty and Penman that hung arrond thegither. Nae cunt really bothered us and we never really bothered any cunt.

This lasted for a long time. We had a good laugh thegither. Once we broke intae the school at night, intent on turning the place over. We got intae a class that wis our redgie class, whair ye went first thing in the mornin tae git checked in, and we found our redgie teacher Miss Gray's belt in the toap drawer ay her desk.

Wi started giein each other the belt, really fuckin thrashin each other's hands, much harder than when Lesbo Gray or any ay the other teachers did it. The thing wis, wi wir aw jist pishin oorsels n it seemed tae hurt a loat less. Then Bri had a barry idea. He pulled oot the top drawer n goat that daft cunt Willie tae dae a shite in it. Willie goes n droaps this fuckin steamin crap intae the drawer: then Bri pits it back in the desk. We laugh like fuck fir a bit then Bri goes: — The morn wi come in n noise up that carpet-munchin cunt Gray. She reaches in fir her belt . . .

— Ohhh . . . ya fuckin cunt! Penman laughed.

— Right then, lit's no brek anything . . . make it soas nae cunt kin see thir's been a brek-in. Ah jist want tae go up tae the library but, eh, ah telt them.

Ah poackled a couple ay bird books fae the library: *The Urban British Bird* and *Sherman's Encyclopaedia Of Tropical Birds Vol. 1*.

The next day we noised up Dykey Gray. We just shouted: 'Let's be friends' at some lassies in the class, and kept it up until it became: 'Lesbee Friends.' That sort of thing would have got on Gray's tits if she'd had any: as it was it just pissed her off. She reached into her drawer for the belt. Gray always smashed it oan the table and we were all supposed to shut up and pay attention after this gesture. Gray always said the same thing: The first thing on a Monday morning or the last thing on a Friday afternoon or the middle of the week isn't exactly the best time to try somebody's patience! Always the same bullshit.

— Right! she shouted, opening the drawer and sticking her hand in, — a dreadful, wet morning is not the time to try somebody's . . . She felt for the belt and froze. She pulled the drawer open slightly with her other hand, looked in and then started retching and choking. We were pishing our keks. Bri's face was crimson, his eyes watering. Miss Gray took the drawer out and stuck a bit of A4 paper on top of the shite and her messy hand. She stormed out the room holding the drawer in her free hand. — Bloody animals! Fucking little animals, she sneered, as we let out loud ooooohhhhhsss at her language. Gray then shouted on this snobby lassie called Bridget Hyslop, who Bri had nicknamed Frigid Pissflaps, to open the door and she vanished doon the corridor towards the staff toilets.

Fuckin barry.

Good times for a while, but then came a problem I hud tae deal wi.

But I dinnae want tae talk aboot that yet. I want tae go back, back tae what happens wi the Stork. DEEPER likes, cause Sandy and me see, we managed tae get some mair supplies fae Dawson . . . no . . . that's not right, DEEPER

DEEPER

DEEPER––old 'Fatty' Dawson furnished Sandy and I with bountiful extra supplies of equipment and tuck, as we'd demonstrated to him that the flamingos were being displaced by the Marabous.

— Watch yourselves on that road, Dawson boomed as we left, — there is an abundance of terrorist activity.

Once again we were off in the jeep, and feeling pretty pleased with ourselves. — This is fun, isn't it Sandy?

— Yes, Jamieson said, smiling at me. — And I want you to know Roy, that whatever happens from here on in, I've had the best bloody time of my life.

I blushed with embarrassment and, to deflect this, bade Sandy to tell me another lion adventure.

— Well, there was the occasion when I went into a village completely terrorised by an insatiable maneater. The poor villagers were literally too frightened to leave their tents and food supplies were short, with conditions increasingly insanitary, the rubbish just being thrown outside. One couldn't really blame the villagers, after all, the poor buggers had lost three people in a month to this beast. Anyway, it was about three in the morning and myself and my team were soundly asleep in our billets, when the door was violently burst in and before my chaps knew what had hit them, one of the men, who went by the name of Mojemba, was seized by a large lion who proceeded to drag him out of the hut by the thigh. Anyway, I was in a tetchy mood, awakened by the blasted commotion, so I quickly grabbed my rifle and dispatched a bullet into the region of the brute's heart. I was very lucky, obviously haste rather than accuracy had been my priority at the time.

— Nonsense, Sandy, I told him, — you're a bloody good shot.

— Nice of you to say so Roy, but I was never particularly

renowned for my shooting ability. This one, though, was certainly on target, because the animal instantly dropped Mojemba and bolted into the surrounding bush.

Villagers found the beast's body at the break of dawn; it was some seventy yards from the hut. It was nothing more than a mangy old lioness, driven to maneating by desperation. But the thing about this episode was that poor old Mojemba saw this attack on him as a sign of his own failing, a lack of vigilance on his part.

— But surely that's exactly what it was, I said.

— Yes, but I couldn't simply leave the fellow there, bleeding to death and bleating away at me; sorry Bwana this and sorry Bwana that . . . so I told everyone else to leave us while I personally tended to the poor wretch's wounds. I cleaned his thigh with hot water and syringed the lacerations with disinfectant to prevent blood poisoning setting in.

— Good show.

— Thankfully, in this case the precautions proved effective and within six weeks the boy was able to walk again. Hunting duties proved too arduous for him after such a trauma, so I made the lad my personal manservant . . . he was a damn good one too, Sandy's long forked tongue . . . wisnae forked, it was a normal tongue.

Fuck   up   This isnae working. Okay, okay.
                  up   What was the problem that ah hud tae
Fuck   up   sort oot?
              up   The problem.
Coming up
                    Caroline Carson.

Caroline Carson. She had always acted as if her shite didnae smell, but she never bothered me. I thought she wis a nice lassie. It was about a year later when I was in the second year and was put in one of her classes, English, I think. She must've been minding about the time she was there wi Hamilton n Gilchrist n The Big Ride when they terrorised me. Every cunt fancied her and she must have thought her looks bought her immunity, like she could dae what she

wanted. One time in the class, she flicked the back of ma fuckin ear.
It wis sair, bit it wis mair the humiliation. I was always sensitive
about my ears.

It wis they laughs in the class. Always they fuckin laughs.

Nae cunt laughs at Roy Strang.

I knew where she steyed and I followed her hame eftir school. I
ran ahead ay her, cutting through the back of the supermarket and
across the back greens and I was waiting for her in her stair. I heard
her talking to another lassie for what seemed like ages, but
eventually she came into the stair alone. I was straight on her and I
had her pinned against the wall of the darkened stair recess with ma
Swiss army knife (again purchased from Boston's of Leith Walk)
pressed at her throat.

— What ur ye daein? What ur ye daein, Roy? she whimpered,
fuckin shitein it. That wis the first time she'd spoke tae ays: the first
time the cunt hud said ma name.

I enjoyed the look in her eyes. Enjoyed having the knife at her
throat. Enjoyed the power. That was it wi the power, I remembered
thinking, you just had to take it. When you took it, you had to hold
onto it. That was all there was to it. My cock was stiffening in my
pants. Everything seemed to be so bright. There was no sound. I
seemed to smell pish, then burning. My mouth, chin, lips, hands,
feet: they all seemed to tingle. — You fuckin flicked ma ears! What
dae ye say!

— Sorry . . . she bleated softly.

I spoke slowly into her ear as she cringed away from me, too
immobilised by fear to try any more ambitious movement. — Roy
Strang is ma fucking name. Nae cunt fucks aboot wi me . . . lift up
yir skirt, I commanded, pushing the blade tighter against her thin,
white throat.

She lifted it.

— Higher!

I put my hand inside her cotton panties and tugged them down
onto her thighs. It was the first fanny I'd seen in real life, though I'd
seen plenty in wank mags. — A ginger minge. Jist as ah fuckin well
thought. Ah'd wanted tae see if ye hud ginger pubes like, ah smiled.

The daft cunt produces a forced, wretched parody of a smile back for me.

— What's fuckin funny? Eh? Think *ah'm* fuckin funny? I spat through clenched teeth, pointing at myself.

— Naw . . . she pleaded.

I stood close to her then moved onto her, and started rubbing up against her till I came, talking like they did in the wankmags, my hot breath on her frozen, terrorised face: — Slut . . . slut . . . dirty fuckin slag . . . you fuckin love it ya dirty wee cunt . . . I felt like Winston Two. My hot wallpaper paste filled my pants. That was it; I'd had my first ride, even if it was only a dry ride. A dry ride was what the aulder laddies in the scheme called it when ye didnae get it up a lassie's fanny, ye jist rubbed up against them.

I stood apart from her saying, — You say anything aboot this ya fuckin ginger-pubed wee cunt n you are fuckin well deid! Right!

She stood rooted to the spot with her hands covering her eyes. — Ah'll no say nowt . . . she gasped with fear, nearly greetin, as I departed. I turned back to look at her pulling her pants up. To think I'd wanked over that. She was just a daft wee lassie: hardly any tits, barely any hips. I was going to get a proper ride soon, and it wid be with a real woman.

That was another problem sorted.

I found schoolwork easy and nobody fucked me about. I'd occasionally skive off to watch Wimbledon or the World Cup if my auld man was on the dayshift. It was great having the hoose tae masel. I remember I got really into Wimbledon that summer: this unseeded big cunt with a powerful serve, I cannae remember his name, he was just blowing away all the top seeds. He got as far as the semi-finals. I remember that snobby auld Dan Maskell cunt referring tae the boy as a 'dangerous floater'. That was me, at the school and the scheme: a dangerous floater. I was too anonymous to be one of the big hard cunts, but I carried an air of menace and I was a risky prospect to fuck aboot with. The hard cunts knew this, and so did I.

Rather than stake my place as a top dog in the school or scheme crews, I avoided them, assembling my own team. I wanted to be the top fuckin brass. The punters I hung around with were misfits. They were either too cool, like Pete, too smart, like Brian, too spaced-out like Penman, or too scruffy and thick like Dexy n Willie to fit in with the other crews.

That summer I was desperate for a ride. I must have been really desperate because I captured this baby-faced cunt called Alan or Alec somebody . . . Moncur, I think, in the laddies' toilet. The guy wore a grey duffel coat in the winter and a school blazer in the summer (this is Craigey wir talkin aboot!) and was always neat and tidy, the kind of cunt who seemed as if his Ma still dressed him.

This Dressed-By-His-Ma-Cunt was quite pally though. He sort ay befriended us for a bit as I think he probably got that much stick at school he was looking for mates who'd protect him. On one occasion he played along at being jocularly mesmerised by me as I pretended to hypnotise him:

— . . . hyp - i - no - tise . . .
. . . hyp - i - no - tise . . .

. . . ye could tell he was shitein it but, his eyes like the windaes oan a computer. What wis oan display looked awright, but there was a lot more stacked behind it, a lot more gaun oan behind they lassie-like eyes. I lifted my leg and let my knee surge intae the cunt's groin with force . . .

. . . now your balls are paralysed . . .

. . . he gave a sick, sharp, animal shriek as he bent double in agony. I led off a cold, smirking chorus as we savoured the pain and trepidation which filled his eyes.

Tony had done that to me. One time in the hoose. But Tony wis awright; he never really battered me much. It was mainly Bernard he battered, and that was barry; seein that fuckin poof get battered.

But the funny thing for me was that I always felt a bit shite eftir I did something like that. It made me feel sad and low. I suppose I just felt sorry for what I'd done. The funny thing was though, that I felt sorry *in general*, never to the *particular person* I'd abused. I just hated them even more. But eftir I did something like that I'd try to make it up by doing a good deed, like giving up my seat oan the bus tae an auld cunt or daein the dishes for my Ma. It was just when I did something like I did to the Dressed-By-His-Ma-Cunt I always felt alive, so in control. So while I felt bad aboot it eftir, it was never enough tae stoap ays daein it *at the time*.

One day ah wis in the laddies' bogs at the school, wi Bri n Penman, whae wir huvin a smoke. Ah never bothered wi fags. We were jist fartin aboot in thair when whae should come in but the Dressed-By-His-Ma-Cunt. I felt a dryness in ma mooth as my eyes feasted oan the Dressed-By-His-Ma-Cunt's worried, rabbit-like expression. My throat seemed to constrict and my lips stuck together soas I had to free them with my wet tongue.

— Captured! I roared, pointing at him, and bundled him at knifepoint into one of the cubicles.

— Strangy! Whit ye daein in thair, ya cunt! Bri shouted.

— Keep fuckin shoatie, Bri . . . keep fuckin shoatie . . . I gasped.

I forced the Dressed-By-His-Ma-Cunt to wank me off. — Slowly . . . ah'll fuckin kill ye . . . slowly . . . I commanded as he pulled gently on my cock, his eyes wide in fear. Despite the banging and laughing from the boys ootside, I was aroused enough tae blaw my muck ower the sappy fucker's black blazer.

I put it away quickly, then opened the door.

Penman and Bri fell about laughing as the tearful Dressed-By-His-Ma-Cunt finally emerged whimpering from the cubicle, followed by me with a wicked smile on my coupon.

But while all my pals laughed at this, they looked at me sort of differently for a while, as if I was a poof like Bernard. I blamed the Dressed-By-His-Ma-Cunt, and nursed a violent wrath. If that cunt hud never looked like an insipid, fruity wee lassie he would never have made me make a cunt ay masel like that. I hated poofs. I hated the thought ay what those sick cunts did tae each other, pittin their cocks up each other's dirty arseholes. I would castrate all poofs.

Shortly after this, the Dressed-By-His-Ma-Cunt was talking tae his pals in the playground and he fairly squealed as my elbow made a strong, cracking contact with his face. I never bothered to look back and watch the blood spill heavily from that girl mouth, but Dexy and Bri assured me that it most certainly did.

I hated that cunt.

However, the reaction of my mates had made it even more important that I got my hole properly likes, for the first time. Fortunately, I was soon into a proper shag. At night we used to hang around the school gates with a group of lassies, and would fuck about, feeling them up. There was one who was gamer than the rest, a lassie called Lesley Thomson. She was nothing special to look at, and she was a total scruffbag, but she had barry tits and a good erse. A loat ay the other lassies were really too wee: nae real tits or erse. I would separate her from the group and go across the playing fields to the gates at the other end of the school with her. After a few dry rides, I worked up the confidence to fuck her properly.

I got the budget room key from Tony. It was only the block caretakers and the binmen that were supposed to have them but my auld man had one because he was the sort of unofficial security guy for the building. It was council policy to encourage responsible tenants to get involved in the upkeep of the area. However, Tony kept Dad's key as he used the budget room to take lassies for a cowp. Tony was a fuckin total shag artist. Even though he had a flat in Gorgie, he'd still come doon tae oors and use the budget room tae fuck aw the local slags fi the scheme that he didnae want hassling him at his pad.

I was pretty good pals with Tony at this time, and I'd sometimes go up to see him in his flat. It was barry; he'd give me beer and I got to smoke dope with him. I never really liked it, but I kidded on I did cause it was good of him tae let ays try it. — Dinnae tell Ma or John, he'd laugh.

It was Tony who really telt ays everything aboot lassies. — If thir slags ye jist grab a hud ay the cunts. If it's a decent bird ye stey cool fir a bit and chat them up, then ye grab a hud ay them.

The budget room was the place where the rubbish chute led to a giant aluminium bucket, which dominated the cold bleak room. The block's central electricity meters were also in here. There was a manky auld mattress on the floor, doubtless used by Tony. I wanted to fuck Lesley standing up, though, as I was used to that through the dry rides. I got her up against the wall and started to feel for her crack. To my surprise, the actual hole was a lot further down the slit in the bush than I had thought. The pictures of women's fannies in the wank mags were deceiving. I never liked the ones where the genitals were exposed in too much detail; they were like raw, open wounds, totally at odds with the smiling, inviting faces of the models. I bet they were highlighted with paint or gloss or some shite like that. I had bought my first wank mag from Bobbie's Bookshop: this was the very same occasion on which I bought ma last Marvel comic mag, the *Silver Surfer* likes. The wank mags did have some use; at least ah didnae try tae fuck Lesley up her arsehole. I had grown up thinking that was the norm for sex, because of Tony saying: Ah'd shag the fuckin erse oafay that, every time a lassie walked past him. It took the wank mags tae pit me right oan that one. They did have their uses.

It took a while to get it in. I remember being surprised that it actually did go *up*, as opposed to straight in likes. Her fanny was wet and slimy but a bit tight and I had to bend my knees. After a few thrusts I shot my load inside her as my legs buckled and I fell onto the mattress. It was my first proper ride; my first wet ride. Being honest, it wisnae *that* much better than a dry ride, but at least I'd done it. I felt equals with Tony; both men of the world. I went to school next day with a confident swagger. Aw these cunts who called me Dumbo Strang; sitting in their bedrooms wanking over Sue Storm, The Invisible Girl in the *Fantastic Four*, while there was me, the ugly cunt who was getting his hole. It was funny, I used tae hate the thought of Sue Storm getting shagged by that Mr Fantastic Cunt, that Reed Richards. She could've done better for hersel than that boring cunt, though I suppose he had the power tae alter the shape and dimensions ay any part ay his boady. If he could dae it tae his cock then she'd be in fir a good fuckin time. I suppose they didnae call the cunt Mr Fantastic for nothing. If she had a sair heid though, she could jist vanish.

I'd talk to Tony about getting my hole; bullshitting about the number of shags I'd had and the things I'd done. I think he knew

I was making most of it up, and I knew that he knew, but he let me go on and said nothing as it amused the both of us and passed the time.

Lesley Thomson though; she began to disgust me, she really did. The truth was that she always had. She wore these manky white socks which used to make me feel aroused but soon just made me feel clarty. She had that unmistakeable stale-cake smell of the scheme scruff. I hated the way she just stood there, never moving, always looking vacant and stupid. I fucked her a few times that summer, always vowing that each time was the last time but eventually succumbing to the temptation to shaft her again and hating her and myself for it.

There wis one time when she tried tae take ma airm, this wis durin the day, ootside the gates at the school, likesay ah wis sort ay gaun oot wi her. I had to slap the slag's pus thair n then. I had tae dae a bit crawlin later oan, but, soas I'd git ma hole. — Wir gaun oot thegither, ah explained tae her stupid face, — but just at night likes, right? Durin the day we dae oor ain thing.

The slag *seemed* tae understand.

While I was up to all this in the scheme, I was sticking in at school. The next year I went into hibernation to study for my O Grades. Dad insisted that ah wisnae tae be disturbed and Kim was enlisted to bring my tea up to my room on a tray. Although Tony was in a flat by this time, so there was mair room, Bernard was made to sleep on the couch so I could have the room to myself. It always surprised me that Bernard didn't move into a flat, he was out the house often enough with his queer mates.

John was adamant that no sacrifice was too much during my study time. He was proud that a Strang was sitting six O Grades, and he and my Ma would embarrass the fuck out of me by telling every cunt.

I passed all six. They wanted ays tae stey oan n take highers, but I wanted a job soas I could get some cash thegither n get a place ay ma ain. There was another party at the house to celebrate; mostly the auld man and auld girl's pish-heid mates who staggered back too fucked tae realise what they were celebrating. There was the inevitable sing-song. Dad serenaded Ma wi 'From Russia With Love' and 'Moon River'. She sang 'Nobody Does it Better', tae him.

> Nobody does it better,
> Makes me feel sad for the rest.
> Nobody does it half as good as you do,
> Baby you're the best.

Dad glowed coyly, his eyebrows rising marginally over those thick frames in a Bond-like gesture. I felt a bit sick.

I held out and got my ain way, immediately leaving the school to take up a traineeship as a systems analyst at the Scottish Spinsters' Life Assurance Company in George Street. I'd always been into computers, at the school n that likes. Ma and Dad were pished off at first that I wisnae steyin oan but they bursted with pride when they heard that I'd got what people termed a good job with prospects. I'm sure Dad saw it as a vindication of the Strang genes.

— Kent ye hud brains, son, he would continually tell me. — Computers, thing ay the future, he would say knowingly, as if he was privy to some secret information that had evaded the rest of the human race. This statement became an almost obligatory utterance in my family at any reference to me, replacing 'six O Grades' and 'university material'. So that was me set up.

I remember my first day at Scottish Spinsters'. I was impressed to the point of being overawed by the building. It was completely new on the inside, but it had retained its grandiose Georgian facade and opulent reception area with marble pillars, and the original oak-panelled rooms and corridors. This was where the boardroom was situated and where the high-up cunts had their offices. This older part of the building led onto an ugly newly-built structure which housed a series of bland, identical offices decked out in pastel colours and lit with migraine-inducing neon strip-lights.

I shared an office with four others. The door was marked SYSTEMS CONTROL and it bore three names; Jane Hathaway, Derek Holt and Des Frost. Myself and Martine Fenwick, the other trainee, were not considered senior enough to have our names on the door. It was that sort of a place. In the office across the corridor was a guy called Colin Sproul, who was our section head.

If the building impressed me, I never really thought that much of the cunts I worked with. Jane Hathaway was like the supervisor, Senior Systems Control Officer, she was called. She was quite overweight with longish brown hair, and glasses which reminded me of the auld man's. There was haughty malevolence aboot her; she was a sad cunt who seemed to thrive on exercising her power over the men in the office. She'd get you to take something doon tae the photocopying for her (which wisnae really ma joab) and then say: —Thank you, young man, in a patronising, jokey sort of way. But she was quite a snidey cunt because she never overstepped the mark to the extent that you could confront her and tell her to fuck off; she just nipped away under the surface, her asides leaving a bad taste in your mooth though you could never be quite sure why.

I got the vibe that Hathaway had the hots for Martine Fenwick, who was a trainee like me, but, unlike me, had been to the Uni. English literature or something: fuckin waste that, eh. Fenwick was an exceptionally skinny lassie with no tits whatsoever. I sometimes used to glance doon her open blouse when she was demonstrating something on the VDU, just tae see if I could spy a *bit* ay tit. But naw, it was like her bra was just an elasticated vest which housed only a nipple. She was a really nervous lassie. Hathaway and her used to go all girlish when they spoke sometimes, it was like that was their patter; and Fenwick would start giggling nervously and jerk and twitch and have to put her knuckles between her teeth to stop herself laughing like an imbecile. She was a gawky lassie, in no way a shag, yet she had a strange, obscure sexuality and I inexplicably used to wank about her.

Hathaway seemed to give Derek Holt a hard time. Derek was an ordinary guy; married with two kids, liked a pint at lunchtime, good at his job, would never blow his own trumpet. He was intae fitba and was a season ticket holder at Tynecastle. I'd sometimes spraff with him aboot it. I was never really intae fitba then, it was just something tae talk aboot. Hathaway seemed to find this guy deeply offensive, like he was some kind of caveman; she'd look at him with withering distaste and her tone would go harsher when she addressed him. Perhaps it was because he wasn't what she was; English, middle-class and a lesbo. Holt never really seemed to notice her behaviour though, or if he did he didnae bother.

Des Frost was quite a smooth cunt. He fancied himself but was detached and didnae get involved. I could tell that he gave Martine Fenwick the hots in a big way.

Anyway, that was the cunts in my office. I didnae really have much time for any of them, but they never bothered me much, eh.

Even though I wanted to find a flat, life in the hoose had got better. I was bringing in money and was treated like mair ay an equal than a silly wee laddie. Sometimes I'd go up the pub wi Dad and Tony and Uncle Jackie and some of their mates. I felt great at times like that. A lot of the auld cunts crawled up my erse, John Strang's laddie, they called me. Winston Two would sit curled at our feet as we sat with our pints and dominoes.

For as long as I could remember, I had fantasised revenge on that fuckin dug for the savaging he gave my leg as a sprog. The animal learned to keep out my road, but I made sure I was never caught kicking him. Winston Two was revered in my family. Kim used to take him out a lot and she had composed a banal and nauseating mantra which was always sung affectionately when the animal had something in his mouth. It went:

> Winners, Winners, Winalot,
> Winners Winners, what you got?

This moronic rhyme quickly gained cult status in my family and it was repeated endlessly by everyone. Kim obviously took this gift for shite poetry from Bernard, who was particularly keen on her daft composition. I hated the way they all idolised that fuckin dog.

One evening I found myself alone in the house with the beast. The old boy had been dozing by the electric bar fire and was slowly coming around. I had been watching him, the rhythmic flare of his nostrils, the rising of the flap of skin at the top of his nose as he slept. I was imagining his long head as the ball on the penalty spot in the European Cup Final between Hibs and A.C. Milan. At the end of an exciting but goal-less contest, the boys in emerald green were awarded a penalty kick which their new signing, Roy Strang, confidently stepped up to take.

Winston's jaw crackled PHAKOH as I caught the bastard a beauty. — Strang . . . one nil! I said crisply, in a nasal English commentator cunt voice, — end shawly nahow the Chempeons' Cup is on its woy to Aistuh Road! The beast let out an injured yelp then whined pathetically, cowering under the sideboard. — Winners . . . Winners . . . I cooed in breathless affection, eventually enticing the terrorised creature back to my side. — You are going to die, Winners, I said soothingly, — as soon as I find a way to get you away from here: You.are.going.to.die. I stroked the old boy as he panted in servile contentment.

I quite enjoyed my new job. I was a bit in awe of all the snobby cunts there, but some of them were okay and the work was easy. Most of all, I enjoyed the salary. Dumbo Strang, making mair poppy than any of the cheeky schemie peasants who had once tried to torment him. My social life, though, was a bit of a drag. I found it harder to get my hole. I wanted a class bird, no just knee-trembling some schemie in a rubbish room. There was plenty of tackle at the work, but it was mostly snobby fanny, or what *ah* would call snobby fanny, and I felt too shy and self-conscious to talk tae them. So there was no action at all. I had never really fancied the idea of taking drugs, apart from a blow with Tony. Pete, Penman and Bri were always oot ay thair faces on something or other. Although I had the odd pint wi Tony or the auld man, drink did little for me, and I wasnae really intae getting pished. I'd seen alcohol as the drug of too many of the plebs I despised. So I suppose I sort of came to the conclusion that the best possibility for me in having a good crack was with the cashies. I had gone to a few Hibs games as a kid with Tony and my Dad, but always got bored quickly. Fitba seemed a drag to me. I identified it with my own lack of ability; too uncoordinated thanks to my gammy leg, courtesy of Winston Two. However, Dexy and Willie were running with the baby crew, and I started listening to some of their stories with interest.

But all this is nonsense.

Let's get DEEPER.

9 The Praying Mantis

Sandy toked hard on the spliff and inhaled powerfully. We were driving Dawson's shabby jeep out towards the Emerald Forest Park. I was at the wheel. I watched the dark, urban landscape of Jambola Park's dank and dingy parent city come to an end as a lush green hill appeared before us. Two young women came into view, hitching by the side of the road. One had honey-blonde hair, streaked by the sun. She was a little overweight, but very pretty. The other one had dark, cascading hair, lovely almond eyes, and a beautiful twisted pout to her lips. She was gorgeous.

— Stop! Sandy shouted, nodding over at them.

I increased speed. — Slags! Fuckin slags! The last thing we want are fuckin slags in tow tae spoil it fir every cunt, I snarled, surprised at the words that were coming out of my mouth.

What the fuck is this?

— We would've been well in . . . Sandy moaned.

— Plenty of opportunity tae get a ride . . . I mean, plenty of opportunity to enjoy the consort of attractive young ladies after we take care of business, Sandy, I said. For some reason I hated those women. The slags gave me the fucking creeps. Hitching like that. They deserved to get . . .

No.

In here I'm doing all the things I didn't do out there. I'm trying to be better, trying to do the right thing, trying to work it all out.

Sandy is not amused. He's well pissed off at me for not stopping. He starts prattling away, his hurt suddenly taking on a more

abstract, conceptual bent: — Justice, he urbanely remarked, — is not
a commodity we enjoy to any great extent. Yes, we strive towards
it, but it seems to be the miserable lot of our wretched species that it
persistently evades us.

I ignored him. We'd just had this conversation. When we first got
into the town we had hit a bar where we watched some disturbing
televised pictures of children starving to death. It was some famine,
or a war, or whatever. I took it that Sandy had been moved by this,
because he came out with exactly the same sort of stuff about justice.
— Yes Sandy, I had agreed, — those poor starving children; a rather
shabby show all round.

— Actually, I was thinking about the infamous handball incident
in the Airdrie v Dunfermline League Cup Semi-Final at Tynecastle
in September 1991 where a controversial refereeing decision . . .

That was what he'd said then. Now, he's saying it all again,
slavering that same shite in ma fuckin ear. I shook my head. Why did
he have to bring this up? I'm losing control, I'm fucking well losing
it here. — I think I've heard this story before, Sandy . . . I wasn't
taking this from a cunt who wasn't real, just a character I'd created in
my own mind, based vaguely on the outline of a footballer. Nothing
is real, but everything is. I have only my perception to determine
what reality is, and in here that perception is so vivid it makes up for
my lost senses.

Sandy sulked and took the wheel after we stopped for a slash and a
cup of stewed tea in an outlying village. On the other side of the
Green Hill was the Emerald Forest Park. I picked up my copy of
YOUTH IN ASIA, the book Dawson had given me. A cursory
glance at the contents revealed a deeply philosophical work in which
the author strove to find paths of self-deliverance.

Though far from a light read, it was just what I was after;
I would recommend it to anyone grappling with
the practical issues of personal political

action which one is faced with   rise – Hiya son.
after indulging in philosophical   rise
discourse. At which point do   rise Whae's that . . . Sandy . . .
we transfer our energies   rise
from analysis to action   rise – Eh's lookin better the day, though, eh no Vet?
in the pursuit of   rise
change? We   rise – Aye, eh does.
need to do this to rise

Father is here. John Strang. Mother seems tae be here n aw. Verity Strang, nee Porteous. I'm starting to remember.

The game.

DEEPER

    DEEPER

           DEEPER – – – – – – – – I feel the sun on my face and see Sandy smiling at me. I feel a wonderous, euphoric warmth towards him; it's as if we've taken some MDMA capsules together and the whole world stops and ends at the positive force of love we feel in and around our bodies. We embrace.

After a long silence I say, — I'm sorry, Sandy. I lost the place a bit back there.

— The jeep's rather . . . eh, fucked, basically, he says, changing the subject to spare my embarrassment as we break our hug.

I stand back from him and my senses are overwhelmed by a montage of images in which I see my fist slamming into the twisted rubbery sick queer face of a poof . . . it's Bernard . . . no . . . it's Gordon, his sweet, pukey breath is now in my ear and my spine trembles . . . what the fuck . . .

Concentrate: get a fuckin grip.

Better.

Better.

I notice that we're no longer in the jeep but lying in our underpants by the side of the lake. I enviously give Jamieson's, muscular, athletic footballer's legs the once over. I've treated him badly during this hunt for the Stork, which definitely seems to have lost its momentum of late.

When Sandy looks up at the sun and exclaims, — It was never a penalty, I now fully understand what he's talking about. I've been trying to stage things too much in this little world of mine, trying to exercise total control over this environment, instead of trusting myself to react to events with dignity and compassion. So what if my two worlds are coming closer together? It may be the way I get closer to the Stork. Rather than cut Sandy off, I decide to go with it.

— I'm tempted to agree Sandy, I tell him.

He points to his bare chest, — I've been vindicated by the cameras. I curse that decision every fucking day of my life, Roy. It destroyed my best ever chance of a medal. It destroyed my place in the record books, my shot at footballing immortality. They had no right to do that to me. He gasped in exasperation. — What gave him the right? No man has the right . . . Tears rolled down Sandy's tanned cheeks.

No man has the right.

Where did I see that?

Where did I see that? I'm a little fazed, so I break into a nervy rant, — Come on Sandy, that type of setback's part and parcel of the game. Anyway, look at Scottish football and its dreary toytown sectarian status quo: pro-Rangers, masonic, bigoted, servile and backward. We're talking Scotland here, for God sakes . . .

SCOTLAND. NO. THIS IS SUPPOSED TO BE AFRICA OR SOMEWHERE OR EVEN INSIDE MY HEAD WHICH IS NOT A COUNTRY, IT HAS NOTHING TO . . .

I look at Jamieson, open-mouthed for a second. Fortunately he is too lost in himself to notice my gaffe. — Sandy, consider forgiveness. Consider human error. He may have just made a mistake.

Sandy thought about this, then turned to me in a state of some shock. — . . . Just a mistake? he said.

— Yes Sandy, human error.

Sandy looked up at me, a light in his eye and a smile on his face, — Yes! Of course! It was just a silly mistake. Only a game of football, twenty-two daft overgrown laddies kicking a baw around. No harm done.

up — — Darren Jackson's solitary strike was enough to put No harm do — — coming Hibs into another League Cup final where they will face Rain-chirs. . .

— Ah'm gaunny pit this oan fir the laddie, the laddie's no wantin tae hear aboot fitba. Ma says.

— How dae you ken that but, Vet? Ah'm askin ye! How dae you ken whit the laddie wants tae hear?

So would ye like tae have fun, fun, fun,

How's about a few laughs, laughs, laughs,

Let me show you a good time . . .

DEEPER

DEEPER

DEEPER — — — — and now Sandy and I are drinking cocktails in a bar which is in a city which is possibly Nairobi or somewhere in Africa, not beautiful enough to be the Cape and this is all wrong because these two slags we saw on the road are in here and Sandy's being all smarmy and saying: – Can I buy you ladies a drink?

The slags flash predatory smiles at us.

I cut in, – No, you two slags can fuck off. This is just me and Sandy, mates like. We don't want youse cunts spoiling our adventure, spoiling our mission, spoiling our fun! It's just boys! Boys only, boys only, boys only!

I hear myself squealing petulantly at them. I fear that I've made a fool of myself in the bar, but it unsettles the women as they have dropped their disguise and are now giant praying mantises with blonde and auburn wigs, lipstick smeared on those deadly pincher-like insect jaws.

— Look Sandy, see them now, I smile, triumphant and vindi-cated. — See those fuckin slags as they really are!

Sandy turned away from them and smiled at the white, silver-haired barman, — These so-called ladies will not be joining us after all. He gave him a nod and a wink and the barman picked up a baseball bat from behind the bar.

— You leave. Now you leave, he shouted at the insects. They made some whirring mechanical insect sounds and backtracked awkwardly towards the door. As they exit onto the street they leave the door jammed open. We can see people passing by on the pavement outside. The draught is cooling.

I feel a great admiration for Jamieson and the way he equipped himself in circumstances which were obviously difficult. I consider whether or not to tell him so and then I think, the hell of it, yes I will, when I see something outside, shuffling awkwardly past the pub, in a slow, crippled, waddling walk.

Sandy sees it too. He throws back his drink, — Quick, Roy! It's our fucking Stork!

We storm out into the street and pursue
the creature down the road and follow it   up   — Naw Vet, hud oan, this
into an alleyway – – but I'm coming   up   is the tape fir the boy . . .
up here naw – – naw – – naw – – – – – up

And now he's singing his New Year special:

From Russia with love . . .
I fly to you,
Much wiser since my
Goodbye to you . . .

SOME CUNT SWITCH OAF THAT FUCKIN TAPE

> I've travelled the world
> To learn I must return
> From Russia with love.

I remember when Matt Monro played the Bird's Cage at the Doocot up Ferry Road. Matt's career was on the slide by then, but Ma and Dad really enjoyed that night out. Ever since that Bond movie and that song he'd been Dad's hero and the auld man did a passable imitation of Matt.

> I've seen faces, places
> and smiled for a moment,
> But oh
> You haunted me so.
> Still my tongue-tied
> Young pride
> Would not let my love for you show
> In case you'd say no.

— This is great though, eh Vet?

— Aye.

— We'd better be makin a move but, thirs the tea tae git n a new David Attenborough series is oan the night. Like ah sais, a new David Attenborough. It's goat the birds in it. The secret life ay the Barn Owl's the first yin. See what yir missin, Roy! Any other news fir the laddie Vet, like ah sais, other news?

— No really, everybody's fine.

— The only other news is that ah nivir voted Tory this time, in the local elections like, as a protest against this fuckin poll tax. Mind you, ah should be protestin against the fuckin Labour council; it's these cunts that keep it sae high. Ah voted SNP, no thit ah believe in Scottish independence. The Scots built the empire n these daft English cunts couldnae run it withoot us. That's ma philosophy anywey. Right Vet, ye fit?

— Aye. Tro, Roy.

— Cheerio, son.

They switch off the tape and leave as the nurses come to attend to me. I am turned over and given an enema by Nurse Patricia Devine.

At one time this would have been a fantasy.

10 Bernard Visits

Bernard has come to see me in the hospital. He comes in every few days or weeks or months, I think: time has no meaning in my state. Bernard comes to read his poems to me. At last the sad queen has found a captive audience.

The only interesting thing about Bernard's visits is that he alone actually seems to believe that I can hear him. When the others talk to me their tones are strained, forced; full of self-obsessed pity, confessional and self-justifying. Bernard is the only one who seems completely at ease. We were never so at ease with each other. Why is he being so nice to me?

— Mind South Africa, Roy? Johannesfuckinburg, he spits. — I fuckin hated it there. Mind you, there was bags of talent. Ah hudnae really come oot then but. That was the one waste, these boys of all races . . . but of course, you scored more than me in that department, he giggles, — You mercenary wee closet rent-boy you.

EH? WHAT THE FUCK ARE YOU OAN ABOOT YOU SILLY FUCKIN QUEEN . . .

— Oh aye. Ah kent aw aboot you and Gordon. Poor old Uncle Gordon. Fascist prick.

How the fuck . . .

— Oh, he tried it on with me too. With me first. Disappointed Roy? Oh yes, I'm a queen alright lovey, but a damn sight more choosy than that. I mean, it's a bit like you and Gran, both hetero's, right? Well, I'm assuming, possibly naively in light of your track-record, that you wouldn't go down on her arid old cunt. Right? His voice is teasy, jesting, rather than malicious.

FUCK OFF YOU HIDEOUS QUEER . . .

— No more than I'd take Uncle Gordon into my gob. But you did, didn't you, eh Roy? What else did that sick low-life do to you, Roy?

DID AH FUCK . . . WE DID NOWT . . . IT WIS A WANK, THAT WIS AW . . .

— Sorry Roy. That was out of order. Do you mind ay South Africa though? I still think of it now. It inspired a few poems, that year did. Remember when Gordon took us to Sun City for that weekend?

I remember that. We took a short flight down from the City of Gold to the African Vegas, in the nominally independent homeland of Bophuthatswana. Gambling was, of course, illegal in the Republic. The Sun City jaunt was a little package Gordon put together to get John and Vet down there to do what he always tried to do; make them feel inadequate by showing off his wealth and his many business interests.

I remember it okay. It was a great time. We stayed in the Cascades Hotel, the most expensive and luxurious in Sun City. As the name of the hotel suggests, water was its principal theme. Its liberal use of the stuff produced rich, tropical, landscaped grounds. Kim and I spent ages wandering through this homemade rainforest, with its waterfalls, streams, paths and bridges. We were the only kids there and it was like our own private paradise. We found this little clearing by the lake where we would just go and sit, and pretend that all this was ours and we never had to go home. I was a bit of a cunt, and I'd make Kim burst oot greetin just by saying that we would be going back to Muirhouse. I wish I hudnae joked aboot it. Like me, she loved it in South Africa. But these gardens, they were like the promised land. In fact, the hotel grounds were a microcosm of the whole of Sun City. Vast quantities of water had been used to create this literal oasis in the desert, which had been landscaped imaginatively with flowers, lawns, exotic trees and streams all over the place.

It was a wonderful few days.

— with Tony and I being old enough to go out to the casinos and all that shite with Mum, Dad and Gordon

it was paradise

— the sickening greed and avarice, the front-line of South African exploitation, the playground where the settlers enjoyed the fruits of the wealth they'd ripped off

SHUT UP YOU FUCKIN POOF, IT WISNAE LIKE THAT, IT WAS BRILLIANT

— but even worse than the casinos was the fuckin cabaret. You and Kim were the lucky ones, tucked up back at the hotel. I had to sit in silence as we watched Doreen Staar's show. She was crude and extremely racist. I wrote a poem about that time.

OH GOD, SURPRISE, SURPRISE. HERE WE GO.

He bursts into a lisping rant: — This one's called: Doreen Staar's Other Cancer.

Did you see her on the telly
the other day
good family entertainment
the tabloids say

But when you're backstage
at your new faeces audition
you hear the same old shite
of your own selfish volition

She was never a singer
a comic or a dancer
I can't say I was sad
when I found out she had cancer

Great Britain's earthy northern
comedy queen
takes the rand, understand
from the racist Boer regime

So now her cells are fucked
and that's just tough titty
I remember her act
that I caught back in Sun City

She went on and on about
'them from the trees
with different skull shapes
from the likes of you and me'

Her Neo-Nazi spell
it left me fucking numb
the Boers lapped it up with zeal
so did the British ex-pat scum

But what goes round
comes round they say
so welcome to another dose
of chemotherapy

And for my part
it's time to be upfront
so fuck off and die
you carcinogenic cunt.

— What do you think then, Roy?

He asks as if I can reply. He knows I can hear him. Bernard
knows.

Bernard

— Went doon a fuckin storm at the club.

Bernard

I thought it was one of your better efforts.

part three

On
The Trail
Of
The Stork

11 Casuals

I first met Lexo on the train from Glasgow Central to Motherwell. I was sitting with Dexy and Willie, out the road fae the top table and the top boys. This was my first away run with the cashies and I was determined to make an impression.

Dexy and Willie had been running with the boys for a while, rising from the baby crew. At first their stories bored me; they seemed exaggerated and I couldnae take their versions of the events, far less their supposed roles in the proceedings with any real degree ay seriousness. However, I got intrigued enough to check out some of the vibes at the home games where you had a substantial casual visiting support, and this was only really games against Aberdeen, and I became hooked on the adrenalin.

It was when Aberdeen were down with a huge crew that I was first bitten. The sheepshaggers had just signed that Charlie Nicholas cunt fae Arsenal, the soapdodger, and there was a heavy atmosphere. These cunts fancied their chances. I did a bit of mouthing and jostling up Regent Road, but there were too many polis aboot for any real swedgin tae take place.

On the train, on this dull Wednesday night, we were assured that it would be different. Dexy, Willie and myself were eager lieu-tenants, laughing sycophantically at any jocular top boy who played to the gallery, but remaining stern, impassive and deferential when a psycho held court.

Lexo went around the train giving a pep-talk. — Mind, nae cunt better shite oot. Remember, a cunt that messes is a cunt that dies. We're the hardest crew in Europe. We dinnae fuckin run. Mind. We dinnae fuckin run.

We didnae have tae wait long before meeting up with the

Motherwell casuals. They were upon us at the station and I was
shit-scared. I didn't know why; it seemed as if I'd been surrounded
by latent and manifest violence all my life. This was different
though, a new situation. It's only now I realise that behaviour always
has a context and precedents, it's what you do rather than what you
are, although we often never recognise that context or understand
what these precedents are. I remember thinking; swallow the fear,
feel the buzz. That was what Lexo said. Then I saw this thin,
spectacularly white guy, almost albino, just charging into the
Motherwell boys and scattering them. I steamed in swinging,
kicking and biting. This cunt I was hitting was hitting me back but it
was like I couldn't feel a thing and I knew that he could because his
eyes were filling up with fear and it was the best feeling on earth.
Then he was on his arse. The next thing I knew was that I was being
pulled off one cunt by some of our boys, and dragged away down
the road as polis sirens filled the air. I was snarling like a demented
animal, wanting only to get back and waste the cunt on the ground
for good.

At the game I was trembling inside with excitement. We all were.
We laughed with liberating hysteria at any banal joke or observation
made about the swedgin. I don't remember anything about the
match, except wee Mickey Weir running up and down the wing,
trying vainly to play fitba, surrounded by claret and amber giants
and a blind referee. We lost one-nil. Back on the train with a police
escort to Glasgow then Edinburgh, the match was never mentioned
once. Aw the talk was aboot the swedge.

Lexo came over to us. Dexy, looking sheepish, got up to let him
sit beside me. Hovering over the table, he was dismissed as Lexo
snapped, — Nose fuckin botherin ye, cunt?

He departed looking like a timid dog. Dexy had not acquitted
himself well in the swedge tonight.

— Fuckin wanker, he smiled, then shouted back down the train,
— Ghostie! C'mere the now, ya cunt!

The albino-looking guy named Ghostie came and joined us. You
would never think to look at him that the cunt was particularly hard,
but every fucker knew him as a crazy radge. He was on-form at

Motherwell. He'd been first in, he had given me the confidence. I'd never seen anything so fast, so ruthless and powerful.

— Whit's yir name, pal? he asked.

— Roy. Roy Strang.

— Strang. Got a brar?

— Aye, Tony Strang.

He nodded in vague recognition. – Whair ye fi?

— Muirhoose.

— Schemie, eh? he laughed.

I felt anger rise in me. Whae the fuck did this wide-o think he wis? I tried to control it. I knew who he was. Ghostie. The Ghost. I'd seen him in action; only briefly as I'd been too involved myself, but enough tae ken that ah'd never mess wi the cunt.

— Me n aw, he smiled. Fi Niddrie. Stey in toon now, though. Cannae be bothered wi the fuckin scheme any mair. Ye ken satellite dishes? he asked.

— Aye.

— Whit dae they call the wee boax oan the back ay the satellite dish?

— Eh, dunno likes.

— The council's, he laughed. I was pleased to join in.

That was the start of my cashie activities. The season was in its infancy and I was already known tae the top boys.

I was arrested at Parkhead for breaking a Weedgie's jaw; fortunately I managed to sling my knuckleduster. Our strategy for Glasgow games was to merge with the crowd and just start laying into every cunt to panic them. All it took was organisation and bottle. The organisation was really just about timing, moving at the right time. I stiffened some stupid fucker for the crime of being a total spaz-wit with loads of badges of the Pope and IRA on his scarf, but a couple of polis came straight after me. I ran through the crowd, but one sneaky soapdodging cunt stuck a leg oot and I lost my balance and fell and was huckled.

Ma and Dad were fucked off at the court case.

— Ah'm no wantin you gittin intae bother, Roy. Ye could lose yir joab, son. You're supposed tae be the sensible yin in the faimlay,

Dad mused. He was in a strange position; concerned, but gratified that all those boxing lessons hadn't gone to waste. — Ah kent wi shouldnae huv come back here. We should've steyed in Sooth Efrikay.

— Aw, c'mon, Dad . . .

— Dinnae come oan Dad me. Like ah sais, Sooth Efrikay.

— Like ah sais, he droned on, — ye could lose yir joab. They dinnae grow oan trees nowadays, eh. Specially no in computers. Thing ay the future.

— Aye, right.

— N whit fir, eh? Whit fir? Ah'm askin ye! Fir they fuckin casual bampots. Ah mean, it's no as if thir even interested in the fitba these cunts. Ah see yis aw at Easter Road. It's aw designer labels wi these cunts, like ah sais, fuckin designer labels.

— Shite.

— Aw aye, ye kin shite aw ye want tae, bit ah've read aw aboot it. In the *Evening News*. Fuckin mobile phones, the loat. Ye tryin tae tell ays that's aw rubbish, eh? Ah'm askin ye!

— Aye. It's shite. Pure shite.

I was less scared of the auld man now. He seemed a sadder, weaker figure, broken by his brother's death and the end of the South African dream. He now worked as a store detective in John Menzies.

I was getting on, leading a compartmentalised life. The weekends it was clubs and fitba with the boys, and I had been shagging a few birds. Joining the cashies had been a bonus on that score. Although I was never happy with the wey ah looked, being a cashie I had access to aw the fanny I needed. Sometimes just skankers likes, but a ride's a ride. It was something to do eftir the swedgin; it was better than no gettin a ride. That fucks up a cunt's self-esteem. Too right. At work I was getting on alright, doing well in my day release in computer studies at Napier College. I enjoyed setting up programmes to run policies: it was a challenge and the money was okay. I still resolved to get into a flat in town and away from my family. The thing was that I was spending a lot of dough as well, mostly on clathes. Nearly every penny I had went on new gear.

The rumours about me being a cashie started to circulate at the work. It was a busy time for us and the newspapers were on our case. Big-time soccer violence in Scotland had always been aboot really thick Weedgies who never went to church knocking fuck oot ay each other to establish who had the best brand of Christianity. We were big news because we were different; stylish, into the violence just for itself, and in possession of decent IQs.

I enjoyed the notoriety. It was good seeing all the straight-peg cunts at my work look at me with respect and trepidation. I just kept quiet. Even when that nosey dyke cow of a supervisor Jane Hathaway tried to bait me by reading out incidents from the paper on a Monday, I just kept quiet. Nae cunt had the bottle tae come right out and ask me if I was involved. More than the notoriety, I enjoyed the sense of enigma.

There was plenty of opportunity tae make money wi the cashies, but I was only really interested in the swedgin. There was less risk in that. I sussed out quickly that the polis werenae bothered too much aboot crimes against the person as long as you never bothered posh cunts or shoppers. When you started tryin tae extort dough fae the pubs, clubs n shoaps, that was when the cunts got nippy. There wis nae wey ah wis gaunny dae time.

There was a big do at the Pilton Hilton, the Commodore Hotel; Tony was getting married to this lassie called Hannah. He brought her roond tae the hoose one night and announced it. She looked really nice, even though she was obviously up the stick. She was moving intae Tony's flat. I was surprised, because I was sure I kent her from somewhere.

— Aboot time ye wir settlin doon, John said, raising a glass of whisky. He insisted we all drank some as a toast. — Like ah sais, ye cannae beat the mairriage stakes. Didnae dae me any herm! He winked at my Ma who gave him a cloying smile.

Bernard said something simpering and Kim started tae greet. Ah jist said: — Nice one Tone, slapped the cunt oan the back and forced the rancid whisky doon wi loads ay lemonade.

At the wedding I got a right fuckin shock when I saw who one of the bridesmaids was. She was dressed in a long peach dress, matching one worn by another lassie and these two wee lassies. It was The Big Ride; Hamilton's shag. She was Hannah's sister, which I suppose made The Big Ride my in-law, or something.

I had clocked her in the church and I couldnae stop looking at her at the reception. I was staring at her. We were introduced, the two families. They'd aw been up at oor hoose before but I had been oot, I never really took any notice.

— So you're Roy, she said.

The fuckin boot didnae even recognise me.

I kept staring at her. As the night wore on, I never took my eyes off her. Eventually she came over to me. — Is thir something wrong? she asked, sitting down beside me.

— You dinnae mind ay me, eh no? I smiled.

She looked quizzical and started mentioning names. Most of them meant little to me, just cunts I vaguely knew through the scheme and the school.

— You used tae go oot wi Stuart Hamilton, I told her.

She blushed a little bit. — That was ages ago . . . she simpered.

— Did eh fuck ye, aye? I asked, looking her up and down. Good tits oan it like.

She screwed her face up and frowned at me. Her prettiness collapsed into ugliness. She was fairly heavily built as well, much broader than Hannah. She'd be a fat sow in a few years' time. Some lassies just kept getting bigger; it was like the daft cows didnae ken when tae stoap. — What? she said weakly.

— Ah mind ay you. You n Hammy n that Gilchrist cunt. Ye pilled ays up ootside the chippie in Muirhoose.

I saw her face register vague recognition.

— Aw . . . c'moan . . . that wis ages ago . . .

— Aye. Too right it wis fuckin ages ago. Like tae see yis dae it now. Whair is that cunt Hammy these days? Ah've been keepin ma fuckin eye oot fir that wanker.

— Ah dinnae ken, ah jist hung aboot wi um whin ah wis younger . . . that wis ages ago . . .

— Ye married? I asked.

— Used tae be, she said.

— Aw, ah goes, makin ma voice aw soft, — did yir felly find oot ye wir a slut? Wis that how eh kicked ye intae touch? Hus Tony fucked ye yet? Ah bet eh hus.

Her features seemed to draw in towards the centre of her face. — You're fuckin tapped, son, she hissed. — Fuck off! She stood up and started moving away. I just smiled. Then she came back and said: — We might be married intae the same family, bit ah dinnae want tae talk tae you. Jist stey oot ay ma wey. You're fuckin sick!

— Fuck off, ya fat hoor, I sneered, drinking in her rage as she turned away.

I kept noising her up during the reception. I was having a great time. — Hoor, I whispered in her ear every time I passed her.

One time she cracked up and confronted me, — You're fuckin spoilin ma sister's big day, she whispered in a harsh hiss. – If ye dinnae fuck off, I'll tell Tony!

— Good, I smiled. — Go ahead. It'll save me tellin um that his sister-in-law's a fuckin hingoot . . . Benny! I shouted, as my Uncle Benny, my Ma's brother, came across. The Big Ride departed.

— Ah wisnae crampin yir style thair Roy, wis ah? Benny asked, raising an eyebrow. — Tidy piece.

— Naw, nae danger. Widnae touch it wi yours, Ben. A right boot: really pits it aroond. Fanny like the Mersey Tunnel, I laughed. Benny joined in.

Later on I saw the daft sow starting tae greet. She left wi another lassie just eftir that. I went over to the married couple and enjoyed a dance with the beautiful bride. I then escorted her back to the handsome groom and gave her a peck on the cheek. — You're a lucky man, Tony.

— Ah ken that, Tony smiled.

— Great do this, by the way, Hannah, I said. — Your folks have done us proud.

— Aye, it's just a pity aboot Sylvia.

— Your sister? What's wrong wi her? I asked with fake concern.

— She's away. Wisnae feeling well.

— That's a shame.

I enjoyed that wedding. Dad got pished and punched this radge who was, apparently, trying to preach socialism at him. That was the only real upset. I also found Kim necking with this daft cunt in the corridor. — Dinnae tell naebody, eh no Roy, she said, obviously hoping that I'd broadcast to the world that she had a fuckin boyfriend. Bernard sloped off early, no doubt to indulge in the practice of arse-banditry. I ended up pished with my Uncle Benny and the two Jackies.

Not a bad night. I never saw The Big Ride again, although I asked after her regularly.

The house was too crowded, even wi Tony away. Kim had her own room and I was in a room with Bernard. That was bad patter; sharing a bedroom with a poof. Sometimes he'd move oot for a bit, but he always came back. Fuck knows why. I never figured out why he stayed for so long. I never figured out why *I* stayed for so long.

Bernard was constantly blowing my cool. I fancied myself as a hard cunt and it was fuckin shan to have *that* for a brother. It made me sick to listen to his lisping, camp patter as he read out his poetry. He always recited it to my Ma, who was embarrassed by it, but as a teacher had once described Bernard as 'gifted', she gamely encouraged him. That was years ago, in the primary, and he'd done fuck all since but ponce about. He worked as a barman in a queers' pub in the city centre and sold jewelry on a stall at Ingliston Market.

Posing in the fuckin stair, he'd read his shitey poems tae aw the young fanny who seemed tae fag-hag him:

> The situation that is life
> sustainable, yet renewable
> its elements building blocks
> in a completed construction
> yet which cannot be identified as such
>   in isolation

> To persecute me for my sexuality
> is to pander to the slavedeck of false illusion
> when the tapes play mixed messages
> through mediums yet to be discovered

> Avanti! I scream, my Italian blood
> courses through my veins
> not to be denied

Aw this wis weird enough, but we'd sometimes get it after our meal on a Sunday, if the auld man went tae the pub. Ma would cook up things like curry and rice, always with chips or tatties and two veg oan the side ay the plate.

One Sunday I asked Tony and Hannah, rather casually, I thought, about Hannah's sister Sylvia, The Big Ride. To my shock my auld man said: — Ah think Roy's goat a wee thing aboot Hannah's sister. Heard ye mention her before, like ah sais, heard ye ask aboot her before.

— Naw ah nivir, I replied. It wasn't that I was being shy, I just couldn't recall mentioning the sow in front of them.

— Aye ye huv, like ah sais, mentioned hur before, he teased, his jaw stretching downwards like Mr Fantastic's. His smile just got broader and broader and as his teeth were exposed, he started to take on the appearance of the Alien in the films of the same name.

In Muirhoose nae cunt can hear ye scream . . . well, they can hear ye, they just dinnae gie a fuck.

He held that radge expression and I felt my face go red and I got a bigger beamer than I had in the first place.

— What a beamer, Tony laughed.

— Aye, right, I snapped.

Laughter filled the room, Kim's shrill tones effortlessly dominating the rest.

I felt my head pound and my pulse quicken. The smell of the food was vivid and intense. Ah'm fuckin Roy Strang. Ah'm fuckin . . . I took a deep breath and pulled myself together.

— Went beetroot rid, so eh did. Like ah sais, beetroot rid, my auld man laughed, jabbing fork into space.

— You'll be the next yin tae git mairried, Roy, Kim said in her banal, nasal way, — cause it'll no be me, that's fir sure . . .

Her nauseating intervention had the desired effect of getting everyone to focus on her romantic life. I suppose I should have thanked her. I resolved to shut up about The Big Ride. I had been weak and had obviously broken, albeit unintentionally, one of my own key rules: say nowt tae nae cunt aboot anything.

When Tony's bairn came, he seemed tae spend mair time back at oor place than ever. For some reason he started to come oan his ain oan a Sunday fir dinner. I think Hannah went tae her Ma's wi the bairn. I don't think he liked her family but I never worked up the bottle to ask him what he thought of The Big Ride. That was out of the question now. I was sure he'd fucked her, or at least tried to. This was simply because, knowing Tony as I did, I couldn't imagine him *not* trying it on with her. Equally, it was hard to imagine The Big Ride not giein him his hole if he did try it on.

Tony would sit in an armchair, glancing up fae the set as Bernard lisped oot his poems. There was one time he looked up and said derisively, — Poetry, schmoetry, pulling the ring on a tin of export. He was browsing at the highlights of the Dundee United v St. Johnstone match on Scotsport. In the words of the commentator it turned out to be a 'game of few highlights'.

— You understand nowt, son, Bernard simpered.

— Ah understand that your poetry is well short ay piss-poor, Tony smiled.

— So we're the world expert on poetry now, ur we Tony? So tell us all, where did you acquire this expertise? Tony, world expert on everything. Armchair renaissance man. As *au fait* with darts as he is pool, Bernard hissed in a derisive manner as I heard a key turn in the door. John had come back early from the pub.

— Ah ken what's shite and what's no. Your poetry isnae shite, ah'll gie ye that. It needs tae improve a hundred per cent before it can be elavated tae that category.

John had come in and sat down and he started slapping his thighs. — Eh's goat ye thair, Bernard. Ha ha ha. Like ah sais, goat ye thair. Yill nivir beat oor Tony whin it comes tae words, like.

— I refuse tae be drawn intae a war of words with stupid people, Bernard said condescendingly, exiting with a camp flourish. I suspected that he was enjoying this performance and felt a twinge of admiration for him which I quickly stifled, reminding myself that he was a sick, diseased beast.

— Hi! John shouted. — Whae're you fuckin well callin stupid! Ah'm askin ye! TRY GITTIN A PROPER JOAB INSTID AY DAEIN AW THAT POOFY SHITE THIT NAEBODY'S FUCKIN WELL INTERESTIT IN!

The front door slammed loudly.

— John! Tony! Vet moaned. — Ye cannae keep gittin oantae the laddie. Leave um alane. At least ehs poetry's hermless. No like some ah could mention, she looked over at me with a sulky pout.

— What's that supposed tae mean then? I asked.

— You ken. They bloody casuals. Yill end up in the jail. You wi that joab in computers n aw. Thing ay the future.

— That's right, Vet! That's fuckin well right! John snapped. — Fuckin casuals. Jeapordisin a fuckin good joab tae hing aroond wi they radge cunts. Computers n aw, like yir Ma sais, the thing ay the future. You want tae buck up yir ideas, son. Like ah sais, buck up yir ideas.

I looked at him coldly. — Ye ken what ah've been daein at work fir the last six months? Ah set up this programme tae call up files when a man reaches retirement age at sixty-five and a woman at sixty. That was aboot a week's work. Fir the past six months ah've been tryin tae train doss-brained cunts how tae operate this simple procedure, which is like gaun tae the toilet, daein a shite but rememberin tae take yir keks of first n wipe yir erse eftir.

The reverence that people who know fuck all about them have for computers disgusts me. Anyway, for me my work was just a refuge: a place to go where my head couldn't be nipped by my family. By either of my families, I suppose, because the cashies were my family n aw now. I could set anything up; that wis barry, you just got on wi it. I set it up, and some smarmy cunt peyed five times as much took the credit. It didnae bother ays though. What did get oan ma tits wis tryin tae teach the system tae doss-brained cunts.

— Aye, bit it's a still a joab! A well-peyed joab! Dinnae tell ays you're no stuffin money away!

Vet cut in, — C'moan John, that's no fair, the laddie earns ehs keep.

The cunt was on shaky ground here. He was always tapping ays up in the week; cash for fags, drink. — Aye, well right, but that's mair thin kin be said ay some. That bloody Bernard. A fuckin buftie!

— Total fuckin embarrassment, Tony said.

— It's no natural, like ah sais, no fuckin natural, John said. — Yir no tryin tae tell ays that ye think it's natural, tae huv sex wi another man? He looked at us all in turn, stopping at Vet.

What's natural? I shrugged, more to support my mother who looked quite upset, than Bernard, who I didnae give a toss about.

— Jist as well eh nivir came fae me, John said.

Cheeky cunt him, with Elgin still at the GORGIE VENTURE FOR EXCEPTIONAL YOUNG MEN, me in the casuals and Kim, perennially a few years behind in her school work, now working at the baker's. Ally that to our hall-of-mirrors look and he's got a fuckin nerve thinking that he's spawned some sort of master race.

Vet looked coldly at him, — Might as well huv come fae you.

— What's that meant tae mean? Eh? Ah'm asking ye! What's that meant tae mean?

— Your fuckin faithir, that's what that's meant tae mean!

This was a sore point with Dad. His old man had been put away for interfering with young boys. Nae cunt really talked aboot it.

— Whit aboot ma faither . . .

— He went that wey.

— MA FAITHER DIDNAE GO ANY FUCKIN WEY! MA FAITHER WISNAE A WELL MAN! Tony and I had to restrain him as he raised his hands to Ma. I'd forgotten his strength and he took me out with an elbow to the nose. The pain was overpowering and my eyes kept filling with water. In no time he had Tony wrestled to the ground and was holding him by the hair, threatening to put the boot in.

— Dinnae Dad! I shouted, trying to stem the blood, tears and snot that leaked out of my face.

He let Tony go, and pursued Ma into the kitchen. She had

grabbed the kitchen knife and was screaming: — COME OAN THEN YA FUCKIN SHITE! AH'LL FUCKIN KILL YE!

I ran upstairs to their room and grabbed his shotgun from under the bed. I thought about going back downstairs and confronting him, bolstered by the weapon, but he was radge enough to try and take it from me, and then somebody would be well fucked. I locked myself in the toilet with the gun, and didn't leave until the screaming had died down.

I heard the noise of the front door slamming. I put the shotgun back. Tony was alone downstairs. — Ma and John's gone up the pub. Aw lovey-dovey again. Ye comin up? He asked, clicking off the telly at the handset.

Was I coming up? No. I was going deeper. Deeper into trouble. Deeper into the Marabou Stork nightmares.
DEEPER
            DEEPER
                        DEEPER ---- into the narrow alley with Jamieson, following the stench of the diseased, decaying carrion on the ugly, waddling bird. The alley is dark, the air is surprisingly cold. Something is moving in the shadows amongst the large, stinking rubbish piles. Something very evil and nasty.

— Expose yourself, you sick, twisted demon! Sandy screams into the darkness. — You think you can destroy the game!

— No fucking chance of that, Johnny Stork! I hiss — Sandy and I are wise to your foul plans. We know that you want to destroy the colour, the noise, the fun and the gaiety associated with . . .

The words stick in my throat as the large predator emerges from the shadows.

Sandy moves forward, but I'm
rooted to the spot. I feel   eh   what the fuck is this
something cold and wet on the   eh   – I know you felt that, Roy.
side of my face and smell perfume eh   My little sleeping beauty . . .
                                                              it's her, that crazy
                                                              sow that's coming for
                                                              me . . . naw . . .

— I'll bet you felt that, Roy, I'll bet you felt me kiss you then.

Patricia. Thank fuck. What are you playing at ya daft cunt?

— You know what I think, Roy Strang? I think all you need is to feel wanted, to feel loved. Let me in, Roy. Let us all in. You're surrounded by love, Roy. Your family, your friends. Let us in.

FUCK OFF YA DIPPIT CUNT!

DEEPER

                    DEEPER ———————— but not too deep. Not back to that fuckin alleyway with the Stork. No yet. But naw, I didnae go up the pub with Tony that night, didnae go tae see my Ma and Dad. I sat in on my own, enjoying the rare feeling of having the hoose tae masel. It gave me time to think.

I had been having some minor hassle at work. That cow Hathaway confronted me aboot my activities with the cashies. I'd been done and fined for my part in what I thought was a minor swedge, but which the papers called a riot. Hathaway called me through into Colin Sproul's office.

Sproul was an intense, tormented looking guy. It had been him who had interviewed me for the job when I'd first started. He always came across as a fair-minded cunt likes. It was blatantly obvious that he had been pushed into staging this daft performance by Hathaway.

— Eh . . . hello, Roy. We just wanted a little word with you, Jane and I.

Hathaway gave me a toothy false photo-flash smile.

I nodded.

— Your work's been excellent, Sproul began, — absolutely first class, he beamed with an almost awestruck smile. He shook his head in mock disbelief, — I still don't know how you managed to incorporate that geographical cross-referencing report into the S.S. 3001 system. That was genius.

I felt my face redden with a simultaneous surge of gratitude and resentment towards Sproul. I was about to say something when I looked at Hathaway's face. She was livid and she couldn't control it.

— Yes, it was rather well done, she said briskly, — but I'm sure that Roy would acknowledge the tremendous support and assistance he had from the rest of the team.

That was bullshit; I'd developed that procedure in complete isolation. I said nowt but.

— Oh quite so, Sproul nodded.

Hathaway's face took on a slyer demeanour. — You see, we want people to be able to get on at Scottish Spinsters', to develop with the organisation. You understand that, don't you, Roy?

— Aye, I said. .

Sproul smiled benignly, — You see, we're a very old institution Roy, and still pretty conservative in our own way . . . some would say a little too conservative . . . he turned to Hathaway, looking for some sort of endorsement, but got only a sharp glare of disapproval, — . . . but that's by the way, he nervously coughed. — Your work, though, is excellent, excellent. And while you're outside this building, outside office hours; what you do is your own concern . . . but at the same time . . .

Hathaway smiled grimly, — It's come to our attention that you're a member of a soccer hooligan gang.

— Eh? I said incredulously. Soccer hooligan gang. Stupid fuckin fat dyke.

— We're not accusing you of anything, Roy. It's just that certain rumours have been circulating about you, rumours which could be detrimental to your future career progression, Sproul told me.

— Aye, I sometimes go tae the fitba likes. Ah dinnae get involved in any bother though.

— Roy, said Hathaway, with a sombre tone and expression, — we've seen your name in the papers. You broke a man's jaw, it said.

I gave her a tired look, and shook my head wearily. — I'm sick tae the back teeth of these rumours. Yes, I was at a match in Glasgow with some friends. It can be quite rough through there at the games and these men, obviously drunk, started spitting at us when they heard our Edinburgh accents. We just walked away. One guy though, he followed me and started kicking me. I lashed out in self-defence. Unfortunately, that was the part of the incident witnessed by the police officer. Surprise, surprise, the Strathclyde Police took the word of locals over a man from Edinburgh. I thought, though,

that my own employers would be a wee bit more inclined to give me
the benefit of the doubt on this issue.

I saw Sproul's eyes light up and his lips stretch into a grin.
Hathaway looked dejected. She wanted old thick schemie Roy
Strang to hang himself, but naw, I wasnae gaunny gie the cunt the
satisfaction.

The following week I got arrested at Middlesbrough at an English
second division match. We were just doon for a bit of mischief.
There was little happening at Hibs v St. Johnstone; the baby crew
could handle the Fair City Firm wankers with ease. We had headed
south for a wee break and turned over a pub. I bottled some cunt.

I remember Lexo saying to the barman, — Eight Becks, mate.
Then he noticed a squad of scarfers come in from a bus. — Naw,
make it Grolsch, eh, he said. He turned to me and winked, —
Heavier boatils, eh.

They certainly were.

Thank fuck that one didnae make the Scottish papers.

So things were sorted for a bit. It was going well, I reflected, as I
sat alone enjoying the solitude in the house, stroking Winston Two.
— I'm not a bad Hibby-Wibby Boysie-Woysie, am I, Winners? No!
No! I'm just Roysie-Woysie who does the computey-wuteys, eh? A
firework exploded outside; Winston Two whimpered and ran under
the sideboard. It was Guy Fawkes' night soon. Winston hated
fireworks. It was something tae think aboot. I was still up for
wasting that cunt ay a dug and ah wis intae daein it really soon.

That night Ma, Dad and Tony came back pished. Kim came in
later, her neck covered in purple love-bites, an even more far-away
and vacuous look on her face than normal.

— Ye should've bought him a packet ay crisps, Tony smiled at
her.

She self-consciously touched her neck and smiled, — Aw this?
Dae ye notice it? Kin ye see it that easy?

Dad looked angry, but said nothing. I watched as his knuckles
went white gripping the armchair. When Kim went up to bed, he
turned to Vet and said: — You want tae huv a word wi that lassie.
Actin like a slag, like ah sais, a fuckin slag . . .

— Dinnae be fuckin silly, John. She's a young lassie bichrist.

Eventually Ma turned in, leaving John, Tony and I in the front room. John looked at us emotionally, it was as if he was almost ready to cry. — That's some fuckin woman. Your mother, he pointed at me, then at Tony, — your mother n aw. A fuckin great woman, the best yir ivir likely tae find. His voice got higher. — Youse remember that! Whativir else yis dae, yis eywis treat that fuckin woman wi respect, like ah sais, respect. Cause that's the best fuckin woman yis are ivir likely tae see in yir fuckin lives! Your fuckin mother!

— Aye Dad, Ma's sound . . . I said sombrely.

— Like you say John, she's the best, Tony nodded.

Dad stood up and went over to the window. His voice took on a compulsive, mocking bent as he thumbed over his shoulder at the outside world. — Ah ken whit they cunts think ay us. Ah ken aw they cunts. Ken what they are? Ah'll fuckin well tell ye what they are, he slurred, — Rubbish. Not fuckin quoted. That's these cunts: not fuckin quoted.

He had always been paranoid about the neighbours and had started to keep a dossier on the other occupants of our block and the one behind us. He had recently bought a personal computer from a mate down The Gunner, and I was press-ganged into showing him how to set up files on the neighbours. I didn't want to encourage him in this pointless lunacy, but to refuse cooperation would have caused a bigger scene. Dad would watch the neighbours' comings and goings and record their *modus operandii* on his files, some of which became quite detailed.

I enjoyed having the odd look at them:

15/5 BROWN
Father: Arthur   *Mother: Frances*
Children: Maureen (10 ish) and Stephen (6 ish)

Arthur works for GPO. Seems not too bad. Frances seems a nice woman, clean. The two wee yins are always well-dressed. Arthur sometimes plays darts at The Doocot.

Verdict: Decent people; no real threat to security.

15/6 PEARSON
Father: Alan (no longer living there) Mother: 'Fat Cow' Maggie
Children: Debbie (16) Gillian (14) Donna (11)

That fat stupid cow tries to monopolise wash-room. Dirty cunt who does not wrap rubbish before putting it in chute. Caught her twice. Ignorant person with dirty mouth. Always ready to phone police. Alan Pearson a thief. Sold Jackie useless CDs at The Gunner. Lucky for him he has done runner. Debbie is a cheeky cow with a mouth like the mother's. A real slut, the kind of lassie who will end up in a ditch by the side of the road one day. Have told our Kim to keep away from this whore. The other sister is going the same way. The wee one is nice but should go into care before she turns out like the rest.

Verdict: Scum. Maximum security threat, repeat, maximum security threat.

While Dad's behaviour was obviously unhealthy, he actually seemed better after getting the computer, the effort of keeping up and monitoring the records seemed to dissipate a lot of his destructive energy. On this night, however, he was drunk and wound up. I kept thinking of Ma singing that Bond song, 'Nobody Does it Better'.

Like heaven above me,
The spy who loved me
Is keepin all my secrets safe tonight.

Tony raised his eyebrows at me as Dad started to pace up and down the living-room like a caged beast, muttering curses under his breath. Just as he seemed to be settling down, he sprang to the window and threw it open. He shouted into the night: JOHN STRANG'S MA NAME! FUCK YIS AW, YA CUNTS! ANY BASTARD IN THIS FUCKIN SCHEME'S GOAT ANYTHING TAE SAY TAE ME OR MA FAIMLAY, YIS KIN SAY IT TAE MA FUCKIN FACE!

— Take it easy, Dad, I said. — Yi'll huv the fuckin polis roond, eh.

He shut the window and said to me and Tony: — People in this scheme huv been makin a loat ay allegations aboot this faimlay. Well, ah want tae hear what these allegators have goat tae say for themselves!

— Ah heard they were gettin a bit snappy, Tony mused.

I started sniggering as John looked coldly and uncomprehendingly at him. — Eh? he said.

— The alligators John, Tony said, opening his jaws wide and making exaggerated snapping motions.

There was a tense silence for a couple of seconds, then John's face burst into a smile and we all started laughing, Tony and I with relief as the tension drained away. — Huh, huh, huh, no bad Tony, no bad. It wis the great man hissel that sais thit ye cannae deal wi the maist serious things in the world if ye cannae understand the maist amusing.

Aye, right.

My auld man then stroked the servile Winston Two. — We'll show the cunts, eh boy? The Strangs, he said softly, — we'll show aw these cunts. We'll come shinin through. We eywis fuckin do.

The next day I bought some fireworks which I kept in my desk drawer at work.

Apart from nosiness and the odd bit of useful information it provided (I'd decided that I'd try and get a ride off Debbie Pearson, who was Kim's pal: Tony'd already been there) I had little interest in the auld man's daft obsessions. Anyway, the cashies was my time. The violence was brilliant; different from in the hoose. The excitement, the buzz, the feeling of your body charged up with it all. You could prepare for it with the cashies, get psyched up n that, but you didnae want tae live like that at hame. Ye wanted somewhair whair ye could shut the door n forget it aw.

I liked clubbing, but I preferred a swedge rush to anything. I didnae like drugs. I had a fuckin bad time on acid. We were up this club, this place at The Venue oan a Thursday night. A loat ay the boys were intae it: techno upstairs and garagey hip-hop doonstairs. I hated that kind of music, cause ah wis mair intae indie stuff, but I went along cause the boys were intae it and there was plenty spare fanny floating around. I took a tab ay acid and I sort ay freaked. It was awright at first, but it jist goat stronger and stronger and ah couldnae keep the bad thoughts oot ay ma heid. I wis thinking aboot that poofy cunt Gordon n believing that there were dugs coming and they wir gaunny tear ays apart. Ah kept seein the heid ay that flamingo in the stork's mooth and it wis shouting oan ays tae help it, in a sad, sick voice.

Ali Dempsey, one of the boys in the cashies, came n talked ays doon. — Yuv goat tae remember Strangy, it's aw jis a distortion ay light n sound. That's aw acid is, nae matter how bad it seems. It's jist the distortions ay light and sound n your imagination fires up tae fill in the gaps.

— Thir's shite in ma heid, Demps, I gasped. — My heart must be beatin too fast . . . ah'm gaunny fuckin peg oot here man . . .

— Naw yir no. It's cool. Jist stey cool. It's awright.

Demps kept it gaun fir ays. He talked ays doon. Then he took ays back tae his flat n sat up wi ays. Sound cunt Demps. Anywey, that wis me finished wi drugs.

The boys tried tae git ays tae take an ecky, bit ah wis jist intae Becks, eh. Besides, clubs wir jist a place tae come doon n talk aboot the swedge n mibbe bag oaf wi some fanny as far as ah wis concerned. Ah loved swedgin. It was easy, n aw; once you got beyond your second or third pagger, once you learned to get past your fear and pain and just go with it, just keep going, keep swinging and booting at anything that came your way, and inspect the damage later. I never got hurt badly; a few bruised ribs and a deep cut above the eye once at Pittodrie.

There were much harder cunts in the casuals than me, and guys who were much better swedgers. They knew that, and so did I. What I had though, was the attitude that marked out most of the top boys; it wasn't even bottle. It was not giving a fuck about anything.

As I've said, one of the best aspects of being a casual was the fanny. Most of the boys were good-looking or average looking guys. While I was ugly and knew it, I lost a level of self-consciousness as my status as a swedger increased and I did more shagging than most. I'd wasted a lot of time in my adolescence, after I'd shagged that dog in the budget room, just looking at myself in the mirror, wondering why my head was too big for my body, and why my body was too big for my small, stumpy legs. The answer was staring me in the face over the top of a *Daily Record* at breakfast time most mornings. I was the auld man's double. So I'd wasted a lot of time and now I wanted it more than maist cunts. I had access to half the decent fanny in the toon.

One afternoon, I finished work early and picked up a juicy bone for Winston Two at a butcher's in Leith Walk. I got home before everyone else and the beast cowered as he saw me enter. It was strange to think that I'd taken a mauling from that pathetic old thing.

— Winners . . . I panted, and the beast took this as his cue to relax and wag his tail. He gave me his head to clap and jumped up on his hind legs with his front ones resting on the kitchen worktop. His tail wagged and his tongue lolled as he scented the bone with that juicy meat covering it. — Yes, it's your's boy, isn't it, all for Winners . . . a present for Winners, I told him, as I hammered some six-inch nails through the bone and the meat. I put the bone in my Adidas bag and zipped it up. — Later boy, later, I told him as he sniffed at the bag. He continued sniffing. My boot made contact with his side and he let out a yelp and scuttled off.

Just then Ma came in from work. She did the dinners in an old people's home now. Kim got in shortly after her, with some cakes from the baker's. She said that she was going to take Winston Two oot for a walk before tea. — Winners needs to stretch his legs across the wasteland. Yes he does, yes he does, she said, crouching down and frolicking with the panting beast.

— Ah'll git ye doon the road, Kim, ah've goat some records tae droap oaf roond tae Bri, eh. I held up the Adidas bag.

As we walked I noted that a few strays were wandering over the wasteland. One was a filthy brown dog which howled constantly like a wolf. — Listen tae that, I said distracting Kim.

— It's an awfay shame fir they stray dugs thit thuv no goat good homes like Winston, eh Roy, eh it's a shame? Sometimes ah wish that we could take aw they dugs, just sort ay adopt thum aw, eh Roy?

As she babbled looking over to the strays, I slipped the bone out of the bag. Winston went straight for it.

— What's Winners found? Kim asked.

— Dunno, looks like a bone, eh, I replied.

— C'moan Winston, that's no fair cause you git fed enough n thir's aw they perr starvin dugs . . . you're a lucky boy Winalot . . . Kim bleated as the dug went crazy over the bone. — Winners, Winners, Winalot, Winners, Winners what you . . .

Kim's expression turned to one of horror as Winston yelped and a nail shot out through his top jaw.

The beast stormed off across the wasteland yelping and shaking his head and was instantly pursued by the group of strays.

— WINSTON! WIIIIGGHHHNNNNSTIN! Kim bellowed, but the dog ran around in agony, pursued by the snapping pack, unable to drop the bone.

The strays set upon him, unable to distinguish between his cut, bleeding jaws and the tender meat which hung from them.

They ripped his face apart.

Kim started screaming and kicking at them, and I had to join in and help in case the stupid cow got torn to bits herself. Eventually we managed to drag Winston Two away. That brown bastard that howled was particularly persistent, but I caught the cunt a beauty with a segged-brogue heel stomp to the body and he staggered away whining.

The vet stitched Winston Two's face together, but he had lost one eye, part of his nose and a lot of the skin and flesh on one side of his jaw.

— Poor Winners, Kim said sadly as the wretched, forlorn creature squealed piteously as it recovered from the anaesthetic, — but you're still beautiful to us! Yes you are! Yes you are!

Everyone was in shock at what had happened to the much-loved family pet. — Daein that tae a defenceless animal, my Ma snarled. —What kind ay sick mind does that?

— A Japanese mind, I heard myself smirk softly from behind the newspaper. Thankfully nobody picked it up.

John totally freaked when he found out what had happened to the dog. I knew that the signs were bad, because he listened to me and Kim's account of events in total silence as he stroked the sad, mutilated beast at his feet.

After his tea he went out to the wasteland and killed four of the strays with his bare hands. I followed him downstairs to witness the sight. A group of kids looked on in awe, and one wee lassie started greeting as John, displaying treats, enticed dog after dog to him, then strangled them to death or snapped their necks. He was helped by Uncle Jackie and a mate of their's called Colin Cassidy, who was a nutter. They held the dogs while John's huge hands ripped the life from them. The only one which wouldn't come was that wicked brown cunt, it kept well out the way. I felt somehow pleased that it had escaped but I suppose I felt a bit guilty at the carnage I'd caused. I liked animals. Birds especially, they were a symbol of freedom, flying like a bird n that. But I liked other types as well, though I was less keen on domestic pets than on animals in their wild state. I felt myself almost choke as I observed the broken bodies of the four strays lying in isolation from each other on the wasteland.

— Council cannae control fuckin vermin, ah fuckin well will, Dad said to me. — Tae quote the great man hissel: in war ye dinnae huv tae be nice, ye only huv tae be right. Cassidy nodded sagely, and Uncle Jackie tried to get me to go for a pint with them but I headed back up the hoose, turning to watch their backs receding, Dad in that thick brown coat, as they wandered down tae The Gunner.

12 Kim Visits

Things are getting a bit fuckin heavy in this nut ay mine as the control breaks down and the memories come back. Nae two weys aboot it: it's a fuckin radge scene. I try to hide in my little cubby-hole in the darkened well, beyond Sandy and the horrible Storks, but still out of range of the loathsome reality in that sick world on the other side of the trapdoor above. This refuge of mine is becoming more precarious though. I sense it to be like a little platform, a small ledge, jutting out from the side of the hole. It gets shakier and narrower every time I sit on it. One day it'll crumble and I'll be faced with the stark choice: climb out into the real world or fall back into fantasy land.

I would until recently, have unreservedly chosen the latter, only now, it's not my fantasy world. I now have as little control down there as I did in the real world . . .

— Hiya Raw-oy . . .

The dull, nasal tones tell me that my sister Kim is visiting me. I can expect a monologue concerning some guy; it'll consist of either unrealistic, unbounded optimism, or be a sorry tale of woe, but it'll be delivered in the same sick, bleating voice.

—Ah'm seein this new felly n eh's a wee bit aulder n it's likesay eh's mairried n eh's goat two bairns bit it's likesay eh's gaunny leave hur cause it's likesay eh disnae really love hur any mair n it's like, eh loves me now n wir gaunny git a flat somewhair . . .

Yeah yeah yeah

—. . . wi him huvin the mortgage n the bairns n wi his responsible position in the civil service n aw eh sais

Get a fuckin brain, ya daft sow

—. . . bit ah'm like, still sortay seein Kevin n aw, well no really seein um bit wi met it The Edge n ah wis a bit drunk n a really only went back tae his place tae see this leather jaykit thit eh goat bit one thing sortay jist led tae anothir n ah jist sortay ended up steyin the night, ken wi Kevin likes. . . it wis jist like ah kinday felt sorry fir um bit ah sais dinnae think thit this is sortay like us gaun back oot thegither cause it's no, cause ah've goat a new felly now . . . bit the thing is, Roy, ken it's like ah've sortay missed another period again n ah dinnae ken if ah'm, well, ken, that wey, n if aham whae's it is ken, Roy? Cause ah've been wi Kevin n the new felly, bit thir wis this other laddie ah met one night it Buster's n we went back tae his fir a perty so ah'm no really sure . . . bit that's jist sayin like, that's jist supposin ah am . . .

You *undoubtedly* are, you daft cunt. Is it Tony's mutant bastard you're carrying again, Kim? You fuckin stupid sow. The budget room, I'll fuckin well bet. Standing up or on Tony's pish-saturated mattress . . . the smell of rubbish . . . the flies . . .

— . . . the bairn's daein fine though, Roy. Kevin's Ma's goat him the now, jist fir the weekend, cause as ah sais tae Ma, it's likesay Kevin's Ma n that are entitled tae see the bairn . . .

Kevin. Kevin Scott. Poor fuckin doss cunt Kevin. Mairrays intae the Strangs. What a total fuckin radge of the highest order.

Clickity click, clickity click . . .

Somebody's coming, Kim. I can sense them. Yes, I can hear those nursey shoes clacking on the lino.

— Hello . . . sorry, we're going to have to disturb you while we see to Roy.

— Aw that's awright, ah wis jist talkin tae um aboot some things . . .

Kim's fuckin verbal equivalent of the Chinese water torture is interrupted by Nurse Patsy DeCline, who has come to give me a good seeing to. Just as well: I'm too tired and too frightened to even try to hunt the Stork just now. The whole thing is becoming far too draining. It's too much, all this bullshit, just too much. But I have to see it through. I'll just sit here on my little ledge, recoup my strength, work up the bottle, and then it's back to the fray.

13 Marabou Stork Hunting

Damn and fucking well blast this shit . . .

There's something in my throat. I try to scream from the narrow alleyway in the festering slum town but the words seem to be stuck. This confounded throat!

The cornered Stork has a bundle in its mouth. It's not going to go down without a fight. Then it mumbles something as it springs to life and stampedes past us, but Sandy fells it with a powerful sliding tackle. As the beast's thin legs buckle and loose feathers fly, Jamieson springs to his feet and swings around, his palms outstretched, with an innocent expression on his face. The Stork is rising behind him.

— Play to the whistle, Sandy! No foul! I yelled. This is SFA rules and we are wearing the blue shirts.

As Jamieson turned, the Stork, which was well over six-foot tall, jabbed at his shoulder with its massive beak. Sandy screamed in pain and fell backwards. I drew my machete and advanced, but the creature turned and ran; flapping its great wings which spanned the alley, building up speed and managing to take off, rising slowly out of the close and into the main street, where it narrowly cleared a bus, before vanishing over the rooftops.

To our great fortune, the beast had dropped its cargo. Approaching with caution, I picked up and tentatively unwrapped the bundle to reveal a foetus, the size of my hand, bloody and prawn-like. — We have to put this devil-child under the sword, Sandy, I said. I took my machete and thought about who, or what, could have spawned such a thing. It had a large head which twisted inwards from the forehead to squashed features, curving out to a big, flat chin. It looked at me in a pleading kind of way, softly shrieking.

I didn't have the heart to machete it. Instead I put it on the ground and recovered the jeep. Reversing into the alley, I backed over the bundle not once, not twice, but three times. There was a squidging sound and I left the vehicle to examine the flattened package which now oozed a dark liquid.

— Whatever you do Sandy, don't look.

It was not a baby. It was

a fuckin weird bastard   up   — Poor Dempsey, Roy.
coming up — — — — — — — up   You remember Dempsey, don't you?

Even though there's something of the cad
About the boy . . .

DEEPER
        DEEPER
                DEEPER — — — — — — — — — — — — — —
— Deeper into shark-infested waters. What the fuck are we doing here? Sandy seems reluctant to put on the scuba gear as we take our boat out along the coastline, determined to enter the Emerald Forest Park by another route. Our efforts to locate the beast's nest on the shores of Lake Torto had proved fruitless. The creature could always spy our approach and move the site of its nest accordingly.

Ghostie had the Evening News *coming round to talk about his life as a casual. He sent a couple of the baby crew out to Thins and Waterstones to shoplift some guerrilla warfare and military strategy books. They came back with a big pile; Che Guevara, Liddle Hart, Moshisma, all that stuff.*

— Goat tae gie the media the right impression, he smiled. — Wind the daft cunts up tae fuck.

He made sure he had the mobile phones ready, out on display. We started using the mobiles just to keep track of where the other crews were heading, but in reality, the thick cunts were so predictable as to reduce the exercise to pure self-indulgence on our part. The sheepshaggers we had a bit of respect for, but the soapdodgers were just as dense as fuck. The hun soapdodgers had even taken tae getting English cunts up to try and give them some sort of organisation. If you had a bunch of Weedgies stranded on a small desert island, they wouldnae be able tae organise a fuckin trip tae the beach.

Fuck.

Fuck . . . where am I here? The sea. The beach. The organisa-
tional skills of the Marabou Stork.

STICK TO THE FUCKIN STORY, ROY, YOU STUPID
CUNT.

— These waters are infected by sharks, Sandy said, still reluctant
to don the scuba equipment and dive. I had anchored on the edge of
the reef and it was a short swim to the shore, but I could smell the fear
from Sandy.

— Infested with sharks is what I think you mean, Sandy, I
corrected, then I began to wonder. — Maybe the term infected also
has relevance.

— I want you to know that I'm a professional sportsman and, as
such, do not use drugs. I certainly don't share needles and I practise
safe sex. I am not HIV. This is so as we know where each other are
coming from, okay?

— As you prefer, Sandy.

— I didn't hunt any lions either Roy, that was just bullshit, he
sneered.

I am losing it badly in here. Losing as much as I did on the outside.
In a strange split second I am back in the alley and the praying mantis
is there, the one with the blonde wig and the lipstick on its insect
jaws and it is holding up a red card. Sandy throws off his strip, close
to tears, and exits the alley, comforted by Diddy, with Dawson
shaking his head in disgust. The mantis is writing his name in a black
notebook, which bears the title: *YOUTH IN ASIA*. Then I feel the
spray in my face and we are back on the ocean.

We struggled into our gear, preparing for our dive into the clear,
light-blue water of the reef. We would make our way to the
shoreline and our alternative point of entry to the Emerald Forest. It
was a risky strategy, as it limited us to the hardware we could carry.

I'm not feeling well here; there's a ringing in my ears and a
strange, sterile smell in my nostrils. The smell of hosp . . . no fuck it,
I'm in control here, I'm in control. Sandy's okay again, he's my
mate, my guide. Me and Sandy, we're hunters. We're the good guys
in this.

Then Sandy said something which tightened my stomach and sphincter muscles and made my pulse race. As we prepared to dive from starboard side he looked at me and smiled, — We're going in at the away end.

14 Winners And Losers

If my auld boy found out that it was me who fucked over Winston Two, the cunt would have killed me. He was even more protective of the beast in its injured state, and he seldom let it out of his sight. Winston wore one of these cone things around his head; to stop the daft cunt from scratching at his wounds with his paws. In the wild the beast would have died. I was all for nature.

Despite Winston Two's suffering, I was disappointed at the outcome. I wanted Winston Two offed for good. To merely mutilate him as he had done to me was not enough. My initial remorse at what I'd done had quickly evaporated and I had to get him once and for all. What made me decide to go for the cunt was this lassie I was shagging.

Julie Sinclair was her name. She steyed up in Drylaw wi her Ma and her sister. She wisnae a bad ride as I recall, and I used tae fuck her in her bedroom then stick aroond and watch the telly wi her and her Ma. I used to sometimes fantasise, no really seriously, just idly likes, about giving her Ma and her sister one as well. Basically, though, I just liked it up at her hoose because you could watch the box in peace.

I didnae have any strong feelings for Julie, but I respected her. She just wanted fucked and went for it in a big way, but she was always in control, you never got intae her heid. That suited ays though; I wisnae bothered aboot getting into her heid and she wisnae clingy like some slags. Anywey, eftir ah'd fucked her one time she asked me aboot the scars oan ma leg. That was what set me thinking about Winston Two again. I remembered how much I hated that monster, and the fuckin family who revered him. I still had my fireworks.

Shagging Julie always made me think of Cramond Island, cause that was where I'd first got intae her. Cramond Island is a small island less than a mile out in the Forth Estuary. You can walk out to it at certain times, before the incoming tide cuts it off from the mainland. There's fuck all to see over there, just a few old pill-boxes from World War Two, full ay beer cans and used condoms.

It was a common tactic of local guys to take lassies over to the island then wait until the tide came in soas that they'd have to spend the night there. Tony told me all about it. I seldom mucked aroond wi Bri and that crowd now that I was a top boy, but one time Bri and I went oot wi Julie and her mate and got 'stranded' on the island and ended up riding them.

That was where I was headed with Winston Two.

I had fortunately accumulated a great deal of flexi-time at my work; I'd been showing the daft cunts in one of the offices how to operate this new set of mainframe computerised procedures I'd installed. My eyes were stinging from constant exposure to the VDU and an eye-test revealed that I needed glasses. There was no way that ah was gaunny be a specky cunt though. Not only would it have been something else to be self-conscious about, I would have looked the spit of my auld boy.

Fuck that for a game ay sodjirs.

I got contact lenses fitted.

The day I took time off to get the lenses sorted out, I decided to go back hame and get Winston Two. I hadn't told anyone that I was taking the day off, and I made sure that nobody, except Winners, would be home.

We walked through the scheme and crossed over by the golf course, passing the Commodore Hotel and going down the esplanade onto the foreshore. I had a large spade I'd bought from B&Q, its head wrapped up in a carrier bag. I felt a little sad when I looked at the dog with the plastic bucket on his head. It was no life for an animal. I began to think of Winston Two as a puppy, and now as a loyal chum. It might have stopped me had the whistling east wind from the north sea not cut through me, particularly stinging my old scar tissue as it swept down the Forth Estuary.

I had my spade, I had my bucket and here I was at the seaside.

It was still quite early, an autumn morning, and Silverknowes beach and the foreshore were deserted. The tide was going out.

I marched Winston Two over to the island, his paws making indentations in the soft sand. The human footprints and the paw prints would soon be washed away.

We reached the island and I tied the dog up to a rusty hook which conveniently jutted from the side of a concrete pillbox.

The bleak wind whistled around us as I removed Winston's cone and taped an assortment of fireworks to his stitched-up face. I bound them tightly around his head with plastic masking tape then put the cone, attached by a separate collar, back onto the beast. I heard him make those almost-empty-Squeezy-bottle noises dugs make when they're shitein it.

As Winston Two struggled, I saw a small bird land on top of the pillbox. It was a robin, that early symbol of Christianity . . .

. . . I thought for a second or two about the meaning of this, about turning the other cheek and Christian forgiveness and all that sort of shite. But nobody believed in that crap anymair. It was you against the world, every cunt knew that: the Government even said it. The wind seared through my denims, stinging my scar tissue again. No, Winston had to go. In Christian terms this was a just war . . .

. . . I looked at the dog for a bit, just looked at him straight on. He was strange; one eye gleaming from the mess of masking tape and coloured cardboard tubes secured to his face, framed by the plastic cone. The funny thing was, he had now stopped that fetching but futile scrape with his front paws and was now just lying down on his side, panting softly.

He seemed almost contented.

My boot cracked heavily on the schemie fashion-accessory's fur-lined rib cage . . .

JUST WHAIR AH WANTED YE
CHILD-KILLING CUNT THAT YE ARE
ME FUCKIN SCARRED AND CRIPPLED FOR LIFE

DINNAE HURT WINSTON DINNAE TELL
THEM IT WAS WINSTON

FUCK YOU FAITHER
FUCK YOU
DUG SHOULD HAVE BEEN DESTROYED
IS THAT HOW MUCH AH WIS WORTH, HOW MUCH AH
WIS VALUED?

DESTROY
DESTROY

Winners . . . Winners . . .
here boy
here boy

Wots wong bwoy?
Huh bwoy?
Winners my woyal fwend . . .

I lit a couple of fireworks where the blue touchpaper was exposed
around his face and, following the instructions for safety, stood well
back. Winston Two unfortunately chose to disregard the instructions.

THAT WAS CWUMBSY OF YOU BWOY
There was a small explosion, and a splatter of red blood
discoloured the clear plastic cone. The dog struggled but was silent. I
was trying to work out what was happening and went closer when a
screaming rocket shot a sparky orange trail out from Winston Two's
face . . .
. . . it was like Krypto, Superboy's dug . . . the dug had heat
vision . . . he should have let me put that cape on him . . .
. . . Winston Two thrashed blindly against the leash . . .
. . . then there was a larger explosion and the dog just toppled
over as bits of charred flesh and blood shot out of the cone. I winced
and moved out of the wind as I caught the scent of an almost
overpowering smell; fainter, though, somehow different from

Gordon's. Worried at the noise, I looked over to the mainland, but the foreshore was empty. On the other side there was a small fishing boat, but it was too far away, over by the Fife coast.

It was like Winston Two had no head at all; just a large, black, charred cinder in a wrap-round piece of melting plastic.

> Who did this tae ye Winston, eh boy?
> Show me boy
> Show me who it was

Winners
Winners

> Who do'ed it?
> Who do'ed dat to Winalot?
> Tell us who it was, boy
> Tell us

Winners Winners
Winalot
Winners Winners
what you got

Winners Winners Winners.

Loser.

> Who do'ed it?

> But you can't tell
> and that is
> just too bad for you
> you silly cunt.

I whistled Roy Rodgers' 'A Four-Legged Friend' as I dragged the corpse of the dog, stinking and smoking at one end, across to the other side of the island, the side invisible from the Edinburgh coast. I pulled the body down onto the wet sand and started digging with my spade. I removed the round metal tag with WINSTON on it, and the address overleaf. What was it that the auld boy said about the dug's namesake: in a war ye dinnae have tae be nice, ye just have tae be right.

I looked at the hole I'd dug and cast my eye over the body, before glancing across at the Fife coast. The tide would be in soon. I almost shat myself as I heard a shuffling noise and looked down to see the body of the beast shaking violently. Without thinking I kicked it into the hole and started shovelling the sand over it. Some of the sand was instantly displaced, but I kept shovelling and the movement subsided and the struggle seemed to cease.

I climbed back to a vantage point and watched the tide come in, lapping up to the edge of the island, covering Winston Two's grave, then I ran over to the foreshore side. I had to move swiftly to avoid being cut off as the water started to cover the uneven shelves of sand around the island.

I slung my spade in the woods by the River Almond, which reached the Forth estuary at the old Cramond village. Then I went for a coffee at the small cafe in the village. An old biddy came in with a yappy wee dug, one of these wee bits of fluff on a string. The animal sniffed at me and I patted it indulgently. — I love dogs, I told the wifie.

I sat for a while, drying my trooser bottoms against the radiators. Then I left and threw Winner's tag in the Almond and headed back up towards the scheme, stopping off at the Commodore for a pint on the way. I walked up to Silverknowes and had another pint in the golf club. Then I took a bus up town and looked aroond the shoaps, getting a no bad top oot ay X-ile, before heading home at teatime.

When I got in, they were all back. I tried to merge in the general air of gloom that filled the house although it was some effort. I kept hearing the auld man's voice: — But eh widnae jist vanish like that . . . the dug couldnae jist vanish oaf the face ay the earth . . .

Yes he could, Father.

Yes he could.

Winston made a mistake. He fucked aboot wi Roy Strang. Nae cunt fucks aboot wi Roy Strang.

Dad's investigations, which took the form of threatening and cross-examining locals, harassing the Drylaw polis, sticking up badly photocopied pictures of Winston (the black smudge he came out as in the copies looked uncannily like him just before he died) in shops and on lampposts, and freaking when kids ripped them down; all this failed to yield fruit.

Winston Two had gone.

Dad swore that he'd never get another dog again, but he was knocked out that Christmas when Kim and I got him a German shepherd puppy. Unlike his previous two Alsatians, this was a bitch.

He called it Maggie.

Maggie was, is,   up   — Another bowel movement, Roy! Doctor
a nice dug. Never   up   Goss is going to be very pleased with you,
did me any – – – coming up   Patricia says. — You're looking so well
                                  these days. As a reward, I'm going to put on some more of your
                                  mum's tape. She's got a good voice.

Please no Patricia, just talk to me, tell me who you've been shagging or what you've been watching on the telly, anything but that fu . . .

                    Even though there's something of the cad
                    About the boy . . .

         — I wish I had a voice like that.

DEEPER
                    DEEPER
                                        DEEPER – – – – – – – – – – – – – – –
– in through the away end. The water, we've been right through the water, but I only feel wet up to my ankles. Crazy.

Jimmy and I scale up to the top of the Green Hill. It's a long, arduous climb, but its summit affords a perfect view of Lake Torto. We get out our binoculars. There is a breathtaking display of pink as we watch the flamingos in the water. You could hear them, that toot-toot trumpeting sound. Like the horns of continental football supporters or fairground cars . . .

Just then Sandy says, never taking his eyes from the scene, —
Look Roy, to the left.

There were a group of about a dozen Marabou Storks waddling
along the shores of the lake, heading straight towards the flamingo
colony.

15 The Flamingo Massacres

The Marabou Stork is one of the major dangers to the Greater and Lesser Flamingo. It walks along the shore, causing flamingo flocks to pack in panic; it then makes a short flight and stabs a selected flamingo in the back. Once disabled, the flamingo is drowned and then torn to pieces and eaten by one or several Marabous in three to four minutes.

The intervention of the Marabous has had a serious effect on colonies of Greater Flamingo by causing mass desertion (one recorded instance of up to 4,500 pairs by seventeen Marabous). Flamingos tolerate and may even repel from one to five Marabous, but six or more, always six or more, cause mass desertion. Nature is so specific in its arithmetic.

When it came to swedgin, we always broke up intae groups ay between six and ten. At the Underground at Ibrox we came upon the beasts. They were colourful, those scarfers. Ridiculous, but colourful, in their red, white and blue attire. Their badges and their buntings; Ulster and aw that wanky shite, needing an excuse, a silly toytown reason to muster up the kind ay force we'd learned tae love fir its ain sake, tae have on tap. They were yesterday's thing. They looked around nervously as we walked in our groups throughout their midst. We had nae colours; we wir here tae dae real business. No for the fitba, the bigotry, the posturing, the pageantry. That was just shite tae us. We wir here oan business.

The air was filled with the loud screeching cries of panic and death. Through binoculars, Sandy and I witnessed the carnage over at the north shore of the lake. Things were happening fast, I was losing track. More than that, I was losing control. I kept remembering something else, kept seeing something else . . .

We scattered them and gave pursuit to a group ay young blue Christmas trees who looked as if they had come fae Fathell, Lanarkshire. These bloated, beery ugly Weedgies ran cowering intae a pub, but there wis nae escape for them. They looked different from us. Even though I'd always regarded myself as fairly hideous, those creatures were beyond the pale. We steamed in and wrecked the boozer. Ghostie had a Weedgie over the pool table and wis trying tae sever his meaty hun heid oaf wi a broken gless.

— Ah'll take your fuckin face oaf ya fuckin Weedgie cunt! he screamed.

Dempsey was trying to cram a bar ay soap intae the rat-shagger's face. — Get a fuckin wash ya smelly soapdodging Weedgie cunt . . . dae yous cunt's nivir fuckin wash . . . slum-dwellin fuckin trash!

Lexo had taken a couple ay thum oot, one interbred hun's face bursting like a ripe tomatay shot by an air pistol as his chunky fist made contact wi it. — Whair's aw the fuckin Glesgay hard men now, eh? Fuckin queers!

I had opened up one skinny hun's coupon with my sharpened carpet tile knife (Boston's of Leith Walk) and then knocked him over and was booting fuck oot the cunt under the juke-box on the waw. Ah remembered the auld man's records, Churchill's wartime speeches, and recalled him saying that the Germans were either at your feet or at your throat. It was the same with the rat-shaggers. Back doon tae they cunts and they're fuckin swarming all over ye, stand up tae them and they're shouting mammy daddy polis . . . I felt a bit bad about using the blade, no because ah had any reservations about improving hun features through plastic surgery, but because bladework was sneaky, like Weedgie shitin cunt's patter and we were intae toe-to-toe stuff in our crew. The jukie was playing Dire Straits' Romeo and Juliet, so obviously brain-dead mutant hun music . . . ah turned tae the half empty pub, only maist ay them wir shitein it tae leave, wi Norrie and Jacksie oan the door n ah shouted, — ROY STRANG'S THE FUCKIN NAME! REMEMBER THAT FUCKIN NAME! ROY STRANG! HIBS BOYS YA FUCKIN CUNTS! EUROPE'S NUMERO UNO! FUCKIN RAT-SHAGGIN BASTARDS!

What the fuck . . . I see a Marabou Stork, not our one, stab a young flamingo, then, after thoroughly sousing its prey under-water, swallow it whole.

Lexo turned tae the bar staff; an auld guy, a fat wifie n a younger guy, who wir just standing thair, shitein it, and went: — Six fuckin Becks then, cunt! Tae take away.

They served him and the wide cunt peyed for it as well. No tae have done so would have lowered us tae the level ay the soapdodger. We were, after all, Edinburgh snobs . . . but ah wisnae getting as much ay an adrenalin rush as ah used tae. We'd been daein too much ay this. Ah picked up a pool cue and jumped on the bar, thrashing the gantry and its bottles. There's something aboot the sound ay broken gless . . .

I was really losing it badly, and I was about to scream: STOP! JUST FUCKIN STOP ALL THIS when I saw our one, our Stork, and he saw us. The creature lowered its neck and made a short run, flapping to take off. It looked awkward and ungainly but continued its laboured ascent until it gained access to thermals where it rose rapidly to such a height it became almost invisible.

— Damn you, Johnny Stork, Sandy cursed.

Despite our quarry's getaway, I felt a strange elation in my bones. This was our beast's turf; the bugger would soon return.

— *LIT'S HIT THE FUCKIN ROAD! Lexo roared, his neck straining, his face seeming tae be just one big black hole. He dispensed the Becks as we left the pub in ruins and its terrorised occupants nursing their wounds. Ghostie turned tae ays as we exited the pub and stole doon the road.*
— *That wis no bad. Just under four minutes, eh, he said, pointing tae his stopwatch.*

. . . I'm seeing clearly again . . . we noted that quite close to us another couple of large Storks had insinuated themselves into a pack of squawking vultures who were devouring the unrecognisable corpse of an animal. It looked like the body of a woman.

not like the body of a woman

no

no . . . it must have been something else. One of the Storks had a scrap of meat pirated from it by a large Tawny Eagle . . .

Another Stork stood on the outskirts of the group, running in frequently to snatch dropped morsels, but its bolder friends were in there with the vultures, tearing at the carcass with them. One was even attempting to dominate those other scavengers, with some success. In fact, the vultures' aggression seemed like posturing. They were scared of the Storks.

— Vultures appear aggressive, but have evolved elaborate threat displays to ward off rivals, Sandy observed, tuning into my thoughts as if by telepathy. — That way they avoid the risk of a fracture of the ulna in combat . . . the ulna of course, being the inner of the two principal wing bones.

A broken bottle shattered behind us as a crowd of huns shouted at us. We turned and steamed in and they ran like fuck.

— Yes Sandy, I nodded, cleaning one of the lenses on my binoculars, because I can't trust my vision, — although the ulna is the larger of the wing bones it tends to fracture more frequently than the radius due to its lesser elasticity. Indeed, if I recall correctly, one survey showed that around twenty per cent in a pack of white-headed vultures had shown evidence of a fractured ulna.

Ah still hud the fuckin pool cue in ma hand; a mingin rat-muncher who had been left behind in his mates' retreat tried to block ma swing as I heard the bone in his arm crack and his shrill squeal fill the foosty Weedgie air . . .

— Yes, smiled Sandy, — it's amazing that they can survive.

— Fortunately, although it's one of the largest flying birds, the vulture has a very small bone weight, approximately seven per cent of its body weight . . .

— . . . thus enabling the creature to live off its reserves until the bones heal . . .

— Look Sandy! I cut in, — Over by the far shore!

Some Storks were circling around a wisp of smoke which came from the other side of the Green Hill.

— It's like they're flying over a settlement . . . Sandy said.

— Yes, but the only settlement there is Fatty Dawson's lodge in the Jambola. Let's check it out!

part four

The
Paths Of
Self-
Deliverance

16 Respect

It's coming back to me. It's all coming back. I wish it wasn't but it is.

I don't suppose any of us stopped being on trial. It was her own fault; she fuckin well asked for it. Her and Lexo's; her the big fuckin teaser and him the fuckin sad pervert whae couldnae git a fuckin ride in a brothel wi a Gold Amex stuck in his keks. If ah hudnae got in wi that crowd, nowt would've happened, ah widnae huv goat involved. Except that she'd still've goat it fae some cunt, the wey she cairried oan. Nowt fuckin surer.

The first time I set eyes on her, I knew the type exactly. The Caroline Carson type; her that was at school wi me. Slags like that have to be taught a lesson, or they'll pish all over you. Fancied herself as the top girl, a big fuckin cock tease. Hung aroond wi the boys but nae cunt could git intae her keks. Lexo n me had talked aboot her, one eftirnoon, over a few Becks, as you tend tae dae. I think we were in The Black Bull, eh.

— A fuckin total ride that wee cow, he said.

— Legged it? I asked.

— Like fuck. Nae cunt's been up that sow, far as ah ken. KB'd every cunt. Tell ye one thing, see if she comes up tae Buster's next week n comes back tae Dempsey's perty, she's gittin her fuckin erse shagged. Even if she is a virgin, her fanny'll no be tight enough once ah've fuckin gied it a few strokes, he laughed.

I laughed along with the cunt.

I was thinking about the time I once went to get her up for a slow dance at Buster's. The music that night was dead loud likes, but I shouted, — Ye want tae dance? at her. She stood up and I followed her ontae the danceflair. The slag just kept walking, right across the flair tae the lassie's bog while ah stood thair like a radge in the middle ay the danceflair, every cunt sniggerin away. This was *me*, Roy Strang. A fuckin top boy we're talking aboot here. I remember that night, cause that was the night ah slashed that cunt Gilchrist.

Ah minded ay that time awright, as ah sat n spraffed wi Lexo. — The boys are entitled tae a line up, ah sais tae him.

She reminded me ay that time at school; aw they fuckin smart cows, aw the fuckin same. Well naebody takes the pish ootay me, nae cunt. I thought of her finally getting it, watching her hurt, watching her bleed, watching her say please.

Say please, you fucking slag, say please to Roy Strang. That's ma fuckin name, n nae cunt takes the pish. Say fuckin please, you bitch whore slut

say fuckin

The hoor must think that I never saw her look at me with Pauline, Ghostie's bird. Thought I never noticed her sniggering at my inverted face, my ears like a taxi wi the fuckin doors open. Of course, it was all behind ma back. Once we came back from South Africa and I'd chibbed that fat cunt Mathews, then taught the Carson slag a lesson, it was always behind ma back. But the point was that they were still at it. I didn't hear or see them, but I knew they were still at it. I just sensed it, felt it. They all had to fuckin learn who I was; aw the cunts. Like that cunt who thought he was hard at school, the cunt Gilchrist fae Pilton. He was the guy whae wis wi Ferguson, n Carson n The Big Ride; that fuckin soft fat slut that time at the chippy. I had just come back fae a trip doon tae Millwall wi some ay the boys. A barry time, we went pure fuckin crazy in London. It wis a brilliant swedge at New Cross: ootside ay the sheepshaggers they were the best opposition we'd ever had. We'd been spraffin aboot it, gettin hyped up remembering it, when I ran intae the Gilchrist cunt on the Mile, mouthin it wi his mates.

He wisnae the worse. He wis naewhere near the worse. But he wis thair, right thair in the pub whair I let him sweat for a little. Then I broke his nose by stickin the heid oan the cunt, and opened up his cheek with my Stanley. (Purchased where I always buy my weapons). It was just ma wey ay saying tae the cunt: My name is Roy Strang: mind that night wi the chips ya cunt?

All I'm looking for is a bit of respect. It's my fuckin entitlement.

Yeah, I fuckin saw her stolen stares when we went oan tae the Red Hot Pepper Club. Making me aware of my short legs, my big heid, my ears, every fuckin defect in my skin. Making me feel like a freak.

— Hi Lexo, if yir up fir gang-banging that wee sow, mind n cut ays in oan the action, I smiled.

— A sow's goat tae realise that if they hing aroond wi top boys, they huv tae dae the biz. Examples must be made, he grinned, his mouth cutting a crescent in that square head.

That wis it. That wis the extent ay our plotting; a daft, half-pished bit ay fantasising in a pub. Ah didnae ken the cunt wis serious: ah didnae ken he'd talked tae Cally n Demps aboot it.

It wisnae as if ah wis intae daein anything. I'd enough problems wi fanny as it wis; I'd made a bit of a cunt of myself at the work, eh. It was that Christmas; it wis pretty strange. There was this lassie called Sheena Harrower who worked at Scottish Spinsters'. She went to Buster's and knew some of the boys. I never ever went to work dos, but I wis spraffin wi this Sheena lassie in the canteen and she sais she was going. I fancied getting into her keks, but another couple of boys, Demps was one, I think this guy Alto was another; they'd been talking aboot tryin tae leg it n aw. For that reason I thought it would be better if I fired intae her at the Scottish Spinsters' do; leave the field clear n that. It seemed too good an opportunity tae miss.

She never showed up. I found oot later that that cunt Demps had met her in a pub the night before and fired in first. So that was me oan ma fuckin tod at a Scottish Spinsters' Christmas perty. It was really weird, seeing aw they straight-pegs oaf thir fuckin tits oan alcohol. Maist ay them wirnae used tae it and they were aw totally ratarsed.

Well, ah just fired back some cans oot ay boredom. It wis Scottish & Newcastle beer which wis shite; ah jist drank Becks normally, but it was there. They had this punch n aw, which wisnae bad. Before long ah wis a wee bit pished. In fact I must have been really pished because I was necking with Martine Fenwick. I don't remember how we got started. It was radge because we never really goat oan n she wis a few years aulder than me, but she wis bevvied n aw.

I had some fuckin root oan ays; I jist wanted tae blaw ma muck in Fenwick, then split from the whole depressing scene. I thought about getting her back tae the office and intae the walk-in storage cupboard where we kept boxes of computer hardware and stationery. There was a table there and I'd be able tae gie her one across it. The problem was that the slag was intae letting me tongue her in public, but when she sussed I was trying to get her away, she knocked me back. My head was pounding like ma baws by this time, and I kept smelling this strong scent of urine. I snarled an insult at Fenwick and hit the bar.

After a couple of drinks, I pocketed this cheap plastic lighter which I spied lying on a table. Then I went for a wee wander through the deserted offices. Rummaging through one of the stockrooms I found some inflammable spirit, for cleaning electrical equipment. It was ideal.

I rejoined the party, which didn't last much longer before fire alarm went off and loads of drunken cunts staggered out into the street. Two fire engines came and doused the blaze, but only after it had gutted several offices. One doss cunt who had goat drunk and passed out was taken tae hoaspital suffering fae smoke inhalation. It served the dippit cunt right as far as ah was concerned. The fire damage was substantial and it led to a memo from the Personnel Director, banning the use of office premises for Christmas perties. For me that was sound, I had nae interest in these cunts' perties.

Shortly after this I was promoted. Jane Hathaway got a better job elsewhere, and, as they put it, 'took' Fenwick with her. Des Frost took over as the supervisor and I got his job. That was me made up to full Systems Analyst. It meant mair dosh, but I was just daein the same job really. It showed me how exploited I'd been in the three years I'd been there as a trainee. We got two new trainees, both young guys, one of whom was involved with the baby crew. There was a better crack in the office.

A few months later it happened.

We were up at Buster's again, and having a good night. Even in

the disco when Lexo nodded ower at her dancin and sais tae ays: —
That cunt's ours the night, I just thought it wis like, wishful thinkin.

She looked so fuckin cool and proud   up   – Up a little bit, eh Roy?
the way she danced, her hair aw sort   up   FUCK OFF
ay long and flowing, her mouth in   up   I've seen faces, places,
that pout that seemed tae spit out   up   And smiled for a moment,
contempt for all the world, her   up   But oh
lithe body twisting to the music.   up   You haunted me so.
She hud that clinging top and   up   Still my tongue-tied
short skirt on, the fuckin cock   up   Young pride
teaser – – – deserved it up her – – up   Would not let my love for you show
                               in case you'd say no.

NO

DEEPER

DEEPER – – – – – Can't get deep enough to get at the Stork – – – –
only her – – – – because we were all pretty out of it . . .
   Aye.

We were all pretty out of it when we got back to Dempsey's. Lexo
stuck a trip on her, and she was out of her nut. It was a crazy time.
There was one tape deck set up in the front room blastin oot aw
that fuckin techno shite, and in one ay the bedrooms we had the
stuff ah wis intae; the Stone Roses n Happy Mondays n aw the
indie stuff. Lexo nodded over to me and then Ozzy, who moved
across tae her. Ah don't think she really knew what was happening when Ozzy ushered her into the bedroom. By the time he got
her there, Lexo and I were waiting, with Demps, who locked the
door. I remember she was still giggling, until Lexo pushed her
onto the bed. Demps and Ozzy held her down and Lexo put a
knife to her throat.

The realisation ay what wis happening hit her hard. — Please
don't kill me, she said quietly.

— Open yir mooth n yir fuckin deid, Lexo said. He pulled up her skirt. She struggled a bit, saying, — Please don't, please don't, over and over again.

I said to Lexo, — C'moan Lexo, we've put the shits up her enough man . . .

He turned and gave me a look like I'd never seen before, never suspected a human being could have been capable of. — Gaunny pit a wee bit mair up her thin the shits, eh, he sneered. I was scared: scared of Lexo. If I shat out I was dead. That's what I thought. Demps, Ozzy; they were just laughing.

— Think ay this is yir initiation, Ozzy said.

— Aye, yuv no been done yit, Demps smiled. — The boys are entitled tae a line up.

— Top boy's perks, Ozzy laughed, — cannae say fairer thin that, eh.

— Lexo hit her across the face and pressed the knife against her throat. She stopped struggling and turned her head to the side. He began pulling up her clinging lycra top, very slowly and carefully, almost with tenderness. Ozzy and Demps had her arms up as the top was jerked over her head. — Dinnae want any signs ay a struggle, he laughed. He pulled her bra down and scooped her tits out at the same time. All the time, her face was frozen, her eyes dead, except for a steady stream of tears. Then she let out a scream, but the music was so loud anywey that nae cunt would've heard. Lexo hit her on the side of her face, then tightened one of his huge hands around her neck. — Ah'll cut your fuckin tongue oot the next time you make a fuckin sound, he whispered. We all knew he wasn't bluffing. Lexo was possessed.

Fuckin right the cunt wis.

— Git a handful ay they titties boys, no bad, he said evaluating a full breast in the palm of his hand.

— She's a fuckin lovely piece ay meat, Ozzy smiled, cruelly tweaking her nipple between his forefinger and thumb.

— Only the choicest cuts for the top boys, Dempsey smiled.

Lexo had her skirt down, and he gestured to me to get the shoes off her feet, which I did, then he slid off her cotton panties.

— Ivir hud yir fanny licked oot? he asked. She was back in a trance of fear, but she closed her legs as his hand went roughly between them. Lexo lay with his full bulk on top of her. — Ivir been licked oot? he asked, right in her face.

She tried to talk but started to gag. Her eye make-up was running. She looked repulsive already. Nothing like she'd looked in the club. The fear had twisted and distorted her face. It wasn't worth it . . .

Lexo pulled down his jeans and boxer shorts, exposing a large, spotty arse. Ozzy and Demps let go of her arms and grabbed a thigh each, pulling her legs apart. I could hear her alternating between sad pleas and insipid threats.

— . . . dinnae . . . please Lexo . . . Alex . . . dinnae . . . please . . . ah'll tell the polis . . . ah'll get the polis . . . please . . . don't hurt me . . . don't kill me . . .

Lexo opened up her piss-flaps with his thumbs and sniffed at her minge. Raising his head, he twitched his nose and pulled a face like a wine connoisseur. — Thir's gaunny be a whole loat ay shaggin the night!

He slurped greedily at her fanny for a bit, then steadily, incrementally, with great care soas no tae show any signs ay forcing, he pushed his finger into her cunt, gently working it. Ozzy and Dempsey still had hold of her thighs.

She screamed as he forced his cock intae her. Again though, he was slow and deliberate. Lexo knew what he was doing. The expression on her face was . . . I remember seeing a documentary about some animal being eaten from behind while its face seemed to register disbelief, fear, and self-hate at its own impotence. That was what she reminded me of. The wildebeest . . .

Ozzy and Dempsey were scrutinising her face, Ozzy brushed her long, dark hair aside as Lexo thrusted, — Nae sign ay her gittin turned oan yit, Lexo, he smiled.

— Mibbe ah'm needin a wee bitty back-up here, boys, Lexo grunted. — Strikes me thit thir's three holes here n only one ay thum in use.

Ozzy unzipped his jeans and brought out his cock. He pulled her head to him and, using Lexo's knife at her throat, compelled her to open her mouth.

I was standing in the corner shaking, wondering what the fuck ah wis daein here, as Ozzy had her next, then Dempsey, by which time she'd almost blacked out. When Dempsey was on, someone tried to come into the room. They knocked persistently. Ozzy clicked the door open and stuck his head round it. — Fuck off! Private perty! he snapped.

— Wir gaun roond tae Murray's. He's goat decks, ken, a guy called Nezzo said.

— We'll catch yis up, Ozzy said, locking the door.

Dempsey eventually came, — Phoah ya fucker, he grunted, before pulling out.

— Nice n lubricated fir ye Strangy, Ozzy smiled.

— Ah'm fucked if ah'm gaun in thair eftir youse cunts . . . I shuddered, trying to keep it light. There wasn't a condom in sight.

— Nae cunt shites oot, Lexo growled.

I unzipped my flies.

Ozzy pouted disdainfully at her vagina. — Like a fuckin soapy sponge in thair man, ah'm tellin ye.

I lay on her. I couldn't have got hard anyway, but I lay on her and faked it, thrusting rhythmically.

— Ah dinnae think the earth exactly moved for it thair, Strangy, Dempsey laughed, as I gave a weak grunt and levered myself off her.

— Last ay the rid-hoat lovers right enough, Lexo said scornfully.

I thought we had finished, but her ordeal was only beginning. Lexo wanted to take advantage of the fact that everyone had left the party. — Watch her, he commanded, then vanished. He returned from the back green with a length of clothesline which he rigged up, with a noose on the end, to the large parallel beams in the living-room. The room was strewn with empty beer cans and bottles, overflowing ashtrays and empty record sleeves and cassette-tape boxes. Lexo came back into the bedroom and tied her hands crudely but firmly behind her back and marched her through the empty flat to the living-room. He had her stand on a stool, almost on her tiptoes, with the rope round her neck. He stuck a large ball of cottonwool in her mouth and taped over it with masking tape.

— If she faws ower n hangs, we're fucked! This is ma flat! Dempsey said.

— Fuck it, said Lexo. — If it faws n chokes, wi jist take it doon the coast n dump it. He rubbed his hands together, — Let's hit that all-night chemist's n git some KY. Ah'm itchin tae gie it one up the erse. Its fanny's been well-fucked enough. Will git a couple ay beers at the club first, eh. Thirsty fuckin work this!

He moved over to her and stood on his tiptoes and kissed her chin. — You're ours now, ya sow. Then he put on a theatrical American accent, — Don't go away baby, the boys'll be back!

We just left her there. Ozzy drove us up to the West End and Lexo procured the KY from the chemist. We then drove down to our club at Powderhall. It was a snooker club and it had shut ages ago, but we had a key and Ozzy put oan the jukey while Demps set up some Becks. — Cheers, boys!

Her trussed up like that back at the flat. Choking on the gag, struggling to draw breath. Fearful of even trying to move. Not knowing when we'd be back, whether we'd be back. I wanted this drink over quickly. I wanted to save her.

— Tae slags that huv tae fuckin learn lessons! Ozzy proposed a toast.

— Slags, we nodded in unison, clanking our bottles together.

How did she feel bound up like that, the noose around her neck? Our spunk trickling down her bare legs?

I was shiting myself that something had happened to her. Demps was too; it was his flat. Lexo and Ozzy didnae seem tae gie a fuck. Lexo picked up on my anxiety.

— Dinnae go aw fuckin poofy oan ays, Strangy. It's an education fir the sow. Be the makin ay it.

— Ye dinnae ken that though . . . it might fuck her up . . . she might never be able tae go wi a guy again like.

He looked at me with withering scorn. — The only fuckin reason it'll no be able tae dae it again is cause it's hud the best n the rest jist dinnae fuckin measure up.

Lexo wanted to stay for another drink, but we talked him into heading back. He hit his motor and drove across the city towards

Dempsey's gaff. Lexo stopped the car before we were there though.
— Eh . . . I said weakly. What was he doing?

She had died. She had fallen over and died. We'd killed her. I
knew it. She would just give up, let herself hang. Why fight it?

I knew she was dead.

— C'moan, Lexo! What's the score! Demps moaned.

Lexo pointed to a group of drunks who were sitting on a park
bench in the deserted night street. They were drinking tins of strong
lager. — Goat tae say hiya, eh.

— Eh? Moan tae fuck! I gasped.

— Nice tae be nice, Lexo said, exiting from the car. Ozzy started
to go as well.

We were in no mood for this, no me and Dempsey anywey, but
we got out of the motor eftir them, reasoning that it would be easier
to try to cajole the cunts back in. We approached the winos who
looked cautiously at us.

There were two guys and a woman. One of the boys was bulky
and big with curly silver hair, but surprisingly gentle, furtive eyes.
The other one was a guy who I realised was a lot younger than I'd
thought. His face was discoloured with the drink and the weather, as
well as a lot of scars and scabs. His hair was thick and dark. He had
that slightly bewildered look a lot of drunks who've not had quite
enough to send them away seem to wear.

I wanted back to her. Maybe she'd got free, maybe some cunt
heard her. The polis . . .

— Awright gents, Lexo said and, turning to the woman, smiled,
— and ladies n aw.

The woman wisnae that auld either. She was thin and pale and
probably in her early thirties. She had short greasy-brown hair, but
her clothes looked in quite good condition, and she didn't seem
dirty.

They gave us some cagey greetings.

Ozzy looked at the woman, — What's your name, doll?

— Yvonne, she said.

— She's awright that yin, the aulder guy smiled, raising his can at
us.

— Bet you're a good ride, eh Yvonne, Ozzy asked, winking at her.

The auld guy wrinkled his eyes and puckered his lips, sucking in air, and smiled at me. — Coorse, he grinned. I liked this auld cunt. I had a desire to protect him from the boys.

— Mibbe git Yvonne here back tae oor wee party, eh Lexo. Git some lesbo stuff set up. Ever fucked another bird, Yvonne? Eh? Ozzy asked.

Yvonne said nothing, she just sat on the bench, between the two guys. The auld guy turned away.

— Leave ur, Ozzy, Demps said.

— See if ye wir tae fuck another lassie bit, Yvonne, jist sayin likes; ah mean ah'm no saying that ye wid or nowt like that, but jist sayin if ye wir, jist supposin, eh: wid ye yaze yir fingers or tongue? Ozzy asked, pushing his index finger into his fist and flicking his tongue in and out of his mouth.

The lassie hunched her shoulders up and stared at the ground.

— Fuck off, Ozzy! C'moan! Lit's go! Demps shouted.

I wanted to see her. I needed to see her. We had to go back.

— Mibbe just git a wee kiss bit, eh Yvonne? Ozzy asked. He bent towards her. She turned away, but he kept turning with her and she finally stopped moving her head and allowed him to kiss her on the mouth. Lexo made whooping noises. The other guy had handed him his Carlsberg Special can, which he was now drinking out of.

— That wisnae sae bad, eh? Ozzy said. — Jist like New Year. Wi aw kiss strangers at New Year, in the street n that, up the Tron. Nice tae be nice . . . what aboot a wee flash ay the tit then, Yvonne? Fir the boys!

— Fuck off, Ozzy! I said.

— Shut up, Strangy, he laughed, — ah'm jist giein Yvonne a bit ay a choice. A wee flash ay the tit or she comes back tae the perty wi us. What's it tae be, Yvonne?

The woman pathetically undid some buttons on her blouse and quickly pulled out a breast before covering it again. Ozzy laughed. Lexo looked away in disgust.

Then Yvonne sprung to her feet. It was only then I realised what had happened. Lexo had punched the youngish guy, his huge fist making a bone-crunching sound as it connected with the boy's head. He stood smiling at the gadge, keeping his arms stiff and punching the air jerkily in front of the guy's head. The boy put his hand to his face; he was shaking with pain and fear in the seat. I wanted the daft cunt to stand up and run, or take a swing at Lexo. I wanted him tae dae something, no just sit thair like a fuckin sheep. The auld guy looked away and closed his eyes.

— Nivir saw that one mate, eh no, Lexo laughed. — Too much bevvy. Makin ye slow. Bet ye could've been a contender at one time n aw, eh?

This stupid cunt keeps his hand in front of his face but actually forces a wretched smile at Lexo. Lexo playfully short-jabs the right hand into his guard; — This one . . . this one . . . he says, then he smacks the boy's face with his other hand, — naw, it's that one . . . he laughs, shaking his left. — That one again . . . his left fist again makes contact with a sickening crunch. Then it's the right one.

I'm watching this and I'm ready to put the boot into this cunt on the park bench for being so fuckin stupid and just taking this undignified punishment; just to put him oot his fucking misery quickly. I want to go. I want to see her. The guy's got his head wrapped up in his hands now. Lexo's lost interest. He's watching Ozzy who's necking with the woman Yvonne. I'm shrugging at the auld jakey guy who's looking frightened. I'm trying to send a vibe out that it's okay, that nae cunt's gaunny bother him.

Lexo goes over to him and pulls out his wallet. He crushes a fiver into the jakey cunt's hand. — A drink fir yir mate the morn, eh. Anaesthetic, he smiles.

— Ah wis a coppersmith tae trade. Rosyth, the auld guy says tae him, taking the money.

— Goat the hands fir it, mate. Strong hands, Lexo smiled.

— The Ministry of Defence. The Civil Service it used tae be, he said.

— Ye ken Benny Porteous? I asked.

— Aye . . . ah ken Benny! The auld guy's eyes lit up.

— That's ma Uncle. He wis a coppersmith at Rosyth.

— Ah worked wi Benny for years! Alec, that's me. Eck Lawson. Mind me tae yir Uncle. What's he daein? Whair's he workin?

— No daein nowt. Jist playing the gee-gees, eh.

— Sounds like um! Mind me tae um! Eck Lawson!

— Nae bother, Eck, I said. I wanted to go.

— Moan youse, Lexo snapped and we got back into the car. — What wir you daein wi that auld hound, ya filty cunt? he laughed at Ozzy.

— Could've taken it back, eh. See how the slag liked a jakey boot lickin her oot, Ozzy smiled.

I could see the possibilities racing round in Lexo's head. — Naw, he said. — Discipline's whit's fuckin needed. Gits a wee bit too complicated, polis n that.

— That wis fuckin daft! *They* could've goat the polis. Panel that wino . . . what the fuck d'ye call that? Demps snarled.

We got in the car. We were going back to her. Please let her be alive.

— They'll no git the fuckin polis, ya daft cunt, Ozzy scoffed.

Lexo turned round, his large smile beaming at us. — That wis a jist a wee bit ay foreplay. Git us aw in the mood fir the slag's erse, eh!

I looked at Demps's tense face where we sat together in the back of the car. His mouth was twisted and I could hear his teeth grind but I couldn't see his eyes for his long fringe. We got back to his flat about an hour after our departure.

I was terrified as we mounted the stairs, shit-scared in case she'd tried to struggle free and hung herself.

I was fuckin shaking. I looked at Demps. He looked away.

Ozzy opened the kitchen door. She was there. For a second she was so still it looked as if she had cowped over. I was about to scream as an overwhelming wave of fear washed over me but she turned her head to us, her eyes pleading and panicked. She was still alive.

We got her down, but instead of taking her back through to the bedroom, Lexo lugged the mattress through and stuck it oan the flair.

— Better through here, eh, he smiled, — We'll be able tae watch they cartoons oan that breakfast telly while we gie it the message.

Ah didnae take drugs but Lexo and Ozzy did an ecky and the three ay them took a couple ay lines ay speed each, and we just kept her with us, having her over and over again. I managed one more pretend thrust, but the rest were up her all night. Dempsey and Lexo were up her cunt and arse at the same time, their balls pushed together. — Ah kin feel your cock, Lexo, Demps gasped.

— Aye, ah kin feel yours n aw, Lexo said.

Dempsey had put on a tape of Hibs goals on the video and we watched George McCluskey smash home a beauty against Dunfermline. — A fuckin cracker fi Beastie thair . . . Lexo growled as he blurted his load into her rectum for the umpteenth time that night. When we got bored fucking her in different ways we'd put on a video or some sounds. We watched the film Nightmare on Elm Street Part 2, which Demps had on video.

In the morning, we made her take a couple of showers and steep in the bath, supervising her washing herself thoroughly. She was so compliant, looked so destroyed and wretched, that I felt it would've been better if we'd topped her. She crossed her legs and kept her arms over her chest, like one of the female prisoners in concentration camp films. Her body, which had always looked so good, so lithe, athletic and curvy as she danced in her tight and flimsy clothes, now looked broken and bent, twisted and scrawny.

I realised what we had done, what we had taken. Her beauty was little to do with her looks, the physical attractiveness of her. It was to do with the way she moved, the way she carried herself. It was her confidence, her pride, her vivacity, her lack of fear, her attitude. It was something even more fundamental and less superficial than those things. It was her self, or her sense of it.

We had no right. We didnae realise . . . ah didnae think . . . Get away. Get away from this for a bit. Get

DEEPER

       DEEPER

              DEEPER——————deeper soas I can see Sandy Jamieson, who is now sitting outside our tent on the forested slope which rises in tiers from the lake.

— Ever thought of what you're going to do when all this is over, Sandy old man?

— I think I'll probably end up doing more of the same. I'd like to stay in the game in some capacity . . . I mean, I can't see me pulling pints in a pub. I'd miss the cameraderie of the whole thing . . . oh, it's more than just sharing the bath with a group of other naked men . . . is anything wrong, Roy?

— I think I'll go for a walk, Sandy, eh, try to find more pieces of wood for the fire, I said. I felt nervous and ill-at-ease, I had to get away from all of this.

— Top hole, Sandy shouted and winked as I edgily departed. What was he on about?

I found myself walking deeper into the dense
woods. I crouched down in a clearing and
tried to gather my thoughts. They
kept taking me back though;
taking me back to my   some other world.
memories of some   to   what other world?
other world – – back – – up   A city. A car going
                                        through a city's empty streets.

Harsh daylight.

We drove her into town and she went home. It took her a few days to report it to the police. We'd been rehearsing our story, which was straightforward. We had some bevvy and drugs and had a party. She was up for a bit of fun, and took a couple of us on. It was only in the morning when we started joking that she was a dirty slag, that she got all bitter and twisted and started all this rape fantasy stuff. We got rid of the video we'd watched and the records we'd listened to that night, so that she would make a cunt of herself if she told the polis what we had oan.

We were taken in for questioning, but we were all veterans of being interrogated by the bizzies. There was no way they were going to get anything out of us, especially with our lawyer in attendance. We had employed Conrad Donaldson Q.C. as our defence. Donaldson was the best criminal lawyer in the toon, and he assured us that they had no case. We just had to keep our nerve. Even when we were formally charged, it didn't worry us too much. The polis were a dawdle, their hearts weren't in it; the worse flak I had was from my family.

— Well, that's it now, ma ain laddie, Dad said. — Sick. A sick person. Like ah sais, a common criminal.

— It was her but, Dad . . . well Lexo wis a wee bit over the top, but it wis her . . . she wanted it . . . I pleaded.

I recall Bernard raising his sick queen eyebrows and pouting distastefully. It was fuck all to do with that pansy. I wanted to obliterate that faggot. Ma rushed to my defence though, — Eh's no that kind ay laddie, John! Eh's no that kind ay laddie!

— Vet! Fuckin shut it! Like ah sais, jist fuckin shut it! Dad snapped, his eyes crimson. He turned to me and I felt the re-emergence of a childlike fear as those huge crazy lamps seemed to be reaching right into me, to be probing around in my soul . . . — Ah'm gaunny ask ye this once, and jist once. Did you touch that wee lassie? Did you hurt that wee lassie?

— Dad . . . it wisnae like that . . . ah nivir touched her . . . a wis jist thair whin she pointed the finger at everybody. It wis a perty . . . everybody wis huvin a good time. This lassie, she wis crazy, high oan drugs n that, she jist wanted tae screw everybody thair. Then in the mornin a couple ay the boys started callin her a slag, now ah ken that wis a bit oot ay order, but she goes aw spiteful n starts takin it oot oan ivray cunt. Ah nivir did nowt . . .

— That's whit it wis! Ma screamed at John. — A slag! A fuckin slag's gaunny ruin ma laddie's life! N you're gaunny jist stand thair n take that slag's word against yir ain flesh n blood!

John let the implications of this sink home. He'd always said that the Strangs had to stick together and Vet had captured the moral high ground. — Ah'm no sayin that, Vet, like ah sais, ah'm no sayin that . . . it's no meant tae be like that, like ah sais, it wisnae meant tae be like that . . .

— Eh's a good laddie, John! Eh's goat a joab in computers . . . thing ay the future. Wi eywis brought um up right! It's jist that rubbish eh's been hingin aroond wi, they idiots fi the fitba . . .

Dad's eyes glared like spotlights and his Adam's apple bobbed like a buoy in stormy seas, — We'll see tae they cunts . . . ah'll git ma fuckin shotgun now . . .

Thank fuck Tony was round with one of his kids, wee Sergio, — Naw John, naw. It'll just cause mair hassle gittin involved now. It's up in the courts. It could prejudice the case.

Dad's face twitched as he slowly grasped this. He hyperventilated a little on the spot and I thought he was going to hit one of us. Then he seemed to settle down. — Prejudice the case . . . that's right, Tony . . . aye. Naebody's gaunny dae nowt. The Strangs'll dae thair fightin in the coort. That's whair aw the fightin's gaunny be done, like ah sais, up the coort.

He squeezed my hand, almost crushing my bones in his fervour. — Ah jist hud tae ask son, ah jist hud tae ken. Ah nivir doubted ye though, son, nivir fir a minute. Ah hud tae ask though, son, tae hear it fae yir ain lips, like ah sais, fae yir ain lips. Ye understand that, son?

I nodded. I didn't really understand. I didn't understand fuck all. I didn't understand why I felt so bad. I hated that slag, I hated every cunt: everyone that fucked me around. It was me against them. Me. Roy Strang.

I didn't understand why whenever I thought of her I wanted to die.

Ah never did nowt.

— Wir gaunny clear yir name! We stick thegither, the Strangs. Wir gaunny win! Roy, Vet, Tony, wir gaunny win!

I remember him shaking a clenched fist in the air.

17 Zero Tolerance

It was a long time before it got to court, and it seemed longer still. I couldnae work. I took all my annual leave from work, one month, and I just sat at home. Kim was there with me. She had lost her job at the baker's shop; been caught with her fingers in the till. We sat at home and chain-smoked. I'd never smoked before, just cause everyone else in the hoose did. I hated cunts who smoked cigarettes: fag-smoked cunts I called them. It seemed to me that the fags actually smoked them; covered them in filthy, rancid, tarry smoke.

Now here I was.

I'd never felt so low, so drained. All I wanted to do was to sit and watch telly. Kim talked incessantly, always about guys she had been seeing. It got soas I couldn't make out what she was actually saying, couldn't pick out the words, I could only hear this eeehhheeeehhhheeeehhh, this constant nasal monotone in the background; a dull, relentless soundtrack to my depression.

Whenever I went out, just local like, doon tae the shops, I felt that everyone was looking at me and I knew what they'd be saying under their breath: Dumbo Strang interbred mutant fuckup sick psychopathic rapist vermin . . . I stayed in as much as I could.

But I couldn't stay in forever. It was just so oppressive. I tried to keep in touch with the rest of the boys on the blower. Lexo and Ozzy were eywis oot, swedgin, partying, acting like fuck all had happened. Demps had gone to ground as well. When I called him and he heard my voice, he put the phone down. He stopped answering after that; his line was disconnected a little later.

I felt like a fuckin prisoner in this madhouse. Kim was a pain during the day, but my depression had inured me to her bleatings, which were fuck all compared to the crazy circus which went on around me all evening when Ma came back fae her joab at the auld cunts' place and Dad came in from John Menzies. He was usually late, he took all the overtime he could get. Thankfully Bernard had finally moved out to a flat, but Tony was often round.

One time Dad came in particularly buoyant. — Caught one sneaky wee bastard the day Vet, tryin tae steal comics. Broke doon in tears, like ah sais, in tears. That's how it starts Vet, the criminal classes, like ah sais, the criminal classes.

— Perr wee sowel . . .

— Ah sais tae um, yir no such a big man now ur ye, ya crappin, thievin wee bastard! Like ah sais, no such a big man now!

— That's a shay-ay-aymmme . . . Kim whined, — a wee laddie . . .

— Ah, bit that's no the point, Kim. Ah did that fir ehs ain good. Psychology Kim, yuv goat tae understand, psychology. Ye lit thum away wi it, thill nivir learn. Cruel tae be kind, like ah sais, cruel tae be kind. Should ah huv jist lit um away well? What if somebody hud seen n ah hud loast ma joab? Should ah? Ah'm askin ye? Should ah huv jist lit um away?

— Naw . . . bit . . . Kim protested.

— Naw bit nuthin! If ah hud loast ma joab, then what wid've happened? Thank Christ thir's somebody here whae kin hud a joab doon! Like ah sais!

This kind of shite went oan constantly.

The worse thing about the auld man was that he watched the fuckin telly aw night, he never seemed to sleep. When I'd go downstairs, insomniac myself with depression, I'd find him there, gaping at the box. Any noise outside and he'd shoot to the window, checking it out. His files were increasing; he'd opened up new ones on the block of flats two down from us.

I had another look at some of his handiwork.

23/8 MANSON
Single Parent: Donna (17)
Child: Sonia (less than six months.)

I always feel sorry for young lassies in this position, even if most
of them just do it to get a flat from the fuckin stupid communist
cunts on the council. This lassie seems good and the bairn is
always clean. There is usually a drugs risk in this situation
though, with the scumbags who hang around lassies in such a
situation.

Verdict: Possible drugs threat. Continue surveillance.

Dad had got involved with a local group called Muirhouse
Against Drugs: Brian's old man Jeff was the President; Colin
Cassidy was its secretary. I don't think Jeff knew what he was letting
himself in for, getting those cunts involved. — Ah've goat detailed
files Jeff, like ah sais, detailed files, oan a loat ay cunts in the scheme.
Ah'm prepared tae make them available tae the group at any time,
my Dad once told him.

The anti-drugs group was now all my Dad spoke about.

— Ah think the thing aboot Muirhoose now is it's goat tae the
stage whair the kid gloves huv goat tae come oaf, Jeff. It's nae good
jist drivin these cunts oot the scheme; the council jist sticks thum
back here again. What we need are five good men wi shotguns, like
the yin ah've goat up the stair. Jist go roond n blaw these cunts away,
like ah sais, jist blaw them away. That's what ah'd like tae dae, that's
what would happen in a sane world.

— Eh . . . aye John, Jeff said nervously, — but it isnae a sane
world . . .

— You're tellin me it's no! We've goat ma laddie thair whae's
workin in computers n he's treated like a leper in this fuckin scheme
because ay some slut. Yuv goat aw they junkies stoatin roond,
protected by the polis n featherbedded by the fuckin council! The
shotgun solution's the only one, like ah sais, the shotgun solution. N

ah'll tell ye this n aw Jeff, see eftir ah'd wasted aw that junky trash, ah'd be right up the council n ah'd blaw they cunts away n aw! Fuckin sure'n ah wid. Cause the junkies n the single parents n that, they're just the symptom ay the disease, like ah sais, jist the symptom. The real source ay it is these cunts up the City Chambers. Not fuckin quoted, these cunts!

I couldn't go out but I couldn't stay in; no wi that shite gaun on.

So one day I ventured out and took a bus up the toon. Walking down Princes Street my attention was caught by a series of black posters with a huge white Z on them. They hung from hoardings along the Gardens side of the road.

The first one had:

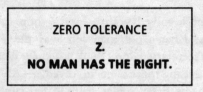

ZERO TOLERANCE
Z.
NO MAN HAS THE RIGHT.

I felt as if I had been punched hard in the stomach. I couldnae get air, the blood seeming tae run right oot ay ma heid. I stood in Princes Street, shaking.

— THEY DINNAE KEN! THEY DINNAE KEN THE CIRCUMSTANCES! THEY DINNAE KEN WHAT IT'S LIKE! I found myself shouting, drawing puzzled, furtive looks from shoppers and tourists who moved to avoid me. A group of Japanese visitors looked on for a few seconds, and one actually took my picture: like ah wis some fuckin festival street theatre. — FUCK OFF YA SLANTY-EYED CUNTS! FUCKIN TORTURIN BASTARDS! ah shouted. They turned away and made hastily down the road, no doubt cursing ays in Japanese.

Composing myself, I wandered on. The whole ay Princes Street, on the gardens side like, was decked oot wi these fuckin Z posters. Each slogan ripped through me like a psychic machete, but I was compelled to read them all:

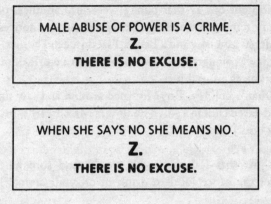

MALE ABUSE OF POWER IS A CRIME.
Z.
THERE IS NO EXCUSE.

WHEN SHE SAYS NO SHE MEANS NO.
Z.
THERE IS NO EXCUSE.

There were other ones; photaes ay bairns. Bairns that had been abused, making oot that what we had done wis like what aw they sick cunts that touch up bairns dae . . . like wi Gordon n South Africa n me . . . when ah wanted tae greet n he sais that ah wis dirty n that nae cunt would believe ays

cause wi that cunt Gordon it wisnae like how ah telt it, it wisnae like that at aw, that wis oan the surface, thir wis another part ay ays . . .

NO

I ran over into Rose Street, and hit the first pub I saw. The young barman looked at me warily; he must have recognised me as one of the cashies. I asked for a double whisky. I threw it back in a oner. It made me feel queasy; I just drank Becks like. I looked around the pub. It was covered in posters for the festival. Aw the fuckin shows that these daft cunts went tae. Then I saw it again. The Z poster, two wee lassies playin:

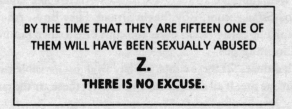

BY THE TIME THAT THEY ARE FIFTEEN ONE OF
THEM WILL HAVE BEEN SEXUALLY ABUSED
Z.
THERE IS NO EXCUSE.

I was straight oot ay that pub. I went into another, perspiring heavily, my temples throbbing. I checked out the notices. Nae Z ones. I ordered a whisky and a Becks. I sat down in a corner. The pub was busy; it was dinnertime. I was too much in a world of my own to notice the voices around me.

— Busman's holiday, Roy? I turned around and saw this white-heided, rid-faced cunt in a suit n tie. It was Mr Edwards, my boss, or rather my boss's boss.

— Eh . . . aye . . .

— It's just that I thought that you'd find somewhere more exotic than the office local to drink in on your annual leave, he smirked.

I never even realised that this *was* the office local. The cunts at Scottish Spinsters' were as boring as fuck; I never socialised with the drab, middle-class twats.

— Eh . . . aye . . .

— Sorry, this is Roy . . . em . . . Roy; Roy from Colin Sproul's section, the cunt Edwards sais tae this big shag in a suit wi tons ay make up, n this slimy cunt in a suit wi dark, Brylcreemed hair n a moustache.

We exchanged nods.

— Roy's people are doing a wonderful job in dragging us out of the dark ages, into a new, exciting halcyon era of advanced technology, is that not right, Roy? he said, in that plummy stage drama voice which is a required accessory for the exercise of Edinburgh bourgeois wit.

— Eh . . . aye . . . , I went, as the others laughed.

— So you're one of Colin Sproul's mob in S.C.? The Bryl-creemed cunt says, like an accusation. That sharp, posh voice, always sounding like a fuckin accusation. Ah felt like sayin: naw, ah'm Roy Strang, cunt. Roy fuckin Strang. Hibs Boys. Ah felt like smashin ma boatil ay Becks ower the cunt's heid, then rammin it in ehs fuckin smug pus.

Bit ah didnae. Wi these cunts, it's like ah'm jist invisible tae thaim n they are tae me. It all came tae ays wi clarity; these are the cunts we should be hurtin, no the boys wi knock fuck oot ay at the fitba, no the birds wi fuck aboot, no oor ain Ma n Dad, oor ain brothers n sisters, oor ain neighboors, oor ain mates. These cunts. Bit naw; we screw each other's hooses when there's fuck all in them, we terrorise oor ain people. These cunts though: these cunts wi dinnae even fuckin see. Even when they're aw aroond us.

— Eh aye, Systems Control . . . was all I could say.

Systems control.

Why was that all I could say? Why did I need my mates to give me a context? Why couldn't I just turn this place over like I did to that working-class pub in Govan? Why couldn't I terrorise these cunts now, now that I had them in my sights, knowing that they'd shite themselves tae death?

— I've a bit of a beef on with S.C. at the moment. You know that death benefits network system your crowd installed?

— Eh . . .

— Uh, uh Tom, Edwards goes, — Roy's on annual leave. He won't want to hear this.

— You're a programmer, Roy? The shag in the suit asks.

— Eh, aye. Systems Analyst.

— Do you like it there?

— Eh, aye.

I fuckin hated it.

No. I didnae. I didn't feel strong enough about it to hate it. It wis jist a place you went to during the day, because they peyed ye tae. While I was there, I just floated around in a void of indifference.

— Roy was just made up recently from a trainee, weren't you, Roy? Edwards grins.

— Eh, aye, I said, feeling this tightening in my chest. There was a strange ringing in my ears, like when the telly's finished. I gulped my drink down. — Excuse me, I'm in a bit of a hurry, I said, standing up. — Got to meet someone.

— Well, she must be nice, you rushing off like that, laughed Edwards.

The shag in the suit looked at me with an expression
which had a mild, playful overlay of flirtatiousness
but which failed to conceal its underlying   baws – – – I'm doing
contempt. I'm out of there, then down   ma   this for you, Roy.
the road to the bus stop – – – ringing   baws   I know you can feel.
in my ears – – – – – my balls – – – – – ma   Why should you be denied
sexual contact? I know what you're feeling; I was on a course on sexuality and the disabled . . . I
want to make you feel, Roy . . . I know they'd say it's unprofessional but it'll be our little secret. I can
make contact with you, Roy . . . you're getting harder with me touching you like this. Would you like
me to take you into my mouth? Would you like that?

No, please don't Patricia, please don't . . . ah dinnae want
any . . .
— That's what I'm going to do, Roy. I'm going to suck you off . . .
No . . . somebody come and help
somebody come
somebody come
somebody
please
come
ooooooohhhhhhhhhhhhhhhhhhhh
— Mmmm . . . it looks like somebody's come! You can make contact, Roy! You're going to
come out of this!

DEEPER
                DEEPER
                                DEEPER
                                                DEEPER– – –
I'm still in the woods, alone. I'm startled to see that there's blood all
over me; I'm covered in it. I draw in a breath. I let a few seconds tick
by. I don't feel hurt or injured. It isn't my blood. It's not mine. I
follow its dark trail into the woods, but I hear a noise in the forest,
the crackling noise of something advancing through the undergrowth and I run.

I run through the bush until I stumble upon the track and follow it
towards the shores of the lake. The beautiful lake. I step into its soft,
lukewarm waters, and wash the blood from my body and clothing.

After a while I emerge from the water in the heat and I'm walking back up the trail towards our camp, when I come across Sandy, looking distraught.

— Roy! Are you alright? What in the blazes happened?

— Sandy . . . I don't know . . . I just went into the woods and I felt suddenly weak . . . I crouched down and sort of passed out. I woke up covered in blood, and it was like some animal had attacked me or something . . . I don't remember.

— My God! Let's get back to camp! Sandy wrapped his arm around me and supported me up through the woods.

We came across the bloodied trail again. — Oh shit, I said, for as soon as we looked up we saw the prostrate, naked body of a young native boy. The body lay half-covered in leaves and shrubbery. The eyes had been gouged out and the genitals mutilated.

— Oh my God, I said. I felt a gagging sensation, that strange dryness in my throat again, but I couldn't be sick. It was only when I saw the discarded blue pants in the bushes that I realised it was the little fellow we'd met earlier.

— The work of terrorists, I'll wager, Sandy said sagely. — I wouldn't even presume to blame our friends the Marabou Storks for this. Mind you, the removal of the eyes look like they've been done by the beak of a Stork or perhaps a blunt knife . . . possibly a purchase from Boston's of Leith Walk . . .

What in the name of . . . — Sandy, this whole fuckin thing . . . it's just fucked man, d'ye realise? It's just fucked!

— Yellow carded. Yellow fuckin carded, Sandy moaned.

What is this shite? What's happening to me?

What happened when I got hame fae the   up – – – Ah mind.
fuckin toon after ah'd seen they cunts   up
fae the work – – – – – – – – – – – – – – – up   Ah mind what
                                                           fuckin happened.

Ah mind what happened awright.

When I got home, it seemed as if there was nobody in. Then I heard voices from upstairs, giggling sounds. When I went for a slash I heard heavy panting from Kim's room. She had somebody in her bedroom; somebody was giving her one. Obviously some cunt fae the scheme.

I made some toast and watched the telly with the volume turned low, but I had to switch it off because one of the lassies in the Aussie soap opera reminded me of *her*.

About twenty minutes later, Kim came down. She looked shocked to see me, like she hudnae heard ays come in. I saw why she was so fuckin bothered, because Tony came straight in after her. He was dressed in a suit and tie, which he was straightening.

— Awright, Roy, he said.

— Tone, I goes.

— Tony came roond for a sandwich, Kim said, in a nervous whine.

Aye, n ah ken whae the fuckin meat wis n aw ya cunt.

— Ah felt really fuckin sick, Tony shook his head glumly. — It's the upholstery oan that new motor: gies ays the boak. Threw up n everything. Hud tae go n lie doon, eh. Then this daft fucker, he nods at Kim, — comes in n starts ticklin ays.

Tony knows how to lie. He's been deceiving his wife with everything for years. He'd stick his cock in anything that moved.

— Ah wis only muckin aboot Tony, jist muckin aboot . . . she says, all clumsy and stagey.

Kim does not know how to lie.

Tony departed after we tentatively arranged to go for a couple of pints and onto the match together next weekend. I couldn't sit there and look at Kim. It was her stupid, large potato head; her fuckin idiocy was just so offensive to me. I went upstairs and when I got to my room I was surprised to find that I wis greetin.

Did anybody else live like us? Did any cunt?

I'd never really gret before; no since I was a really wee bairn. I learned not to as a kid. John and Vet just ignored you, or battered you for it, so there was no emotional currency in it. Now it felt good, therapeutic, just to surrender to all the shite and let it flow out. I wasn't Roy Strang.

I wasn't a top boy. I wasn't even Dumbo Strang either. I didn't know who the fuck I was and it didn't matter.

The only other occasion I ventured outside before the court case was to visit Elgin. I don't know what made me dae this. I had long stopped thinking of Elgin as my brother, that was if I ever had; I always cringed when John or Vet referred to him in that way. To me he was just something that pished, shat and drooled over itself, and asked questions in a secret language that no other cunt had ever learned.

Once again I was as para as fuck on my journey. I could see those cunts, all those fuckin schemie bastards that lived in this shit-pit, all of them staring at me. The word 'casual' on their breath was okay, it meant they knew not to mess, but now it was 'rapist' which was worse than 'Dumbo'.

When I got to the GORGIE VENTURE FOR EXCEPTIONAL YOUNG MEN I saw a boy or a man; I didn't know which, he could have been any age. He had the largest head I'd ever seen. My own, Kim's, even the auld man's, they just paled into insignificance alongside this. Elgin still drooled incessantly, more than ever. I'd forgotten his face, that expression on it, or perhaps I'd never really looked at him before. That was it; all those years in the same fuckin hoose and I'd never really looked at his face, I mean I'd looked at it, but never really seen what was there. All that was human had been sucked out of that face. He just sat on a chair beating out a monotonous rhythm on his thighs.

I didn't even attempt to talk to him; didn't even try to go through the token patronising crap the so-called experts laughingly refer to as communication, as therapy, as meaningful interaction. It was nothing like that for either myself or Elgin. I just sat looking at him for a while. I don't know where Elgin was but I sat looking at him, thinking of my situation and that wherever he was it didn't seem such a bad place to be.

On the eve of the courtcase, John and Vet were dealt another blow. We learned that Kim was up the stick. I suspected it was Tony's, but practically everyone in the scheme had been up Kim: at least that was how it seemed to me. It wisnae her fault. She was gullible, impressionable. No, that's too kind. She was just totally fuckin thick, as solid in the head as the concrete support pillars in a multi-storey car park. John raged at her. — Whae's is it? Ah'm asking ye, Kim! Like ah sais, whae's is it! Tony, who was normally never away fae the hoose, kept a low profile around this time and Kim kept quiet. Her drama, which she seemed to thrive on, didn't really concern me. I had my own problems.

Our brief, Conrad Donaldson Q.C., was supremely confident. He was the best there was. We'd set up a fund for his payment, jointly managed by Ghostie and Lexo's partner in his second-hand furniture shop in Leith, a psycho named Begbie. There were plenty of publicans and club owners only too willing to contribute to Donaldson's legal fees.

Donaldson was a ruddy-faced man with a slack mouth and large, rubbery lips. — Rape's a funny bugger, he told us in his offices in the New Town. — Somebody gets raped, the first thing they want to do is to obliterate all traces of the assailant. They just wash everything away. Then it generally takes a long time until they've recovered sufficiently from the shock to report it. The police's first response is to interrogate the complainant: that generally puts most of them off. Your girlie though, she seems persistent. I can only assume that she's getting some bad advice. She's on a pretty sticky wicket here. Even if the police refer the case to the Procurator Fiscal, in over thirty per cent of such referrals he simply won't initiate proceedings. Even then, only a quarter of defendants are convicted. Most of them get it reduced to sexual assault and almost half don't get custodial sentences. Statistically speaking, the rapist who goes to jail is a most unfortunate sod. The odds are heavily weighted against that happening.

— Thing is, we never raped naebody, Lexo said, smiling and chewing on some gum.

— Quite, Donaldson replied tritely. It was obvious he didn't believe a word of what we were saying.

He explained that there were no real witnesses for the prosecution, nobody who could actually say they had any real evidence to suggest that she'd been raped or held against her will. — It's a minefield for a girlie. Wouldn't touch it with a bargepole if I were her. I don't know who's put her up to this, some dykey feminist group trying to make the unfortunate wench into a *cause célèbre*, no doubt. Well, she has two chances; slim and none. I contend that she can't win; we can only lose. We can only throw it away. So I'm expecting exemplary behaviour from you chaps. Put yourself in my hands and we'll give her a damn good shafting, he said smugly, his smile crumbling around the edge of his mouth in realisation of a poor choice of metaphor.

I cringed and looked away, but something made me glance at Lexo, who just smirked and said softly, — Again.

Demps rolled his eyes and Ozzy laughed.

— One other factor very much in our favour, Donaldson said, anxious to move on, — is the judge. Judge Hermiston's attitudes are very much influenced by his practising of criminal law in the fifties where the dominant school of criminology was the Freudian model. This essentially does away with the concept of the crime of rape by proving that there are no victims. Female sexuality is deemed by nature to be masochistic, hence rape cannot logistically take place since it directly encounters the argument that all women want it anyway.

— Ah believe that, Lexo opined. — Simple whin ye think aboot it. A boy's goat a cock, a bird's goat a fanny. Thir meant tae be thegither.

— Right, Donaldson snapped, distaste for the first time playing across his thick lips, — I think we understand each other.

For the trial we had to move out of being Lexo, Strangy, Ozzy and Demps, top boys. We were now Alex Setterington, businessman (Lexo had his second-hand furniture shop in Leith), Roy Strang, Analyst with a reputable Edinburgh insurance company, Ian Osmotherly, Sales Manager with a busy nationwide retailer, and Allan Dempsey, who was a student. Demps had enrolled to do a Social Care course at Stevenson College before the court case. It gave a better impression than dole-mole.

So it was her word against the four of us. We were described by

Donaldson as 'a far cry from the picture of rampaging soccer yobbos that my learned friend so unconvincingly tried to paint; in fact decent, articulate, upstanding professional young men with excellent prospects, from good families.'

I caught a glimpse of the auld man nodding in stern approval across the court at that statement.

The worse thing for her case was that numerous guys at the party testified to how flirty and out of her face she was. So did several women; top boys' birds we had primed, or just jealous cows cause every cunt fancied her the most.

We had our own skills, our organisation, our cool. Lexo metamorphosised into a large, gentle giant in court; a choirboy with a baleful, slightly nervous and bewildered expression, polite and deferential to the judge.

Most important of all, we had the top lawyer. Conrad Donaldson Q.C. expertly dictated the whole emphasis of the trial. It became like she was the one on trial; her past, her sexuality, her behaviour. She looked really strange in the court. It was the wey she moved. She walked like the centre ay balance in her body had irreversably shifted. It wis like the movement ay some cunt that had come oot fae under the surgeon's knife and who was recuperating from a chronic and ultimately terminal illness.

Donaldson hammered out and established some key propositions:

She danced with several men at the party.
That was established.

Her stammering, plukey, inexperienced Legal–Aid Cunt tried to say that everyone danced with several men, including us, the accused. Most people there were either eckied or tripping, no me though, I never used drugs. I hated the feeling ay being oot ay control. Bad things can happen when ye get oot ay control. Like at the party. But yeah, everybody danced with each other there. It was that sort of party. You could tell that the senile auld cunt of a judge couldnae git his heid roond that concept though.

— When I attended parties, a lady seldom danced intimately with several men, he said.

She wore provocative clothing. That was established.

It was standard Ms Selfish, Chelsea Girl, X-ile type gear. Every woman at the party was dressed the same.

She had sexual experience. That was established.

So did ninety-nine per cent of the people in the court, and she probably had less than any. But allied to her admissions of two previous boyfriends and the posse of cashies we brought in to say that they had aw been there, Donaldson blew her away. I remember the plukey fuck squeaking that her sexual history, false as it happens, had no relevance.

Donaldson shook his head sadly, — My learned friend must concur that it is established practice to allow this line of questioning, sensitively imposed, on the basis that a complainant's previous sexual experience may be relevant to the issue of consent. This is at the heart of the matter surely, the issue of consent.

Then more cashies were filed in.

Conrad Donaldson's next tactic was to ask about 'rape fantasies'; a standard approach, he told us later. This paid off with a vengeance when one guy who had gone out with her, a guy called Bruce Gerber, did her case a lot of damage when he said that she occasionally talked of such 'rape fantasies'. In fact, this was what probably won it for us. — I suppose she did say that she liked teasing guys, liked the danger in flirting, he testified, — I was upset when she started hanging around those casual guys.

— Upset because you felt that she would act on her rape fantasies with these young men? Donaldson asked.

— I suppose . . . , he shrugged, — . . . I don't really know. I just saw that no good could come of it.

— Something must have given you that impression. The impression 'no good could have come of it'. Donaldson prompted further.

Gerber was a bitter man, and a feart one. He kent no tae fuck aboot wi us. — She just . . . she started acting like a slut! he snapped.

The Legal-Aid Cunt, in trying to repair the damage, just made matters worse.

Donaldson then presented an 'expert' who claimed that gang-rape fantasy was a common female sexual fantasy. He circulated lots of academic literature to back this up, even some which he described as 'feminist'. Then our brief concluded: — Witnesses have stated that this young girl, headstrong, emotionally immature, behaved in a way to suggest that she was flirting with this fantasy.

Her brief intervened, — Even if it is accepted what the defence claim, surely acknowledging one's own fantasies is not the same as acting on them. She said no!

— That's not what the four accused say, Donaldson said assertively. — That's not the inferences we're getting from the witnesses. By hanging around with a gang of young lads, by engaging flirtatiously with them, might she not have given out the wrong signals? Was it not the case that Miss X was indeed acting on her fantasies already?

He let that one hang in the air for a while and I could see the straight cunts on the jury absorbing it like dry sponges immersed in a bath full of water.

She was intoxicated and showed flirtatious affection towards several men. That was established.

Every piece ay fanny present did.

She claimed that she was 'drugged', but Miss X took drugs regularly. That was estabished.

Under questioning she admitted to using marijuana. She claimed she never took chemicals. Donaldson pointed out that this established that she did take illegal drugs. That was the bottom line. I saw this blatantly register with the judge, his mouth puckering.

She voluntarily went into the bedroom with Osmotherly. That was established.

She was out of her face after we slipped her the acid. She'd have gone anywhere with anyone.

The thing was, she showered thoroughly afterwards and we took care not to leave any marks. The medical reports were inconclusive.

Donaldson blew their case out of the water. Carefully establishing these key propositions, he built up a bandwagon of unstoppable momentum, fuelled by his flowery rhetoric and grasp of case law, which bulldozed through their defence. I say defence, because as I sais, it was evident right from the start that she was the one on trial. That was just how the whole thing felt. It was mainly just tae dae with the whole setup, but her lawyer was a poor courtroom performer and that made things worse for her. He failed to gain any empathy with the court and made no inroads in trying to attack our characters.

So Donaldson established that there was little evidence of her having had any forced sex. Ozzy claimed she consented to anal sex with him. — I didn't want to do it, not that way . . . but it was as if she was daring us to see how far we'd go. She was very drunk, and I think she'd taken some . . . stuff. I don't really know that much about drugs, but it was like she'd taken something . . .

Lexo, sorry Alex Setterington, admitted to having full intercourse with her, with her consent. — I don't think consent puts it strongly enough. The term I would use would be insistence, he said, putting on a biscuit-ersed face.

Dempsey did the same and Strang claimed that he attempted to, and she was willing, but he was drunk.

I didn't do as well as the others up there in the dock. I was the most nervous. It just wouldn't come out, then I got into full flow and ranted accusingly, — I didn't want to. I thought the whole thing was just . . . sick. It was horrible. If it had just been me and her together, but it was like she wanted everyone. I could've been anybody. She just laughed at me.

Ozzy endorsed this. — She mocked my performance as well your honour. She was out of her head. The whole thing was pretty degrading for all of us. Some of the boys werenae too bothered.

Some guys think: 'a ride's a ride'. No me. I don't like being mocked for not being able to get it up.

All this time she looked like a zombie. She was obviously sedated. It didn't stop her frequently breaking down. I tried not to look at her. Only Lexo looked at her, he looked at her constantly. His face was sad, his head occasionally nodding softly. It was like he was asking: Why? Why are you doing this to us? He was right into his role as the victim.

Summing up, Conrad Donaldson Q.C. said: — It has been established that Miss X was intoxicated and, as people generally are in such circumstances, was not in full control of her emotions. She was belligerent, aggressive and mocking towards the accused. She was out of control, giving sexual favours when under normal circumstances she would not do so. Some members of the jury may feel that one or more of the accused behaved in a cynical and opportunistic manner when presented with an intoxicated and vulnerable young woman ready to give sexual favours, although at the time, as we have heard from witnesses, she seemed anything but the sad and forlorn figure that sits in court today. But behaving with an opportunistic cynicism and showing what many may consider to be a lack of sexual etiquette and concern for others is a far, far cry from the hideous, pre-meditated crimes of drugging, imprisoning and repeatedly raping someone. The jury must, and surely will, find this to be the case.

They did. We were found not guilty.

When I looked at her, she had the expression she wore when we did her over. She crumpled into the arms of her father.

Lexo winked and blew her a kiss. Her brother stood up and shouted at him and had to be forcibly restrained. — That cunt dies, by the way, Lexo hissed to me under his breath, his face quickly snapping back into its baleful expression.

Outside the court my auld man punched the air to celebrate victory. — Ye kin fuckin well say what ye like aboot British justice bit it's still the best in world! Thir's some countries whair innocent laddies wid be rottin away behind bars! Like ah sais, Vet, behind fuckin bars they wid be in some fuckin countries . . . in a wog country or that.

He then collared the triumphant Donaldson and shook his hand vigorously. — Brilliant! Fuckin brilliant mate, he said, — Tae quote the great man ehsel: nivir in the field ay human conflict huv so many owed so much tae so few.

— Thank you, Donaldson said curtly.

— Listen, wir huvin a wee celebration perty later oan the night, doon at oor place. Doon the scheme, ken? Muirhoose likes. Yir welcome tae come along fir a drink. Nowt fancy, like ah sais, jist a wee drink. Doon Muirhoose, doon near Silverknowes like. Near D-Mains, eh.

— Muirhouse . . . Donaldson repeated slowly, — . . . sorry, I don't think so. I'm very busy at the moment.

— Ah kin imagine, mate, ah kin imagine. Anywey, well done. Ah kent that you kent straight away that oor Roy wis intelligent, hud brains like. Eh's in computers, ken? That's whair the future lies. That's what this country needs. N that wee hairy wis gaunny git um sent tae jail . . .

— Well, thankfully it didn't come to that, Donaldson forced a smile.

— Thanks tae you, mate, like ah sais, thanks tae you. Fuckin magic, if yll pardon ma French like.

I had to get away from him, making a tit of himself, a tit of me. I went to Deacon's with the boys for a celebration drink, or at least Ozzy and Lexo. Dempsey went straight hame.

— Easy fuckin meat, Lexo roared.

— Wi wir a bit oot ay order, bit she fuckin asked fir it. Ah mean, she wis lucky it wis cunts like us thit goat a hud ay her, it might've been a fuckin psycho like that Yorkshire Ripper cunt or something, eh. That's the wey she should be lookin at it, Ozzy said.

— That's right. The slag goat oaf lightly, Lexo smiled.

I couldn't get intae it. I left, citing the party back hame as an excuse. I went for a few drinks on my tod, then got back and found that the do was in full swing. There was loads of alcohol around, and quite a bit of blow. Dad had got into it through Tony. It was good for him, mellowed the cunt oot a bit. He didnae count it as drugs. — The star ay the show, he said, his arm wrapping round me like a boa-constrictor, — proved innocent though, son! Proved fuckin innocent! British justice! Like ah sais: British justice! He put on Churchill's victory speeches full blast and after a short while, started to sob. Uncle Jackie and Auntie Jackie flanked him. Shaking with emotion, he shouted, raising his glass, — THIS IS STILL THE GREATEST FUCKIN COUNTRY IN THE WORLD!

Most people nodded approvingly, thinking he meant Scotland. I was one of the few present who knew he meant Britain.

18 Running

I had been applying for jobs elsewhere; away fae this fuckin place. It was a lot harder daein this than it sounds. The way I wis feelin, just filling in an application form was a massive undertaking. I was relieved and surprised when I managed to complete one, and even more surprised when I got a start, at a slightly reduced salary, at a building society based in Manchester. I had to go: had to get away. The money didnae matter.

— Bit how, son? How should you be the yin tae run away! It's hur, that slag, that bloody Jezebel they should be pointin the finger at, no a laddie that's goat a good joab n works hard.

— Works hard n plays hard, like ehs faither, said Dad. He was still working at Menzies.

— It's a good joab ah've landed masel doon thair, Ma. Cannae settle here since aw that fuss.

They aw knew the score at the work. I'd spoken to Sproul and he'd let me take two months' leave of absence. It was no good, though. It had to be a fresh start, away from aw the cunts.

— Spread the wings, eh? Bright lights n that? Tony said. He was up with his kids, Marcello and Sergio.

What bright lights the cunt expected fae Manchester wis beyond me.

— Jist tae git away, start again. No intae hingin aboot wi the cashies nae mair either, eh. Too much hassle.

— Well, that's the maist fuckin sensible thing ah've heard ye say in a long time, Roy, like ah sais, the maist sensible, the auld man said.

— Bit Manchester, John . . . Ma bleated. She hated the idea of any of us not being in close proximity to her. Tony lived nearby and was always here. Bernard, though he had a flat in town, was always falling out with the other poofs he shared with and often crashed at Ma n Dad's.

— Aye, this is her that went away tae Italy talkin, Dad said. He'd never really forgiven my Ma for shooting the craw tae Italy all those years ago, but it seemed to bug him more these days than it ever did.

This started the predictable argument. They went on and on, until Dad screamed: — THAT'S ENOUGH, VET! AH'M FUCKIN TELLIN YE!

CANNAE FUCKIN TAKE THIS . . .

DEEPER

     DEEPER

          DEEPER————————So Sandy and I have seen the circling Storks but they're much deeper into the bush than we realised. It seems that it's not Lodge 1690 that they are flying over, but Dawson's hideaway in the jungle. Nonetheless we make for 1690 as Sandy recounts another lion adventure.

— This type of woodland with its sudden dense undergrowth and its open tracks reminds me of the terrain I encountered when I had a particularly nasty brush with Johnny Lion.

— Yes? I urged, sticking a whole chocolate digestive in my mouth. The biscuits were melting in the heat and had to be consumed quickly. Then I munched on a jammy dodger, the jam section tasting oddly like cough mixture, as Sandy told his tale.

— We were returning to our camp after a month's exploration in the bush. Darkness was falling and we were still some way from our destination. The natives were starting to get a little edgy. As leader, I decided to push on ahead of my bearers and pack donkeys, accompanied only by my loyal dog Gladstone.

I had never heard Sandy mention a dog before. This made me feel uncomfortable but I let him continue.

— Well, Gladders started barking and I looked towards the source of his aggression, discerning a vague form moving in the darkness

out by the reeds alongside this dry river bed which straddled the path
we were following. — Enough boy! I snapped, anticipating that my
faithful companion had sniffed out some game. A second or two
later I made out the shape again. This was no bloody antelope or
some such thing, it was a bugger of a lion and it was running towards
me at speed!

— Fucking hell, Sandy! What did you do?

— I had no time to do anything. I felt a powerful impact, like a
bloody fast car hitting me, and the next thing I recall was that I was
being dragged along the path on my back, my arm and shoulder in
the mouth of this beast, my body and legs being pulled along
underneath it!

— My God!

— As the bugger trailed along, his forepaws kept trampling on
me, causing considerable lacerations to the front of my thighs and
ripping my trousers to shreds. While dragging me along, those
growling purrs emanated from the beast's throat, as if he was a
hungry cat anticipating a meal. Yours truly, of course, being the
tasty little morsel he had in mind!

— Gosh! Sounds like a damn tricky one, Sandy.

— I'll say! There seemed no prospect of escape. Then I realised
that I had my eight-inch sheath knife, which, using my free arm, I
removed from the leather case hanging from my belt. I picked my
spot on the beast. When the animal stopped, preparing to drop me,
either to change its grip or to begin its feast, I stuck the bugger twice
behind the shoulder. He dropped me, but continued to stand above
me, growling. Then, with all the force I could muster, I stuck him in
the throat. His blood cascaded down on me and I realised that I must
have somewhat fortunately hit a large vein or an artery. Well, the
bugger sprang back a few yards and I scrambled to my feet and just
shouted obscenities at him. After a few seconds the maneater walked
slowly away, occasionally turning to growl in my direction.

— Gosh Sandy, that was brave to face down the beast!

— I had no choice, Roy. Valour does not come into it. In such
circumstances, one is operating, as you know, purely on a primal
instinct. With great difficulty, due to my wounded arm, I climbed a

nearby tree. It was as well that I did, for a second lion had got Gladstone and I was forced to watch as he and the one I'd wounded feasted on the poor old boy.

— That must have been heartbreaking, I said. I tried to sound sympathetic but I couldn't help a note of glee creeping into my voice. Somehow I was comforted by the death of Sandy's dog. Africa does something to a man; the heat, the silence as the sun descends behind the mountains, trees or horizon. The silence of an African jungle on a dark night must be experienced to be believed. What this place was doing to *me* was something I'd rather not contemplate.

— I stayed all night in that fucking tree, Sandy carried on with his story. — The natives found me at first light. They took me back to camp and superficially dressed my wounds. It took them a couple of days to get me to hospital. My injuries had gone septic and I had blood poisoning due to the putrescent matter lodged under the claws of the maneater that mauled me. The mauling was nothing to the fever I had . . . blast!

Our jeep swerved dangerously as one of its front wheels hit a rock in the semi-darkness. Sandy quickly regained control and stopped the vehicle for a while to compose himself. In the darkness the deathly silence was broken only by our heavy breathing and the soft noises of a few bats which sipped at the limpid waters of the lake in a series of flying kisses. We decided we would concentrate all our energies on the road. I took the wheel for a bit.

There was a campfire outside Lodge 1690 when we arrived. Dawson was strutting around and I saw two natives seemingly hugging a tree apiece. I realised, on approaching, that Dawson and Diddy had the natives stripped naked with their arms extended around the trees and bound at the wrists.

— Roy! Sandy! You're just in time. Some of our so-called rebel friends here are about to realise what it means to cross Lochart Dawson.

Even from the back and in his naked state, Sandy and I recognised one of the prisoners straight away. — Look Sandy! I said.

— So we meet again, my friend, Sandy smiled, examining the naked figure of Moses, the thief who had stolen all our equipment.

— I should say so! And in circumstances rather more advant-
ageous to us! I sang triumphantly.

Moses looked around at us, his large eyes pleading, — No bwana,
he begged.

— You'll thank me for this one day, Dawson smiled widely,
licking his lips. He went over to the other native and produced a tube
of jelly which he began to spread over the boy's buttocks. I took it
that this was in preparation for the strokes of the lash, but I was
somewhat surprised to see Dawson withdraw his stiffening penis
and apply the jelly to himself. He then pushed a finger deep into the
sphincter of the native. — Tight. The way I like it, he said.

Diddy the dwarf valet whispered at Sandy, — Remember I
always told you to keep it tight at the back.

Sandy ignored him.

— One requires a certain resistance of course, eh Roy? Dawson
turned to me smiling broadly. — After all, it's only through
resistance that one can sense one's own power: in the overcoming of
that resistance. Power always goes on and on until it finds its limits.
C'mon Roy, c'mon Sandy. Drop your trousers and join the queue.

We unbuckled our belts and let our shorts fall. I had a semi but
Sandy was already firm no I've got to stop this . . . — DAWSON! I
shouted, as he was about to thrust his erection into the native.

He stopped and turned towards me.

— We've no time for these games! Time is of the essence! It's the
Marabou Storks! We know where they are.

— This had better be good, Mr Strang, he snapped, scooping his
subsiding erection into his shorts. — Diddy, watch those traitors,
but don't lay a finger on them until I say so!

He gestured to the Lodge and what   up – – – after my Ma and
happened was – – – – I'm coming back up   Dad had that
                                                                    fight it carried on.

It carried on, eh.

Ma sat in the chair like a tightly wound spring, her face flushed.
She sucked violently on a fag and glared at the box. There was one of
these really shitey Scottish television Gaelic programmes on; the

kind where they always have some straight cunt who looks like a fuckin muppet singing some daft song in a language naebody understands with mountains and rivers in the background. I looked over at the auld man and I could see the cunt was wary. Tony and I knew that the auld girl would explode in a bit.

She started emitting a soft, long twisting sound which built up into an almighty scream at the image on the television: — FAAAHKIN HOOR! FAAHKIN DIRTY FAAHKIN JAP-SHAGGING TRAITOR! She leaned forward and gobbed at the telly screen. Greasy spittle trickled down over the image of the Gaelic singer Mary Sandeman.

— Whit ye daein, Vet? Like ah sais, whit the fuck ye daein? Jist a wimmin singing the Gaelic likes, that's aw it is, a wimmin singing the fuckin Gaelic! Whit is it? Ah'm askin ye!

— It's that fuckin slag that goat done up like a Jap and sung that Japanese Boy song . . .

— Naw . . . this is this Gaelic lassie . . . yuv goat the wrong wimmin, Vet . . . like ah sais, this is the Gaelic, a Scottish lassie, no a Jap. Dis that look like a fuckin Jap? Ah'm askin ye; does that look like a fuckin Jap? Dad gestured at the screen.

Ma glared at him and pointed derisively at Mary Sandeman. — That's worse than a Jap! A Jap cannae help what it is, bit that, dressin like a fuckin Jap, glorifyin these dirty, torturin wee bastards . . .

— She disnae dress like a fuckin Jap bit, Vet, it's the Scottish lassie thit does the Gaelic programmes . . .

— Naw, Tony said. – Ma's right. She did that 'Japanese Boy' song. Goat done up as a Jap oan Top Ay The Pops, mind ay that?

— Aye . . . ah mind that yin . . . Dad started to sing, and Tony joined in:

> Won't somebody tell me where my love has gone,
> He's a Japanese Boy.
> I woke up this morning and my love had gone,
> He's a Japanese Boy.

Was it something I said or done?

Ohhhh

He's breaking up a happy home . . .

— Shut the fuck up! SHUT YIR FUCKIN MOOTHS, YA FUCKIN CUNTS! Ma screamed.

— Jist a song bit Vet, jist a song. 'Japanese Boy' likes. John turned his palms outwards in appeal.

This was radge. This was how these cunts lived.

It was time I got away.

But I couldn't get away. Not in Manchester. Not here in my head. Here in my head she'd come after me. She kept coming after me. The nightmares, the Marabou Stork nightmares — — — —

DEEPER

    DEEPER

        DEEPER
           into
              the
                  Marabou
                    Stork
                      nightmares — — —

— — — getting closer to the nest, I told Dawson after we went back into the conservatory of Lodge 1690.

— The Storks have been flying overhead. It seems that the only place they could be is at your secret hideaway lodge Lochart. They've probably taken it over and set up nests there, Sandy explained.

— My entertainment suite . . . Dawson was dumbstruck . . . — a nesting location for these monsters . . . Sadie . . . the Jambola malcontents . . . of course. I see it all now. They've conned Lochart Dawson. Well, let's show . . .

His spiel was interrupted by the crashing of breaking glass and a cacophony of frenetic squawking as one, then another, then more large Marabous smashed through the French windows.

We were unarmed; our weapons were in the jeep outside. We instinctively retreated from the vile, shrieking clatter and I was about to run to the main door when it fell inwards with a crash, framing a monster Marabou Stork. I followed Dawson and Sandy down a set of flimsy stairs into a basement but the Storks continued to pursue us and we were cornered.

The basement was a dank, dark room. You could hear the sounds of running water below the rotting floorboards. A group of giant Storks surrounded us, shuffling closer like repulsive old beggars. A scent of charred, burning flesh filled my nostrils. We were helpless, unarmed. The largest of the Marabous came forward.

— Looks like it's sort ay panned oot tae oor advantage, eh boys, the creature observed.

It tore a large piece from a bloodied flamingo carcass with a ripping sound, and swallowed it whole. Another held the severed neck and head of a flamingo in its beak. I started gagging.

Dawson stiffened his back and pulled himself up: — As a businessman who is seeking controlling interest in this enterprise, the leisure park does not need the likes of you, people who care nothing for the . . .

The Stork's black, beady eyes focused on him, — Shut it, ya fat fuck! Whae's this cunt!

Dawson's eyes widened briefly with
fear before petulance replaced it as
the dominant emotion. Shaking   o
nervously, he whispered under   i   u
his breath, — You obviously   v   s
don't understand the   b   l
process of debate . . . — — — — — o   y   — I obviously had great

difficulty in going to the police. They say they've changed their procedures, but I didn't find a

great deal of understanding there. Must be something to do with the training, eh? Let me

quote to you from the advice given to police officers on the interrogation of rape complainants,

as it appeared in the *Police Review*:

It should be borne in mind except in cases of a very small child, the offence of rape is extremely unlikely to have been committed against a woman who does not show signs of extreme violence. If a woman walks into a police station and complains of rape with no signs of violence she must be closely interrogated. Allow her to make a statement to a policewoman and then drive a horse and cart through it. It is always advisable if there is any doubt of the truthfulness of her allegations to call her an outright liar . . . watch out for the girl who is pregnant or late getting home at night; such persons are notorious for alleging rape or indecent assault. Do not give her sympathy. If she is not lying, after the interrogator has upset her by accusing her of it, then at least the truth is verified . . . the good interrogator is very rarely loved by his suspect.

But the whole thing was Lexo . . . he set it up . . . ah never even . . .

— So Roy, I was reluctant to become a suspect. Suspected of lying about being held captive, brutalised, tortured and humiliated. A suspected and a proven liar; proven in a court of law. I still get flashbacks, Roy. Two years later. These flashbacks are nothing to do with the acid you gave me. Some people have them ten years later. It never really ends, Roy. It never really ends.

It wis Lexo that gave ye the acid! Lexo's fault! Alex Setterington. He's done it tae lassies before, he's probably still daein it. You'll no remember, bit ah tried tae stoap it! AH WIS THE CUNT THAT TRIED TAE STOAP THUM! AH SAIS TAE UM! MIND AH SAIS!

DEEPER, PLEASE PLEASE DEEPER

Oh fuck, I can see light coming through those thin membranes that are my eyelids . . . I'm going to fuckin open them and stare her in the face . . . please no no no no no DEEPER . . . I can smell this disinfectant . . . this is the fuckin hoaspital . . .

— I was a fool, Roy. A fool to go through the process. It was worse than the rape itself. The judge. Worse than a joke; a sick joke played on me. The whole thing was a theatre. A theatre to humiliate and brutalise me all over again. What was it Judge Wild said in Cambridge in 1982: 'It's not just a question of saying no . . .

NO

— it's a question of how she says it, how she shows it and makes it clear.

NO

—If she doesn't want it she only has to keep her legs shut and she would not get it without force and there would be marks of force being used. That was another good judge, just like our Justice Hermiston. So it was my own fault, Roy. I didn't say no the proper way . . .

NO

— . . . I should have kept my legs shut, even drugged, even with that knife at my throat, even with two men pulling my legs apart . . .

NO

NO

I can't wake now

DEEPER

DEEPER

DEEPER – – – Now I'm away from you . . . I'm sliding down the well, past my platform, out of that tunnel of darkness into a clear blue sky above the tropical savannah of Africa, the place of my dreams, of my freedom . . . but it's going dark again and I'm back in this room with Dawson and Sandy, cornered by the Storks.

— There must be some arangement we can come to, Dawson pleaded with the dead-eyed beast, — I'm a man of not inconsiderable personal wealth. I have a family!

The large Marabou turned to its friends and squawked loudly. The air was raw with the sound of their hysterical screeches and floating feathers and dust flew, giving off a vile stench and irritating me so that I sneezed – – – – – – – – – – – – – – – – – – – Eh fuckin moved, Vet! Like ah sais, the laddie moved! It wis like eh sneezed or somethin! Roy! Kin ye hear ays! Ah'm askin ye son, kin ye hear ays!

— Dinnae shout John, the laddie's ill, the laddie isnae fuckin well!

— Bit eh kin sneeze, Vet! Quick! pit the tape oan, the new tape . . . It's goat ays singin Born Free oan it son. Ma favourite film ay all time. Mind, Roy, ah showed ye the video! Like ah sais, favourite film ay aw time that yin: Baw -rn freee — as free is as the wind blows . . . mind ay that son? Matt Monro sung it! Mind! The film Roy, mind; Joy Adamson n her man, whit wis the cunt's name again?

Joy Adamson's man? Based oan a true story! Elsa, the lioness cub, ken bit thit grew up tae be a big lion! Kin ye hear ays, Roy! Born Free! Mind! Vet! C'moan wi the tape!

— Ah'm comin, John!

> I'd like to run away from you,
> But if you never found me I would die . . .

-— That's you singing Shirley fuckin Bassey again Vet, no me wi Born Free. Pit me singin Born Free oan!

I'm going to wake up if I don't go fucking deeper . . . DEEPER

— Bit it's a new Shirley Bassey John, a different Shirley Bassey . . .

— Aye, bit ah wis talkin tae the laddie aboot Born Free. Eh must mind ay that video. Joy Adamson. Eh watched it enough.

— Naw, bit ah dinnae agree wi that, John. The laddie grew up hearin me singing like Shirley Bassey so that's whit we should be playin fir um . . .

— Like ah sais, Born Free . . . n thirs a bit ay me singin Tom Jones oan it n aw. . . Thunderball . . . that wis a James Bond theme tune, like ah sais, Thunderball. Aye. Thunderball.

I'd rather face the Stork than listen tae these cunts . . .
DEEPER
DEEPER

I can't get fuckin deeper . . .

— Here we go!

> He always runs while the others walk,
> He acts while the other men just talk . . .

— That's the one, Vet! Me singin Tom Jones . . . likesay Thunderball n that. Like ah sais, Thunderball.

— Aye . . .

> He looks at the world and he wants it all,
> So he strikes like Thuuuunder-ball . . .

— One ay ma favourite Bond theme tunes ay aw time, this yin. Some chanter Tom Jones, eh Vet?

— Aye . . .

FUCK OFF FUCK OFF FUCK OFF FUCK OFF FUCK OFF FUCK OFF

— A great number, like ah sais, a great number.

— Ah dinnae really like that yin but John, ah like Tom Jones's other stuff . . . last night ah went tae sleep in Detroit City.

— Listen but Vet . . .

Any woman he wants he'll get . . .

NO

NO

He'll break any heart without regret,

His days of asking are all gone . . .

His fight goes on and on and on . . .

DEEPER PLEASE DEEPER

— Ah widnae really class masel as a belter bit, Vet. Ah'm mair ay a crooner, ken? Mair yin fir the soulful ballads like.

— Mibbe git ma tape on now though, John.

— Soulful ballads, like ah sais.

— Ma tape, John.

— Aye, soulful ballads.

PLEASE GO

— Change the tapes now, John.

— Eh . . . aye, bit we huv tae be gaun now, Vet. Likesay need tae be makin a move. Cheerio Roy!

Ma's cheap perfume reeks as she bends over to kiss me.

— Cheerio sweetheart.

Thank you and goodbye.

GOODBYE.

19 Miss X's Confessions

I feel my senses returning. This is beyond perception. I know she's in the room before she speaks; observing me, toying with me. I'm at her mercy in the same way she was at ours. How will she exercise her power? Will she show compassion or is she just the same as us? Is she what we made her? I know who you are, Miss X. I know who you are, Kirsty.

Kirsty Chalmers. Miss X.

But I didn't . . . it was Lexo. I didn't mean to hurt you.

IT WISNAE MA FUCKIN FAULT
The wey you carried oan
asked fir it
wi wir aw pished

```
BLAME THE WOMEN
BLAME THE DRINK
BLAME THE WEATHER

Z.

THERE IS NO EXCUSE
```

I want to go.

You only live twice
Or so it seems
One life for yourself
And one for your dreams . . .

— Your taste in music is strange, Roy Strang. It's fuckin weird, just like the rest of you.

ITS NO MA FUCKIN TASTE, IT'S THESE CUNTS

You drift through the years
And life seems tame,
Till one dream appears
And love is its name . . .

— The funny thing is Roy, Roy Strang, that I actually fancied you. Honest. Crazy eh? I genuinely thought that you were a bit different. Thought you were a nice-looking felly. I know that you were shy aboot your ears, anybody could see that, but I liked them. He looks like Shane in the Pogues, I used to say. I thought that you were tasty. Different, quiet, not full of yourself like the others. Thoughtful. Deep. Ha ha . . . I thought you were deep. Deep in a fucking coma.

DEEPER

And love is a stranger
Who'll beckon you on . . .

DEEPER

Don't think of the danger,
Or the stranger is gone . . .

DEEPER

— I was scared to talk to you though. You didn't show any interest in me, no like the others. You didn't drool. The only reason I hung around with these morons was to get closer to you. How crazy is that then, eh?

This dream is for you
So pay the price
Make one dream come true
You only live twice . . .

DEEPER

I can't get away, I can't get deeper . . . this is fuckin . . . if ah don't watch out ah'm gaunny wake up, gaunny end up right back in thair fuckin world where ah huv tae face aw this . . . and why is she sayin this aboot me, Dumbo Strang . . . why is she tellin these lies, tryin tae fuck ma heid up . . .

—I've decided to get them all, Roy. Your mate Dempsey was just the first. It was so easy. I just waited until he was coming home from the pub, he'd been there a lot lately, and I drove at him at high speed. He was all over the road. Held on for a couple of days as a cabbage, like yourself. I was sad when he kicked it; it would have been nice to have had you all lying before me like the produce on display at a fruit market; the vegetable stall. Then I could inspect the vegetables at ma whim.

DEEPER

—It would be great if you could hear this Roy, although I suppose that's just wishful thinking on my part. Mind you, Dr Goss did say that you were showing greater signs of awareness than ever before and he is hopeful that you'll come out of this one day. I wouldn't count on that though.

I WANT AWAY

—I'll tell you Roy, if you can hear me, you still won't have gathered how much I hate and detest you. I could never really tell you how much. You probably have no idea how you changed my life, how you could have ruined it, if I'd let you. I'll never be the same again Roy. Sex and men. . . it doesnae work for me anymair. I've found something in it all though, Roy. I've found me. I hate you for what you did to me. I understand that hate. What I'd really love is for you to be able to explain how you hated me so much to do what you did. What happened to you? What was your fucking problem, you sad, sad cabbage, you sick, brutalised, fucked-up bastard? Why did you hate me so much, Roy?

I didnae hate ye . . . I wanted you . . . I wanted us to . . .

THERE IS NO EXCUSE

NO NO NO NO

IT WIS LEXO . . . LEXO . . . IT WIS FUCKIN LEXO THAT
INSTIGATED THE WHOLE THING AH NIVIR EVEN
REALLY TOUCHED YE NOWT TAE FUCKIN DAE WI
ME AH WIS FEART, FEART AY LEXO THE CUNT'S A
FUCKIN KILLER

> Make one dream come true
> You only live twice . . .

DEEPER

      DEEPER

            DEEPER----------------
-- and
    it's
        happening now . . . and Dawson's jumping on
the spot and throwing a tantrum about how he doesn't want to die
and because of this we go crashing through the rotten floorboards
and run through a cavernous set of tunnels. — Wait for me, Dawson
wheezes, as we hear the Storks squawking in pursuit.

I run and run until I can see nothing around me or ahead of me.
Then it's like my lungs collapse and I black out. I have a pleasant
image of the two of us, me and Dorie, at a club, dancing together,
really high, I feel the music in me, feel the rushes, the uninhibited
euphoria . . . I awaken and Sandy's kind face pulls into focus in front
of me. Dust kicked up by a swirling wind stings my eyes and my
throat. Sandy's got a shooter. It's a pump-action double-barrelled
shotgun. — We have to go, Roy, he says. I get up easily and I see the
Lodge in the distance. We run towards it.

— Let's get that fucking Stork, Sandy, we're so close, so close to
solving the whole fuckin problem --- coming up --- so close to
the surface--------—A total breakdown, Roy. I blamed myself. For a whole year I was
no better than you, a fucking walking corpse.

WHAT THE FUCK ARE YOU DOING HERE THIS IS JUST SUPPOSED TAE BE ME AND SANDY

SANDY

Sandy

> Diamonds are forever . . .
> They are all I need to please me,
> They can stimulate and tease me,

Sandy

> They won't leave in the night,
> I've no fear that they might
> > desert me . . .

JAMIESON

> Diamonds are forever . . .
> Hold one up and then caress it,
> Touch it, stroke it and undress it,
> I can see every part,
> Nothing hides in the heart
> > to hurt me . . .

WHAIR THE FUCK UR YE, JAMIESON!

20 Self-Deliverance With A Plastic Bag

I couldn't run away from it in Manchester. The nightmares; oddly enough the Marabou Stork nightmares were the worst. Why should that have been? Who knows. Who the fuck knows. The Marabou Storks. I saw them at the Kruger Park in South Africa, the only place in the Republic where you can view them. When that one killed the flamingo, it was fucking horrible. It made me feel queasy. It was the way it held up the flamingo's head, severed at the neck. The flamingo is not a beautiful bird. It is a stupid, ugly-looking creature which happens to have beautiful plumage. Gaze at the flamingo's face, and what do you see?

You see a beautiful bi

You see

The flamingo's blood, her blood. The blood of her on me.

No. There was no blood.

Only my blood. My blood

when he did that to me in

the city of gol – – – – – – den words he will pour in your ear,

But his lies can't disguise what you fear,

For a golden girl knows when he's kissed her,

It's the kiss of death from mis-tah

Gold-fing-ah.

Pretty girl, beware of his heart of gold,

This heart is cold.

I'M NEARLY FUCKIN AWAKE HERE, I COULD OPEN
MY EYES . . .

No.

No way. This is my home. My refuge. Like Manchester.

Manchester was my refuge. I stayed in my flat in Ancoats,
keeping away from everyone, except to go to my work. I watched
videos and started reading again. Not just books to do with my
work, like information technology and software design; books on
politics n that, and no nature books, no ornithology. Apart from that
it was everything really; loads on Africa, imperialism and apartheid.
I wanted to go back, no as it is now but as I imagined it was or as it
could be. Once those fuckin white cunts had been kicked out. That's
all I did in Manchester, I read, and I kept masel tae masel.

Then she came along.

I had seen her at work, even knew her name. She worked in the
Pensions Section. Her name was Dorothy. She always had a smile
for everyone, a smile that just made you smile back. It wisnae a
bland, stupid indiscriminate smile though. It was a real engaging,
searching smile; the smile of someone looking for the good they
know is in everybody and invariably finding it.

It happened when I was coerced along to an office leaving do.
Coerced along by a bossy, domineering middle-aged cow who liked
to organise every cunt's life. There always seemed to be loads of
them in the type of places I worked in. One of those people who
thinks of themselves and is thought of by others as friendly, but who
is anything but, who is another fuckin control freak. As I was new,
or relatively new by that time, this person insisted that I came along.
I would get to know people better. The last thing I wanted to do was
to get to know any cunt. I don't know why, but I went. It was
probably because I was so depressed I didn't have the willpower to
say no, or to contemplate the excuses I'd have to make on Monday.
Roy Strang. Top boy. Ha ha ha.

The whole thing was just another load of shite to get through. I
took my Becks and sat making small-talk, trying to be as inconspicu-
ous as possible. People seemed to be comfortable talking to me for
an obligatory couple of minutes, before deciding to find better

company. It was as if I was wearing a baseball cap with flashing lights that spelt: FUCKED UP.

Then Dorothy came over and sat beside me. She smiled and I felt myself smiling back. I felt some tightness in my chest unlock. — It's about time I introduced myself. I've seen you around. I'm Dorothy from Pensions. Oh bloody hell, that makes me sound ancient. It's Dorothy from Warrington really. I hate it when people say what do you do, and people talk about their sodding jobs all the time. What do you do? I eat, sleep, shit, pee, make love, get out of it, go to clubs, that's what I flamin well do. Sorry, I'm rabbiting ere. What's your name?

— Eh, Roy.

Dorothy was pretty. She had a nice face and shortish blonde hair. Pretty enough to be thought of as plump rather than fat. Not from Fathell, Lancashire. She seemed not to be drunk, but somehow euphoric.

— Look Roy, I'm sorry about this, but I'm E'd out of my face. If I'm in a club an there's good sounds on, I don't bother nobody, I just dance. If I'm in this sort of environment though, I just want to talk to everyone. Life's too short to be all quiet n grumpy, init?

Life's too short. Her enthusiasm was infectious. In spite of myself I was enjoying talking to her. — What dae these things dae for ye?

— Ain't you done any E before? I thought you were all big ravers up in Scotland.

— Naw, ah like the indie stuff mair, ken? No really intae dance n that.

I was a freak. Legs too short. Gimpy, thanks tae fuckin Winston Two. Rest in peace you canine cunt. I'd always wanted tae dance, I mean really dance, tae really go for it, but naw. I never bothered, eh.

— This gear's brilliant. I never drink now, can't stand the stuff and I've never had such a good time in my life, she smiled. She was certainly having a better time than me. I'd had just two Becks, the rest of the night I'd been on cokes. I didn't want to get drunk and lose control. I was looking at the others; their morose, belligerent beery faces. They didn't seem to be having a good time either.

But she was.

A lot of the boys in the cashies took Es, a lot of them didnae. I never saw the point. I'd always liked the Becks, and couldnae get intae that fucking music. It was shite, that techno, nae lyrics tae it, that same fuckin drum machine, throbbin away aw the time. I hated dancing. It was like playing fitba. It put me up there on exhibition; my savaged, stumpy legs, my large body and my long, swinging ape airms. Swedgin had always been ma dancing.

I suppose I'd built up an aversion to any kind of drugs because of the wey my Ma and Dad got through the drink and how it made the cunts behave. That didnae seem to matter now though. I took one from her; fifteen quid, a wee capsule.

— R&Bs, she said.

I was talking away to her, but getting fuck all from the E. I was still enjoying myself, though, until I realised that I was really rushing, really riding the crest of a wave. Then I felt myself rise and the music seemed to be inside me. It was like the music was coming from me. I felt dizzy and queasy, but I'd never known such an exhilarating high. I wanted to shite for a bit, but it passed. The swedgin was fuck all compared to this; I felt I had all the power in the world but it was positive. I felt a bond with Dorothy, or Dorie as she liked to be called. Her face looked so clear and fresh and beautiful, her eyes were so alive. Her hair was a 2 Unlimited number came on the juke-box and I felt the drums thrash through me and the synth slabs lift me out of my seat. It had done fuck all for me before. — Whoaahhh . . . , I gasped.

— You alright? she asked.

— Ah'm sortay startin tae see what aw the fuss is aboot . . .

— Paula, she shouted over at her friend, — Roy ere's just lost his virginity. C'mon, let's get out of here. We need a more memorable setting to do this experience justice.

All I wanted was that music. House, it had to be house. When Dorie told me I would get more of it at a club called the Hacienda, but only far, far, better and blasted through a PA, with brain-frying lights and surrounded by people who felt the same, I was instantly sold.

The club was fuckin awesome. I was lost in the music and the

movement. It was an incredible experience, beyond anything I'd
known. I could never dance, but all self-consciousness left me as the
drug and music put me in touch with an undiscovered part of myself,
one that I had always somehow suppressed. The muscles in my body
seemed in harmony with each other. My body's internal rhythms
were pounding, I could hear them for the first time: they were
singing to me. They were singing: You're alright, Roy Strang.
You're alright, we're all alright. People, strangers, were coming up
to me and hugging me. Birds, nice-looking lassies n that. Guys n aw;
some ay them cunts that looked wide and whom I would have just
panelled in the past. I just wanted to hug them all, to shake them by
the hand. Something special was happening and we were all in this
together. I felt closer to these strangers than I did to anyone. Dorie
and Paula I loved; I just loved them. I couldn't stop hugging them,
like I'd always wanted to hug pals, but it was too sappy, too poofy. I
knew that after I came down I'd still love them. Something
fundamental happened that night; something opened up in me.

I was the Silver Surfer, I looked into the laser lights and zapped
across the universe a few times, surging and cruising with the music. It
built up into a crescendo and Dorie, Paula and I, it was like we were the
world, us and the people around us. I was one with them and myself
and I never wanted to lose it. Even when the music stopped — it was
hours later but it felt like minutes — I was still right up.

I was overwhelmed. All the shite Bri had spraffed, him and some
of the boys in the cashies who we used to say had gone aw soft wi the
ravin, it was all fuckin true and so much more. It was euphoria . . . it
was something that everyone should experience before they die if
they can truly have said not to have wasted their life on this planet. I
saw them all in our offices, the poor sad fools, I saw them in their
suburbs, their schemes, their dole queues and their careers, their
bookies shops and their yacht clubs . . . it didn't matter a fuck. I saw
their limitations, the sheer vacuity of what they had on offer against
this alternative. There would, I knew, be risks. Nothing this good
came without risk. I couldn't go back though. No way. There was
nothing to go back to . . .

. . . like now there's nothing to come up for — — — your eyes only

Can see me in the night.
For your eyes only
I never have to hide.

You can see so much in me,
So much in me that's new
I never felt until I looked at you . . .

Oh fuck, go for it Roy you crapping cunt, go deeper, go forward, go
back to the Stork or stay with this reminiscing because it doesnae
matter, it's the same sad fuckin story, it's always gaunny be the same
sad fuckin story – – – – so go DEEPER

DEEPER

DEEPER – – – and
now Sandy's back, and I'm thinking to myself, fuck them, fuck
them all.
— Let's hold on a bit, Sandy, I say.
— What? he replies, a little bewildered.
— I'm thinking, why should we be in a hurry to do battle with
Johnny Stork? Why should we run to the lodge to try and sort this
out? It's between Dawson and the terrorists and the Storks . . . I
mean, what's old Johnny Stork ever done to us? Let's enjoy our
picnic! It's nothing to do with us. We've got jam here, and honey and
butter, and plenty of that *absolutely* wonderful homemade bread.
We . . .
— Cut the bullshit, Roy. It's got everything to do with us, Sandy
snaps, his face harsh.
— Can't we have just a small picnic here first? Can't it be just like
the old times?
— No it can't be, Roy. It can never be like the old times, Sandy
says coldly.
— Never like the old times, I repeat wearily, — . . . never like old
times. I felt beaten. I just couldn't be bothered. — Okay, let's go.
We start up towards the lodge, but Sandy turns to me and says,

—I'm sorry Roy, I've been a little abrupt. I think you've realised what the score is now. I think we can spare the time to stop off for a little picnic before we go. For old time's sake, he grinned.

— Thanks Sandy, I appreciate it. For old time's sake, I smiled. Sandy was alright, no doubt about that.

he was a proper – – – – – Diamond – – – – – s are forever . . .

> Sparkling round my little finger,
> Unlike men the diamonds linger.
> Men are mere mortals who
> Are not worth going to
> Your grave for . . .

No. Give me the old times . . .

It can never be like the old times – – – – never like it was back in Manchester – – – – after the club that night – – – – because outside the streetlights were brilliant. I suppose I was slightly shiting myself about taking E because of the bad freak-out on acid once, but this was different. I felt totally in control. I'd never felt so much in control.

I had got dead sad when the music ended. My eyes were watering and it didn't matter. I wasn't embarrassed about being sappy. I saw what a silly, sad pathetic cowardly cunt I was, ever to be embarrassed about expressing emotion. But I wasn't even hard on myself; it didn't matter.

Back at Dorie's gaff, we drank tea, and I told them about myself; more than I've ever told anyone. I talked of my fears and insecurities, my hang-ups. They talked about theirs. It was supportive, empathetic; it was good. Not in a smarmy, false-intimacy, middle-class counselling way, or in a big, weird, spaced-out, hippy bullshit trip. This was just punters saying how they felt about life. I could talk about anything, almost anything, the rape and my family were taboo, but that was my choice.

It was no problem. Nothing was a problem.

Every weekend after that I was E'd out my face and clubbing. I had more pals in Manchester in a few months than I ever had back home.

The problem was that it was so good that it made everything else seem shite. No, that's not quite right: it showed that everything else *was* shite. Work was shite; just something to get through.

Eventually Dorie and I started sleeping together. We felt good about each other and there was nobody else involved. It had just been a matter of time. I was worried about sex, because I hadn't been with anyone since the incident. When we first shagged, I was E'd up and it made no difference, so we always made love when I was eckied. One day she said: — You don't have to be E'd up to make love to me you know.

We went to bed. I was trembling, scared of exposing myself without the chemicals. We kissed for a bit and I stopped shaking. We played with each other for a long time, and after we had joined, my cock and her fanny just became the one thing, then it seemed to vanish as we took off on a big psychic trip together. It was our souls and our minds that were doing it all; our genitals, our bodies, they were just the launch pads and were soon superfluous as we went around the universe together on our shared trip, moving in and out of each other's heads and finding nothing in them but good things, nothing in them but love. The intensity increased until it became almost unbearable and we exploded together in an orgasmic crash-landing onto the shipwreck of a bed, from a long way out in some form of space. We held each other tightly, drenched in sweat and shaking with emotion.

To my surprise, it was just as good as it was with the ecky.

Dorie told me after that she thought I was beautiful. I was shocked to find out that she wasn't joking. I kept looking at myself in the mirror. — Your ears are big, but beautiful. They got character. They're distinctive. They ain't as big as you think n all, your head's grown since you were a little kid, you know.

We went to the Hacienda every weekend. There was always a party at somebody's gaff after. To come down we usually smoked grass. Skunk if we could get it. I loved just blethering away, but more than that, I loved listening; listening to all the punters, their patter, hearing about their lives, getting up to all sorts of mischief with each other. I'd take a deep suck on a joint and hold on to it until a large ripe tomato of pleasure blew to smithereens behind my face.

Dorie and I got engaged. It was stupid and cavalier, we had only known each other for a few months. It was bizarre, but I just wanted to make a gesture, to show her how I felt.

Life was okay; it was better than okay. I read a lot during the week, and went with Dorie to watch arthouse movies at the Cornerhouse. At the weekend we clubbed and partied. Some Saturdays I went to the football with a couple of mates, Jimmy and Vince. We'd go down to the Moss to watch the City at Maine Road. The football wasn't as good as at Old Trafford, but the feel to it was better, more real. The crack in the pub before and after was great. Manchester was a brilliant place, it was the happiest time of my life.

Then something happened to knock the bottom out of my world and remind me who I was. It was an article in the *Manchester Evening News*, talking about the successful Zero Tolerance campaign in Edinburgh.

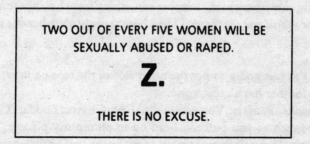

TWO OUT OF EVERY FIVE WOMEN WILL BE
SEXUALLY ABUSED OR RAPED.

Z.

THERE IS NO EXCUSE.

I lost it completely.

At the Hacienda that night I embraced Dorie most of the evening and through the morning; held her tightly to me. I held her as if I could force her love into me, drive the shit out of me, out of my mind and body, but what I was doing was infecting her; infecting her with my hurt, my pain, my anxiety. I could feel the sickness and doubt transmit in our embrace while my chin rested on the top of her head and my nostrils filled with the scent of her shampoo and perfume. The vibrations of doubt came back through her, right up through her skull and into my chin and into my head. She snorted

with irregular discomfort through her nostrils, making a ragged
sound against my neck. I got a duff E that night.

— Don't worry Roy, it don't always happen, Dorie said.

I'd lost it completely. All I could do was try to hide how much I
had lost it.

Then I lost Dorie.

I got more and more depressed. I literally couldn't move. I just
got more and more and more depressed. The doctor said I was
suffering from ME, yuppie flu, that fucking post-viral fatigue or
whatever they call it. For the first time, my relationship with Dorie
was tested and found wanting. We sat in and ate, just fuckin ate, junk
food, while watching videos. I could barely string a sentence
together. We put on pounds, stones. She couldn't adjust to living
with a depressed fuck-up who couldn't go out. Dorie was a party
chick. She just wanted to have a good time . . . maybe I'm being
hard on her. She wasn't that frivolous. She probably knew I was
holding something back, keeping something from her, not showing
her the whole me. Perhaps if I had been straight with her she might
have

No.

— I'm just going to put the other side of the tape on now, Roy.
Your mother has a great voice.

Thanks, Patricia. You sound different. Clearer. Louder. Closer.
Your touch as you pull my head up to plump my pillows. Your
perfume. The disinfectant smells of the hospital. The dimensions of
this small room. I feel them for the first time. The drip in my arm.
The tube in my throat, the one in my cock. It all doesnae matter. I
lost Dorie.

> Nobody does it better,
> Makes me feel sad for the rest.
> Nobody does it half as good as you do,
> baby you're the best.

— Are you as good a singer as your mum, Roy?

I lost Dorie . . .

We agreed to split. I moved into a new place in Eccles.

> I wasn't looking,
> But somehow you found me.
> I tried to hide from your love.
>
> Like heaven above me,
> The spy who loved me
> Is keeping all my secrets safe tonight.

I remember when I left the flat. I tried to talk to her, but the words wouldn't come. Even at that late stage she looked at me as if she wanted to hear words that would have made a difference. I couldn't even think them. My brain felt like it was floating in thick soup and my chest was as tight as a drum. Nothing would come.

— I'm sorry I couldn't help you, Roy. You have to help yourself first though. I'm sorry it didn't work out, she sniffed and couldn't stifle a sob. — I've been through this before and I don't want it again. It's better a clean break . . . I thought you were different, Roy . . .

— See ye, I said, picking up my holdall. I walked out the door and never looked back. I hated the cunt. I fuckin hated

No.

No Dorie fuck Roy Strang silly cunt top boy E head good looking so refined Dumbo Strang

> The way that you hold me,
> Whenever you hold me,
> There's some kind of magic
>   inside you . . .

Oh God what have I fuckin well done

Oh my God

I stayed in.

I stayed in at the weekends, watching videos. Then the worse part of it passed. I started going out again, though not so regularly. When I did go out, I avoided the Hacienda and I took loads of Es. I started taking sleeping pills to come down. I fucked as many lassies as I could; there were plenty at the clubs who were up for a shag. I respected them, there was massive respect, but we never kidded that it was anything else other than sex. There was no bullshit. It sometimes gave the illusion of happiness, but I was not happy, not in the same way. It's just that the pain was taken away. You can either use drugs as a validation of the joy of life or you can use them as an escape from its horrors. You have to become sensitive to the point where one shades into the other. I wasn't, and I went through a bad time.

I must have gone through a bad time because I started writing home. I got letters back. They'd all write on the one piece of paper to me. Before it would have embarrassed me, now it was strangely touching. It was crazy, but it made me want to be near them.

Dear Roy,

Hope everything is well down in Manchester and that your not getting too English! Nane o' that by the way Jimmy or your no a proper Scotsman n you'll no be alowed back up here. (Only joking!) New neighbours upstairs are a wee bit too lippy, Tony and I paid them a little visit and taught them the meaning of the word respect. Had a wee crowd back the other night and had a bit of a sing-song. We were minding of the time one New Year when we got you to sing A View To A Kill. Mind that? You liked that Duran Duran when you were younger! No denying it! I sang some Tom Jones and your Ma did her Shirley Bassey. A rare night. Colin Cassidy and me taught the Hopes dunno if you ken them a junky family in the scheme well we taught them a lesson they'll no forget in a hurry. Suffice to say our frends the Hopes are no longer resident in the scheme. Anyway, hears Mum.

All the best, Dad.

Hello Roy son,

Mum here. God, it doesn't seem more than a year now since you moved away. Time flies, right enough. Everyone is well here, and the big news we have is that Kim is getting married and is going to be a mum. We are all very thrilled. I don't know if you know Kevin, he is an awful nice fellow. What about you? Any sign of a girlfriend?

We had spaghetti bolognese the other day (is it still your favourite?) and that made us think of you. I had what your Dad calls my 'usual wee greet' at the thought of you being so far away and I hope you can come home soon so it can be like old times.

All my love son,

Mum. XXXXX

P.S. Here's a few words from the mum-to-be, the future Mrs Scott.

Hiya Roy,

I shewd be calling you Uncle Roy because of the baby which is going to be born in February and will be called Jason if it's a boy and either Scarlet or Dionne if it is a wee girl

and the wedding will be sumtime in December at the Commidore Hotel and I have chosen a nice dres

Kevin seys that he's looking forward to meeting you and having a pint cause he is a nice felly and I will be glad when you two have met but no arguments about the football cause he's a JAMBO and I have started to support Hearts two because they are the best time. No arguments like cause that's what Tony does who's going to rite something here.

Love from Kim Scott (soon to be the formir Kim Strang.)

XXXXXXXXXXXXXXXXXXXXXXXXXXXXXXXXXXXXXXXXXXXXXXX

XXXXXXXXXXXXXXXXXXXXXXXXXXXXXXXXXXXXXXXXXXXXXXX

XXXXXXXXXXXXXXXXXXXXXXXXXXXXXXXXXXXXXXXXXXXXXXX

Hi Roy,

Tony here. We've got the Huns in the semi at Hampden, that's
next week. A good night out, so get up for it. Hibees on a good
run just now. I'm hoping we don't get any injuries or
suspensions and have to play Joe Tortolano — a good Italian
but a shite player. See you for the semi!

P.S. Hannah and the kids are okay and send their love.

Tony.

I came home to Edinburgh, a glazed-eyed basket case, back into
the now strangely comforting chaos of my family.

I was ostensibly up for the League Cup semi-final, where Hibs
were playing Rangers at Hampden. Nobody gave them a chance,
but they won. I scarcely noticed. Tony's nails were bitten to the
quick in that second half as we stood at the open end of the ground.
Kevin, Kim's felly, was with us. He seemed an okay guy, a bit slow
and bewildered, but harmless. A typical Jambo in fact. John got
stroppy and threatened some guys in front of us with assault for
putting up their flag and interrupting his view. At the final whistle he
crushed one of them in a victory bear-hug. Tony jumped on me,
tearing my neck muscles. I allowed myself to be dragged along and
slapped by everyone near me.

There was a party . . . — — — — — —
— — — — — Me. and. Sandy. Jamieson.

Just the two of us.

At our party. A picnic. A spread of fresh bread, cheeses, farm eggs and mouth-watering preservatives laid out on a pink gingham cloth. It was just the two of us, the way I'd always wanted it to be. ------

------ It was Dorie and me; at the Lake District . . .

Who have I ever really loved?

I don't need ---------- luuuuuurrrrrrvvvvvvve.
    What good would love do me,
    Diamonds never lie to me,
    For when love's gone
    They last onnnnn . . .

DEEPER.

There was a party . . . ------

------ a party after the game at my auld man's. A party at my auld man's. You could have replaced the guests with a series of inflatables that wobble on their bases, with a tape deck built in to spout out clichés:
CHEERY AULD CUNT WITH HALF A LUNG AND GIMPY LEG: — Mustn't grumble . . . aye . . . mustn't grumble
    MUMPY-FACED GUINNESS-GUTTED AUNTIE: — Pit oan an awfay loat ay weight since her hysterectomy . . . pit oan an awfay loat ay weight since her hysterectomy . . .
    VACANT PARTY-CHICK COUSIN: — Hiyaaah . . . Hiyaaah . . Hiyaaah . . .
    BROODING TEEN-PUP COUSIN IN CORNER: — Shite in here . . . pit oan some decent sounds . . .
    WHINGEY UNCLE WITH ULCER: — Ah like it bit it disnae like me . . . ah like it bit it disnae like me . . .
    I thought that it couldn't get any worse but it did. I hadn't told any of the guys I used tae hing aboot wi that I was coming back up fir the fitba. While everyone else had been on tenterhooks at the game's

outcome, my only anxiety at being at Hampden was concern that one of the boys would see me.

Somebody had. The phone went and it was for me. It was Lexo.

— Thoat ye'd be up fir the fitba, he said.

— Aye, barry result, eh.

— Stomped a few hun casuals. Her Majesty's Service. Fuckin wee bairns; shitin cunts. Typical Weedgies; fling a few boatils n cairray a blade bit cannae pagger fir fuck all.

— Keith Wright's heider . . .

— Aye, well they'd better no fuck up against any shite in the final. The winners automatically qualify fir Europe, mind. This is oor chance tae cause real bother, oan the continent. This is one fuckin show thit hus tae be taken oan the road; it'll be a fuckin great crack. Whit did ye no come wi us fir the night?

— Eh, wanted tae see the auld man n that, eh. Nivir see thum aw now thit um doon in Manchester, eh.

— Aye right. Ah need your address doon thair. Git a squad doon fir a wee brek one weekend, eh. See whit fixtures are oan. They tell ays that Bolton's the tidiest local firm, eh. Mibbe pey they cunts a wee surprise visit. Anywey, we're doon the club: oan a loak in. Git yirsel doon.

— Eh, thir's a wee perty oan up here . . .

— C'moan ya schemie cunt, git doon tae the club!

— Eh, aye, right then . . . I went, mainly because it was too depressing watching all those cunts get pished in the hoose with their fuckin alcohol, mainly because that persistent cunt Lexo wid be oan the phone aw night and mornin.

I hit Leith Walk, no knowing where I was going or what I was doing. The town was decked in green and white, songs were spilling out of every bar. It was a Hibbie's fantasy; not a Jambo in sight: they were all skulking indoors contemplating thirty years without a trophy on the shelf. I couldn't get into it though. I realised I should have been at Powderhall and I cut down from the Walk.

The club was heaving with casuals. Some of the teen pups that hung around in the baby crew were obviously now staking top table claims. Their bodies had filled out and their faces had hardened and some were looking at me with a lot less than their customary deference. There had obviously been a few changes. The important thing was to quickly suss out what these had been without getting involved with any radges. I was broken; I'd had enough of all this. I sat at the bar and sucked tensely on a Becks, anxious and nervous in the company of my old mates. Demps still wasn't around.

— Cunt's went a bit ay a straight-peg, eh, Ozzy told me.

Out the corner of my eye I noticed one guy who seemed vaguely familiar. He was blethering to Ghostie. He was a huge bulky bastard with a real mouth and a big swagger. I hadn't seen him with the cashies before but ah sure as fuck kent the cunt fae somewhair. I nearly froze in shock as it dawned on me who it was. His face looked the same but his eyes were different. They didn't flit around softly like they once did. They were now still, intense and focused. I couldnae remember the boy's name: I just kent him as the Dressed-By-His-Ma-Cunt.

I was for the off.

I scored an ecky and went with a couple of fringe cashies who were into clubbing, to this new midweek club at The Venue. I was relieved to be away. It was okay, but I recognised yet another cunt, and this time got an even bigger shock. This boy was well into his dancing. I went up and spoke to him. I don't know who was the most surprised, myself or Bernard. He was really E'd n aw. I found myself, to my surprise, hugging him. Bernard and I had never touched like this before, just exchanged blows in makeshift boxing rings. We farted around on the dancefloor, enjoying the hip-hop beat. I'm mair ay a hardcore than a garagey or hip-hop type ay cunt myself, but this was okay. We talked for a long time and my cashie mates filtered away, so Bernard and I ended up leaving and headed down to Chapps, a gay club near the Playhouse.

— Nivir thoat ah'd see you eckied up, Roy, he said.

— Oan it non-stoap fir the last six months, I told him with a sad smile. Bernard was alright.

Bernard. Aye. He was alright.

— Nivir thought ah'd be in here, though, I smiled, looking around. I didn't like the place. I told Bernard that I thought it was

pretty sad and desperate, the way all those queens cruised each other
out.

— Naw, it isnae really, he explained, — cause here just about
every guy who wants fucked ends up getting fucked. It's much
sadder and more desperate up at Buster Brown's or any hetro place,
cause the number of guys that want fucked is higher than the number
of lassies that want to fuck them. At least here, most people get what
they want.

I thought about that for a while. There was no doubting his logic.
I had to agree. It was easy. I felt good, I was rushing on the E. —
Whoahh man, that ecky . . .

— Well, it agrees wi ye, he laughed.

I looked at him and said, slipping my arm around his neck, —
Listen Bernard, you're alright man, ken? You had the whole thing
sussed way back. I was a fuckin wanker, I couldnae handle anything,
I'm no just talkin aboot you bein a buft . . . eh, bein gay, I jist mean
everything . . . aw fuck, Bernard, I'm really sorry, man . . . it's not
the E talkin, ah've just fucked things up, Bernard . . .

He shrugged. — We aw fuck things up, Roy.

— Naw, bit see when yuv *really* fucked things up, fucked them up
so bad soas that thir's nothing ye kin ever dae tae pit it right; just
nothin man, like it's always with ye? Bernard, see when ye dae
something bad, dae something terrible, it doesnae make ye a bad
person, does it? Ah mean ye can change, right?

— Ah suppose ye can, Roy . . . what's wrong, Roy? What is it?
Yir talkin aboot love, eh?

I thought bitterly about that, — Nah, no love, the reverse ay that,
I smiled, then I gave him a tight hug. He reciprocated.

— Ah nivir goat tae know ye, Bernard. Ah acted like a cunt tae
you . . .

— It worked both ways, he smiled, hugging me again. It felt
good.

— But ah've changed, Bernard. I've allowed myself tae feel. That
means that ah have tae dae something, like tae sort ay prove tae
myself that I've changed. It's like I have tae assume responsibility for
ending my pain and making someone else feel better. Even if it

involves the greatest sacrifice. Try tae understand . . . ah mean, fuck, ah sound like the auld man giein it big licks wi one ay Churchill's fuckin speeches . . . it sounds like ah'm wafflin here . . .

I just couldnae say

— It's okay Roy, he just kept saying, then he seemed tae go sad. — Listen, Roy, I've got the virus. I tested positive. I'm HIV.

I felt as if the life had been crushed out of my frame. — Bernard . . . naw . . . fuck . . . how . . .

— A couple ay months ago. It's cool, though . . . ah mean it's no cool, but that's the wey it goes eh, he shrugged, then looked at me intensely. — But it's the quality thing in life, Roy. Life's good. Hang onto life. Hang onto it, Roy, he smiled as I started to sob. — C'mon Roy, stoap acting like a big poof! he laughed, comforting me, — it's awright man, it's okay . . .

But it wisnae okay.

But me and Bernard, well, we were okay.

The following Friday I arranged to go to the big Rezurrection gig at Ingliston with him and his posse. It was weird, Bernard and I becoming mates. His poetry was still shite, well, that's maybe no fair, but it was certainly patchy. At least he had grown out of inflicting it on people. I actually volunteered to read them. Some of it was to do with ecky and shagging; those were the best ones. The shagging poems would have disgusted me before; the idea of men doing that with each other, men shagging. Now though, it just seemed like two people in love, like me and Dorie. The queenish rants were still a bit hard to take.

Bernard's posse were an okay crowd; mixed gays and straights with a few fag-hags thrown in. The fag-hags were quite pathetic figures. There was something incomplete about them. I spotted it straight away, it was an obscure quality, but I saw it in myself. We had some problems getting sorted with eckies, and Bernard and his posse were just into doing some speed and acid – Supermario's.

I wasn't up for the acid, — No way, man, I said to Bernard. I was remembering my bad trip.

I was remembering someone else's bad trip.

He gave me an as-you-like shrug.

— It's no that, Bernard, it's just that there's too much shite floatin aroond in ma heid tae dae acid the now, ken?

— Fair enough, he said. — I think you're being wise.

But I wisnae wise. I was talking to a guy in the posse called Art, a big fuckin pill-box this cunt, and I got carried away as he talked of his drug experiences. I fired down a Supermario.

At first it was great; the lights, the sounds. We headed for the heart of the bass and I was happily tripping oot ay ma box. Bernard looked fuckin amazing; I tried not to think of him having that fuckin virus in him, he just looked so good. Party chicks checked him out, well fucked off that he was gay. This shag in the posse called Laura shouted in my ear: — I'm madly in love with your brother. It's a shame he's gay. I still want to have his baby. I just smiled. I was enjoying her patter, even hoping that I might be a proxy fuck for Bernard.

Then I looked at the big sign above the stage:

reZurrection

The Z luminated and the slogans came rushing into my head:

NO MAN HAS THE RIGHT

WHEN SHE SAYS NO SHE MEANS NO

THERE IS NO EXCUSE

THERE IS NEVER AN EXCUSE

I felt terrible all of a sudden; just all hot, breathless and shaky. I tried to compose myself, moving through the crowd towards the exit and the chill-out zone. I needed to think. I needed to

A girl smiled at me, and it looked like

It was her

They all looked like her

Then there was a guy. A steward. It was Uncle Gordon. — Ah'm no fucking gaun wi you again, right! Ah'm no gaunny fuckin dae that again! I shouted at him.

— Calm doon mate, eh, a raver shouted at me as the security guy stood bemused.

I ran to the toilets and sat in a trap crying and talking to myself. Some guys came in and talked me down. They found Bernard. I heard somebody mutter, — Cunt cannae handle his drugs.

Hospital Bed LYING IN YOUR HOSPITAL BED IN A COMA STUPID
RELATIVES NIPPING YOUR HEAD CAN THEY
UNDERSTAND WHERE YOU HIDE AND WHAT YOUR LIFE
AMOUNTS TO
Their Africa YOU ARE A
DYING MAN
AND YOU ASK
The Well FOR NO PITY
ONLY UNDER-
S T A N D I N G Capital City Service
WHICH WILL
NOT HELP YOU
OR HER OR Marabou Storks
SANDY OR
BERNARD BUT IT IS STILL AN URGE YOU HAVE, A FUTILE
URGE TO MAKE SENSE OF THIS FUCKING CRAZY SHITE
YOU'RE INVOLVED IN THIS TROPICAL LAND THIS
COLONISED NATION OF YOUR DISEASED MIND
Africa, my Africa . . .

Why no death | IT WON'T HURT ROY, YOUR UNCLE
why only incompetence | GORDON WOULD NEVER HURT YOU
why when you purchase the manual | JUST LIE STILL PERFECTLY STILL NOW
is it that you still can't do it right | ROY, OR THERE WILL BE BIG TROUBLE
in our flat Dorie, mind the time I fucked up | WHEN YOUR DAD HEARS ABOUT THIS
putting up the shelves | SHUT UP YOU LITTLE BASTARD I'M
I had the manual and all the right tools then | WARNING YOU SHUT THE FUCK UP
THAT'S BETTER THAT'S BETTER
THERE THERE THERE

I wanted to die. I thought I would die. It felt like the time. It had felt like the time for a while.

Bernard took me home and I spent a couple of days in bed. Kim indulged me a bit; I told them I had flu. Kim was kind, that was what she was. She was nice Kim, and good and kind. That was Kim; people took advantage, but her and Kevin seemed to love each other, they were obviously happy.

I was upstairs in my old bedroom watching a video of the other semi-final. Dad and Tony had kept on at me to take a look at it. They said there was an astonishing refereeing decision in it. Everyone had been talking about it. I decided to watch it. Dunfermline and Airdrie were competing for the right to get fucked in the final by Hibs. The Pars versus the Diamonds. Airdrie were in easy street, but they didn't win. I didn't wait for it to finish, didn't stop to see the penalty shoot out.

I decided it was time to go.

I had a look at my book again, the one I'd picked up in a radical bookshop in Manchester. It was apparently banned in this country. It was called: *Final Exit: The Practicalities Of Self-Deliverance and Assisted Suicide For The Dying*, by Derek Humphry, published by the Hemlock Society. Their motto was:

GOOD LIFE, GOOD DEATH.

With any luck, I'd achieve half of this. I was dying. I knew it, I felt it. It was beyond transitory depression. I wasn't a psychopath; I was just a fool and a coward. I had opened up my emotions and I couldn't go back into self-denial, into that lower form of existence, but I couldn't go forward until I'd settled my debt. For me it wasn't running away. That was what I'd been doing all my fuckin life, running away from sensitivity, from feelings, from love. Running away because a fuckin schemie, a nobody, shouldnae have these feelings because there's fuckin naewhair for them tae go, naewhair for them tae be expressed and if you open up every cunt will tear you apart. So you shut them out; you build a shell, you hide, or you lash out at them and hurt them. You do this because you think if you're hurting them you can't be hurt. But it's bullshit, because you just hurt even mair until you learn to become an animal and if you can't fuckin well learn that properly you run. Sometimes you can't run though, you can't sidestep and you can't duck and weave, because sometimes it just all travels along with you, inside your fuckin skull. This wasn't about opting out. This was about the only resolution that made sense. Death was the way forward.

I looked up the chapter on 'Self-Deliverance With A Plastic Bag', a chapter I'd referred to many times. As it recommended, I took the paracetamol and applied the plastic bag, pulling it over my head and taping it round my neck.

The bag was clear but it all got foggy.

I was drifting . . .

That was when I saw Jimmy Sandison, the *real* Jimmy Sandison, not Sandy Jamieson . . . who was Sandy Jamieson?

The bag was clear . . .

The bag was clear and I continued watching the telly through it as I drifted into unconsciousness. I could see Jimmy Sandison. Jimmy Sandison, the fitba player. The expression on his face as he gesticulated to the referee made me almost want to tear the bag off. I wanted to help him, I wanted to help all the people who'd ever suffered injustices, even though it was just a fuckin recorded tape of a fitba match I was watching. I'd never seen a man so shocked and outraged at what he felt was a miscarriage of sporting justice.

Never a man.

I once saw a woman who was worse, much worse; I saw her face in court . . . then I saw

DAD PUNCHING ME MA SCREAMING AT ME KIM'S GREETING FACE MY FISTS SPLITTING BERNARD'S MOOTH A MAN TWITCHING ON THE GROUND GORDON WITHDRAWING HIS BLOOD-STAINED COCK FROM A FRIGHTENED YOUNG BOY BENT OVER A WORKBENCH THAT BOY LOOKING AT HIS DISCARDED BLUE SHORTS AN EXPLOSION A HELICOPTER A KNIFE AT A LASSIE'S THROAT A

SCARRED FACE BURSTING OPEN A KNIFE AT A LASSIE'S THROAT THEN

NOTHING

Just a blissful void.

After a long blackout, I woke up lying in a tropical grassland, with Jamieson mopping my sweating brow. We've been companions ever since, sharing an interest in wildlife, particularly ornithology, and a concern for social justice and the environment.

Sandy the Diamond.

Diamonds are forever.

21 Facing The Stork

Sandy Jamieson and I sat enjoying our picnic. Sandy stroked at the mane of a nosy lion who had ambled over to us. I fed the beast some chicken then rubbed its stomach as it rolled over on its back in appreciation. I remembered the Silver Surfer, walking amongst the animals, saying that they were the gentle ones, it was man who was evil and warlike. The Surfer spoke a lot of sense. I like cats; even big ones. I wish we had had a cat instead of a . . .

— Cats are ruthless creatures, and I've had to hunt a few of them down in my time, once they've turned maneater, Sandy smiled. — What I like about them, though, is that they are almost totally devoid of servility.

— I think it's a good quality, I agreed. I looked at the brilliant sun rising up over the distant mountain peak, felt its luxuriating warmth on my bare face, arms and legs.

We sat for a while before Sandy awkwardly cleared his throat. — Hummph. It seems a pity to ruin the picnic, Roy, but the lodge is only a few hundred yards up the road. I think we should go and find a certain predator-scavenger better known in these parts as the Marabou Stork.

— Yes Sandy, as much as we loathe and detest the evil capitalist Dawson, we did enter into a gentleman's agreement with him; the most binding of agreements between gentlemen; namely to rid the Emerald Forest Park of Marabous.

Sandy smiled quizzically. — Whatever happened to the element of personal crusade that seemed to fuel this pursuit?

I shrugged, — I don't really know, Sandy. It's just that when I woke up this morning, it no longer seemed to be so . . . pressing.

We headed up to the lodge, Sandy keeping his gun pointed. We entered stealthily by the conservatory, into the main library. The large Stork was there. But something was far from right.

— — — — I'm here for you now Roy. I'm here to take you away . . .

> Meeting you
> With a view to a kill
> Face to face in a secret place
> Feel the chill . . .

Go away . . . I've got to face up to the Stork . . . please Kirsty. Go away.

> Nightfall covers me
> But you know the plans I'm making . . .

I sang this once at a perty. New Year. I liked Duran Duran when I was a wee laddie. Hungry Like The Wolf was their best yin but, eh.

I'm falling, I feel myself falling — — — Lexo's in here. He's got in. I'm looking at him. He's with Dawson and Jamieson. Lexo is the Stork. But the Stork still stands facing us. Lexo isnae the Stork . . .

Lexo isnae . . .

Jamieson is pointing the shotgun at me.

> Until we dance into the fire
> A little kiss is all we need . . .

I feel as if I can't breathe. —
— — — — — — — — — — — — — — I'm pulling this little tube out of your useless cock, Roy. Can you feel it?

> Dance into the fire
> The fatal sounds of broken dreams . . .

Can ah fuckin feel it?

I'm almost awake. I seem to see everything. It's like my eyelids are now just translucent membrane. I could open my eyes.

I could open my eyes.

I feel a sharp pain in my penis. She has it in her hand. She's squeezing it . . . like Dorie . . . like Patricia . . . but not so gentle . . .

— — — — — I'm going to cut this off and I'm going to stuff it down your throat and watch you choke to death.

It was LEXO, no me, LEXO

> There's crystal tears
> Full of snowflakes on your body
> First time in years
> To change your skin
> From lover's rosy stain
> A chance to find a phoenix in the flame
> A chance to die
> And then we dance into the fire . . .

— Remember when you put this useless shrivelled thing into my arse, Roy? I can't believe how this thing hurt me so much. Well, not as much as it's going to hurt you . . . remember when you put the mirror at the foot of that mattress to see my face as you forced yourself into my arse . . . remember what you said? Do you? You said you wanted me to look at you, and you wanted to see my face. You wanted me to see Roy Strang. You wanted me to feel what happens to any cunt who fucks about with Roy Strang. Now I want to see you, Roy. I want you to see what you've made me, because you've made me just like you. I hid like a sick, twisted vegetable for days, hid inside my flat, frightened of my own shadow. Sleep was an impossibility without the pills. You raped me once, and with the help of the judge and the courts you raped me again. Then I saw those posters, those Zero Tolerance campaign posters. NO MAN HAS THE RIGHT they said, but they were wrong, Roy.

Naw, they were right, I saw them, they hurt me, but they were right . . .

— They were wrong because you *did* have the right. You all wanted to teach me Roy, to teach me a lesson, that was what you said. You did teach me . . .

Naw.

— You taught me that you had the right by simply taking it. The posters were prescriptive, they were talking about a world as it should be rather than as it is . . .

But there's another world Kirsty, it disnae huv tae be this wey . . . we can change it aw, make it different . . .

— I don't know who fucked you up, what happened to make you the sad, wretched excuse for a human being you are and I don't care. It's not my problem. You're my problem, or rather were. Now I'm your problem. Might is right. You *take* the right. I'm taking the right Roy, taking the right to fuck you off, son.

I can feel the cold steel on my cock . . .

— That silly little tube up your cock Roy, taking all the piss out of you. What was it you said: Nae cunt takes the piss out ay me? The nurses do it every day, Roy. They just drain it from you. It would probably be nicer to just leave you, to let you rot away like you've been doing for the last couple of years, but they tell me you might wake up. We're playing Doctors and Nurses now Roy, so let's get rid of this silly fucking tube . . . which one, Doctor? . . . why both of them, Nurse . . .

I feel the catheter tube pulling sharply out of me. It was fuckin Lexo . . . how is it that ah . . .

DEEPER

DEEPER

DEEPER

My throat is burning on this tube . . . it's the tube in my throat . . . take it oot soas ah kin speak . . .

DEEPER

DEEPER – – –

– Sandy still has
the gun pointed at me. But I hear other voices shouting. Their faces
are just at the periphery of my vision but I know who it is, it's Ozzy
and Dempsey and Lexo and they're shouting that she's had enough.

The slag asked for it . . .

What the fuck is this? Sandy! Dinnae fuckin point that at me!
   Shoot Lexo
   He's the cunt that

DUMBO

DUMBO STRANG

The slag asked for it

Her face, like Caroline Carson's

she was just a young
lassie

cruel slags all the same

the slag asked for it

mocking the afflicted

just a young lassie but

they fight back

The slag asked for it

the dog
          cannae go aroond hating fifty per cent
          ay the population
Gordon
          ah didnae want it, ah didnae want that

who do you fuckin hate Roy Strang you hate schemies Kaffirs poofs

Weedgies Japs snobby cunts jambos scarfers English cunts women only you don't do you Roy Strang the only cunt you really hate is

Roy Strang.

> cannae go aroond hatin fifty per cent ay
> the population just because some dirty
> auld cunt fucked ye up the erse as a
> bairn, nae use that, eh.

— AH'M RUNNIN THIS FUCKIN GIG! AH SAY WHIN THE SLAG'S HUD ENOUGH! I'm shouting . . . why am I getting into this . . . it's fuck all to do with anything . . . — Sandy . . . shoot Lexo . . . he's the fuckin rapist. He's a fuckin nutter . . .

I see an image in the mirror, the image of the Marabou Stork. It's on the flamingo . . . tearing into it, ripping it to shreds, but the flamingo's still alive, I see its dulled eyes . . .

THERE IS NEVER AN EXCUSE.

Her fingers are holding my eyes open and I can see her, she's holding open one eyelid at a time and her surgical scissors are snipping my eyelids neatly off, I can feel the cold steel and hear the sharp tearing sound . . .

. . . I can feel her knife hacking into my genitals, thrashing into my chest, digging, trying to find me, but she'll never find me in here . . . and now I'm soaring upwards trying to get out, to fly across the fields of Africa, but I'm stuck on the hospital ceiling looking down at Roy Strang being hacked to pieces by Kirsty . . . hacked by a serrated knife . . . did you get it at Boston's Kirsty . . . ————————
— I'm going to let you feel this, Roy! They say a man can hardly feel it, hardly feel the removal of his prick . . .

NO
NO

I'm suddenly back down in here and I feel the pain and I can't move because of her

— Let you taste it, like I had to . . .

NO

It's my prick . . . the dirty fuckin sow's cut oaf ma cock and she's . . . aw what the fuck, the Silver Surfer never had a cock and the cunt seemed to get by as he soared on his board . . . that's all I ask . . .

— This is going in your mouth, Roy, open wide, come on now . . .

NO

NO

NO

— Do I hear sounds there, Roy . . . I can't hear you . . . what is it you're saying to me, Roy, what are you trying to tell me . . . I know you want this, I know you're asking for it . . . you shouldn't speak with your mouth full . . . you have to learn Roy, you have to be taught . . .

NO

PLEASE

NO

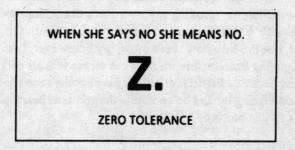

WHEN SHE SAYS NO SHE MEANS NO.

Z.

ZERO TOLERANCE

She's looking into my eyes, my lidless eyes and we see each other now. She's beautiful. Thank God. Thank God she's got it back.

What we took. I'm trying to smile. I've got this severed cock in my mouth and I'm trying to smile. I can't breathe and she's showing no mercy.

I understand her.

I understand her hurt, her pain, how it all just has to come out. It just goes round and round, the hurt. It takes an exceptionally strong person to just say: no more. It takes a weak one to just keep it all to themselves, let it tear them apart without hurting anyone else.

I'm not an exceptionally strong person.

Nor is Kirsty.

We're just ordinary and this is shite.

We both understand everything.

The sun is rising behind me and my shadow spills out away from it, out in front of me. My spindly legs, my large overcoat, my massive beak . . . I have no visible ears, I never really had much in the way of ears, it was always my nose, Captain Beaky, they used to call me at the school . . . it wasn't the ears, my memory hasn't been so good, nor has my hearing but I can think more clearly now . . . I have the gait of a comical scarecrow, I shuffle like an old man who has shat his pants. I'm so tired . . . I spread my large, black wings . . .

She's going . . . don't go Kirsty, stay with me for a bit, see this through . . . but no no no I hear her hastily depart. Then I hear another voice, the hysterical screaming of Nurse Patricia Devine. She's watching me smoking my own penis like a limp, wet cigar, staring with horror into my eyes that cannot shut. I'm getting weaker, but I'm here now. I can move my lidless eyes, I can see my cock dangling from my mouth and I can see the scissors sticking out from my neck . . . Patricia runs to get help but she's too late because Jamieson's facing me and he's pointing the gun and I hear it going off and it's all just one big

Z.